MANNY PORTER AND THE YULETIDE MURDER

By the Author

A Champion for Tinker Creek

Manny Porter and the Yuletide Murder

Manny Porter and the Yuletide Murder

by

D.C. Robeline

2022

MANNY PORTER AND THE YULETIDE MURDER

ISBN 13: 978-1-63679-313-9

This Trade Paperback Original Is Published By
Bold Strokes Books, Inc.
P.O. Box 249
Valley Falls, NY 12185

First Edition: December 2022

Credits
Editors: Jerry L. Wheeler and Stacia Seaman
Production Design: Stacia Seaman
Cover Design by Inkspiral Design

To Richard and Catherine,
my best friends and most important supporters.

CHAPTER 1

Thanksgiving

"I'll tell you again, I'm not leaving here without my Maggie!"

The elderly man's voice sounded thin and reedy, but the words were unmistakable. I imagined him glaring at his tormentors from under sun-bleached bushy eyebrows as they stared down at him, uncertain what to do next.

"I'm going to find Manny," I heard Tristan say, and in a moment, he located me beside the walk-in, inspecting the prep for tomorrow's start.

"Hey, Tristan, what's up?"

"Almost all the tables have been wiped down, and we're starting to set for breakfast," Tristan reported. "But there's an old kook who swears he came in with somebody. He won't get up from the table without them, and we don't know what to do. He's holding us up."

I grimaced at "kook" but decided to let it pass for now.

"Okay," I replied, glancing over the shining stainless steel prep counters, "let's go see." We started walking back to the Romero House dining room.

"Did you—"

"We already checked with the greeter, and she swore he came in alone off the St. Mary's bus," Tristan said.

We arrived at the table to find the scene largely as I imagined, so I adopted a deliberately cheerful voice.

"Ah, Mr. Cooper, good morning. Happy Thanksgiving. What seems to be the problem?"

Cooper's face brightened when he saw me.

"Mr. Porter, I'm glad you're here," he said. "These thugs are demanding I leave this establishment without my wife, and that's something I simply cannot do," he explained. "I told them she left to the ladies', and I'm sure she got caught up chatting with someone on the way back. She'll return momentarily, but they seem to think I'm crazy." He glared at the assembled teens and young adults again.

I set my clipboard on the table and squatted beside Cooper.

"You're not crazy, but we both know that sometimes, not always but sometimes, you're a little forgetful. Am I right?"

"Well, sometimes," Cooper grumbled.

"Like what day is today?"

"I know it's Thursday."

"That's right. And what does Maggie have every other Thursday?"

Cooper paused, then gave a chagrined sigh. "Bingo," he admitted sheepishly.

"That's right, bingo. So, if you'll catch the last St. Mary's bus, I expect she'll be back shortly, and she may have won."

Cooper smiled a little at the thought, then looked around at the young people surrounding us.

"I apologize for any trouble I caused."

"No worries," Tristan said before I could reply.

"That's right. No worries at all. Everyone forgets things sometimes, isn't that right, team?"

The young people gave an assenting murmur, relieved the holdup to their shift was being removed.

"Why don't you go with Tristan here, and he'll make sure you get on the bus, okay?"

Tristan nodded as Cooper began moving with him toward the exit.

"Now, the rest of you, I know the setting team could use some help, and could someone please check on Jenny and see if she needs assistance wrapping up the dishes?"

The group broke up as each returned to their end-of-shift tasks, and I went back to checking that everything was set for the breakfast makers who would arrive at five the next morning.

Ever since Romero House had helped me and my boyfriend, Lyle James, fight off a bureaucratic and legal assault from city hall, we had each tried to do something to help the education, health, and nutrition center. Lyle began servicing the charity's vehicles at his garage, Bonne Chance Motors, charging only for parts and supplies, and I started volunteering to coordinate their dining operation, particularly when demand rose in the fall and winter.

I made my efforts at Romero House do double duty by getting Tristan DeJesus, my barely nineteen-year-old mentee, involved as a volunteer as well.

Now I waited by the kitchen door for Tristan to get his jacket for the ride home. We walked to Lyle's pickup in silence, but after I pulled away from the curb, he spoke up.

"I'm sorry about saying 'kook,'" Tristan said. "As soon as I saw your face, I was sorry I said it. I just get frustrated sometimes, you know?"

"I know. I felt that a lot when I got started. You walk into a situation where a solution looks obvious, but it's not obvious and that makes it frustrating."

"Can I ask a question?"

"No, but you may." I smiled.

"Ha ha. How come you told that man his wife was at bingo? I don't believe anyplace has bingo on Thanksgiving. Where was she anyway?"

I sighed.

"Dennis Cooper is one of our regulars from St. Mary's. A teenager driving drunk ran a red light in 2013 and killed his wife Maggie as she walked across the street. Cooper never really got over it. His memory has started failing, and he forgets that Maggie's not here anymore sometimes."

"Awww, man."

"So now, when we're dealing with him and he forgets, we have a choice," I continued. "We can tell him his wife is dead, so he feels all that grief and sorrow all over again." I pulled to the curb in front of Baldwin House, where Tristan lived. "Or we can let him keep believing he's going to see her in just a few hours."

"But won't he realize it when she doesn't get back after fake bingo?"

"He forgets before then. In fact, he's probably already forgotten he had dinner with us today," Manny replied.

"That's really wild. And sad."

"It is, but it's also an option we can give thanks for having. We don't have to tell him his wife has died over and over again. What are you cooking for the Baldwin House table?"

"Nothing," Tristan said with a laugh. "Ms. Dass let me off the hook for the kitchen because I volunteered at Romero this morning. But I'm the oldest, so I still have to carve the bird."

"You ready?"

"Thanks to YouTube," Tristan said with a grin.

"Viva YouTube!"

Tristan started to open the door. "I got something going on at my internship," he said. "It's no big deal, but could I talk to you about it sometime soon?"

"Sure. Let's make it happen this weekend."

"Thanks, man," Tristan said. Then he bolted out of the truck and up to the Baldwin House door.

I watched my mentee enter the shelter, then I pulled away from the curb.

Tristan was the oldest of Baldwin House's residents, most of whom are formally foster wards of the institution. If you are gay, lesbian, or a transgender person under age twenty-one, living somewhere in the states between Florida and the Carolinas, whose family kicks you out, abandons you, or otherwise can't care for you, one place you can go is Baldwin House.

Tristan had aged out of the institution's formal structure but remained by paying a nominal rent and complying with the rules.

The solution lent him the support of a foundation while getting started, and I marveled at the skills of Arundhati Dass, the shelter's

Indian-born director cum den mother, at keeping the whole place together and thriving.

I parked Lyle's truck back in its familiar spot and headed upstairs. Once I had formally moved in, I didn't have to ring the bell to get in. I rested my right thumb on the little black screen beside the door to start the lift on its clanking, banging descent.

Moving in with him had been a big step for both of us. For Lyle, because it represented the first time he had trusted anyone else enough to allow them into his heart and his home. For me, because I had to adapt to a man who didn't communicate easily and who was often not as forward as I am concerning our sexuality or relationship.

For example, in a couple of hours we would be celebrating Thanksgiving with my parents and extended family at Albemarle, my parents' large estate. In the face of what I considered their continued denial of my being gay, I felt a need to assert it regularly, but Lyle disagreed.

"Papito, your parents aren't stupid," he reminded me with my pet name that morning while he shaved and I showered. "Of course they know we're gay. Especially your father. After all that's happened this year, how is he going to not know we're sleeping together or that you love cock?"

Lyle, as usual, put the topic in the most in-your-face terms.

"You're right, my dad's not the problem. But my mom has a real thing about it. Not only can she not bring herself to the say the words 'Jose is gay,' she hasn't stopped trying to get me married off to one of her friends' debutantes."

"But look at where we are," Lyle said as I turned off the water and stepped around the shower wall to find him waiting with an outspread towel. "Who invited not just you, but both of us to Thanksgiving dinner," he asked as he started a rubdown.

"Mom?" I murmured from inside the terrycloth tornado.

"And who called back later to make it clear we didn't have to bring anything?"

"Mom."

"And anyway, didn't you tell me they have the family matriarch coming this year? That alone was enough to make both your parents want to keep us safely in a closet somewhere, but they still invited us."

He was right about that. My mother's aunt Cici, age ninety-six and allowed to emigrate from Cuba for health reasons, was going to be there too. For Mom, of course, this was a big deal. For my father too. But for me, she would be little more than another bony hand to bruise my cheek and another barrier preventing my parents from fully acknowledging me as their gay son.

"Okay, let's compromise," I said as I finally emerged from the tangle of towel to find Lyle giving me his signature smirk. "So long as no one asks, we won't identify. If Mom persists in introducing you as merely my friend the mechanic who I mysteriously decided to invite to Thanksgiving dinner, so be it. But if anyone asks straight out 'are you gay or is he your boyfriend,' we fess up and let the feathers fly where they may."

Lyle pondered this a second, then agreed. "Fair enough," he said. "If they ask the question, it's on them."

"Okay, but don't blame me if I have to divide my attention between you and some Angela from Little Havana Mom has seated next to me to try her luck," I said.

Lyle laughed. "I won't, but who's to say she just doesn't get swept off her feet by all that Papito? We could hear wedding bells in the distance."

"God, you're impossible sometimes," I muttered as I stalked from the bathroom to get dressed.

"How many people are going to be at this thing, anyway?" Lyle asked as we started the twenty-minute drive to Albemarle.

"If Mom is feeling up to it, a cast of thousands," I said. "Don't try to remember them all. Most of them I see once a year. I'll introduce you to the ones you might need to recall later."

"And there're some, like Aunt Cici, that you haven't even met yet, right?"

"Actually, that's Great-Aunt Cici, since she's my mom's mother's older sister, and no, I haven't met her yet."

I glanced over at him. In honor of the occasion, he wore dark dress pants, formal shoes, and a white French cuff shirt with small gold cufflinks. By contrast, I had on loafers, khakis, and a pale blue polo.

"Except for my dad, you're going to be the most formally dressed man there," I said.

"Did I overdo it?" The touch of anxiety in his voice surprised me. "It's one of my things," he added. "I'm a mechanic and a business owner. But in some situations, it's better to dress similar to a grease monkey and others like an entrepreneur. Meeting my boyfriend's parents formally for the first time is not the occasion to have oil under my fingernails."

"You've always cleaned up quite nicely," I said.

Then, overwhelmed a bit by the day and his presence beside me, I started humming a Broadway tune.

"That sounded nice, what was it?"

"I'm sure you know it," I replied. "It's classic."

I hummed the line again, slower this time.

"Nope. Drawing a blank," he said, and a side look at his face confirmed his sincerity.

"God. Do I have my work cut out for me? That's a line from a song called 'Something Good' that is part of *The Sound of Music*, only about the most famous musical in the world."

"Sorry," he replied, a bit abashed. "I like music fine, but I haven't seen any musicals."

"What? Any?" I couldn't believe it. "Didn't your high school produce *The Music Man* or something as a fundraiser?"

"I went to an all-boys, military-minded school," he reminded me. "We had a choir that sang things like the 'Marines' Hymn' and 'The Battle Hymn of the Republic,' but no musicals."

We drove on a few moments without speaking.

"For what it's worth," I eventually sighed, "I felt grateful to be here with you, and I sought a tender moment before we entered the lion's den." I rolled down my window as we pulled up to the Albemarle gate. "Manny and Lyle," I called out to the wall box, and the entry started to open.

"I'll make it up to you later," Lyle whispered, leering at me. That made me shiver a little because I knew he would.

Lyle parked the truck some distance from the house, and we sat for a moment, watching people arriving in groups of two to ten. We both felt the tension rise.

"We only have to make it through the meal," I reminded him. "And after dinner, if either one of us hears the other use the word 'hippo,' we'll know it's time to start moving toward the exit."

"Hippo? What kind of safe word is that?"

"A perfect one. Can you imagine a conversation arising where we would have to use the word 'hippo' involuntarily? Now, come on."

We left the truck and started walking up the path toward the front door. I could tell my mother had been busy. Her manicured and well-watered flower beds testified to hours overseeing and harassing whatever landscape firm had been foolish enough to expect an easy contract from the Porter house.

On the doorstep, Lyle turned and looked over the grounds before we entered.

"They really are magnificent," he said.

"Be sure to tell my mom that first thing," I said. "That will get you off on the right foot."

We stepped through the door into the entranceway where, to my surprise, we found my Aunt Sammy nursing a cocktail alone.

"Manny, my darling boy, come give us a kiss."

I approached and received her usual rib-bruising hug and a peck an inch below my right ear before she turned her attention to Lyle.

"And of course I'm so glad you came." She tracked him in a vaguely proprietary way. "You know, it's really unfair that you get better looking every time I see you," she said, before adding sotto voce to me, "I'm glad he's your boyfriend and not mine. If he were mine, I wouldn't ever get any work done at all."

"Aunt Sammy, behave," I scolded. "Now you've started him blushing, and he hasn't even faced the family yet."

"Oh, I apologize, dear," she said, looking up earnestly at him. "I didn't mean to embarrass you."

"No, it's fine, please," Lyle replied. "I appreciate the… enthusiasm."

"By the way, where is the clan?" I asked, admiring the quiet in the house.

"The brigade of people under age eighteen are out at the pool, being looked after by one of your many cousins," Sammy said. "Some of them are helping Javier with last-minute meal preparation, and the rest are with the other guests having drinks on the lanai. I was on my way to join them again. Shall we go together?"

She hooked her arm in Lyle's, and we set off toward the back of the house.

"Have you met Great-Aunt Cici yet?"

"Yes," she said, "and she's splendid. In fact, she is so splendid I'm just a tiny, wee, small bit jealous."

"What, you?"

"Sadly, yes me," she confessed. "I'd gotten used to not having to work at being the cool grand dame at family events, and now it looks like I may have some competition." We had arrived at French doors leading out onto the screened space. "But I might be exaggerating too. Tell me if you think I'm right when you meet her." She paused at the top of the short steps. Lyle and I descended first.

My mother spied us immediately and glided over. "Manny, darling, so good to see you!" she gushed.

"Mother," I said. "Happy Thanksgiving."

"And a happy day to you too. This must be Mr. James?"

I stood aside briefly and introduced Lyle. "Isabella Porter, may I present my friend, Lyle James? Lyle, my mother, Isabella Porter."

"Encantado, señora," Lyle said, bowing slightly from the waist.

"Oh, mi corazon, but the honor is all mine." She grew serious in about a second. "You helped bring my son back to us," she said. "I owe you a million thanks."

"I care for Manny very deeply, señora," Lyle said. "It was my honor to bring him safely home."

My mother paused and waved her hand in front of her face. "The conversation grew very serious very quickly," she said. "Manny, come meet Cici."

We walked together to the small clump of people who were gathered at one of the round party tables in the corner of the lanai.

"Cici," my mother proclaimed in a loud voice. "Here is your great-nephew, my son Jose Immanuel." The assembled cousins parted, and we could see one another, her all smiles and wrinkles, piled white hair, green sequined gown, and sparkling eyes. Instinctively I went to her side and squatted to offer my hand. "Encantado," I said.

"Oh, my boy," she murmured and then took my hand in both of hers. "The enchantment is all mine," she said, immediately calling my mother. "Isabella, Isabella!"

"Yes, Cici."

"His eyes. He has Elena's, doesn't he? My boy, has anyone ever told you how much you resemble your grandmother?"

I shook my head no.

"Well, you do. Now stand up. Let me take a good look at you."

I stood and stepped back, allowing her to study me closely with her green eyes.

"Excellent," she said. "Your mother doesn't exaggerate about you," she added. "And who is this giant?" She tilted her head like a bird to look past me at Lyle.

"This is my friend," I said. "Lyle James. Lyle, my Great-A—"

"Aunt Cici will do fine. I haven't accomplished enough good things yet in my life to deserve to be called great."

"I'm pleased to meet you, Cici," Lyle said.

At that point a gong sounded from within the house, signaling it was time to go in for the meal.

The repast, as Thanksgiving dinners go, passed unremarkably. One high point came when the eating had begun to slow, and Cici leaned across the table to ask Lyle and me, in an exaggerated stage whisper, how long we had been boyfriends.

Poor Lyle had been taking a drink of wine then and wound up in a brief coughing fit. I felt the heat of one of my hated blushes.

My mother set her fork down with a clank. "Cici!"

"Oh, calm down, Isabella. I'm ninety-six years old. Don't you think I can recognize young lovers when I meet them?"

She turned to me again. "Well?"

"Right about a year," I croaked, reaching to gulp some water.

"Excellent," she said. "May I ask as to your line of work, Mr. James?"

Lyle had finished coughing after emptying his water glass and another offered by an observant waiter.

"I own my own business, Aunt Cici," he said.

"And what sort of business is that?"

Lyle coughed again. "I'm a car mechanic, ma'am. I own my own garage, called Bonne Chance Motors."

"Oh, that's splendid," she said. "Where I come from, good car service people—meaning they know what they are doing and don't cheat you—are treated like gods."

The other memorable moment came when my father pulled Lyle and me aside as we were leaving.

"Meet me at the garage in five minutes," he whispered.

Intrigued, I led Lyle out the back of the house, down past the pool to the long, shadowy garage building. Dad waited for us outside the third bay door.

"What's up, Dad?" I whispered, though there was no chance of anyone hearing us. "You haven't bought Mom a car for Christmas, have you?"

"Hardly." He laughed. "Even if I bought her a new car, she wouldn't stop using the Lexus," he said. "No, look at this!" He hit a button on the wall, and the door slid open to reveal a new, electric blue Toyota Prius.

Lyle and I stood there, gaping. "Wow, Dad," I finally said. "It's beautiful, but I didn't think you would ever go for a hybrid."

"I haven't," he said. "This is your car."

"What?" Now my mouth truly hung open.

"This is your car. And it's not from Mother and me, although we think you deserve it. It's from the editors and publishers of the *South Georgia Record*. We consider your work through all the ups and downs of the Tinker Creek story to have been extraordinary, as has been the growth you have shown. After we decided last December to start rewarding a journalist of the year, you were unanimously voted to be that reporter this year."

"My God, Dad. I don't know what to say."

"Well, a 'thank you, Mr. Porter,' would be a start," he said. "Since I am definitely making this award as your editor-in-chief, not merely as your father."

"Thank you, Mr. Porter. And thank everyone who voted for me. I'm truly overwhelmed," I said.

"Well, you can drive it home today. All the taxes have been paid. The title and related paperwork is in the glove compartment, and the tank is full. Happy Thanksgiving, son."

❖

Other than driving it home from Albemarle, the first place I took the new car, which Lyle dubbed the Electric Blue Gumdrop, was to Tommy and Daniel's for our annual leftover feast and holiday moan.

We had let the tradition lapse after graduation from college but decided to pick it up again as we contemplated managing our holidays in a new location with new people.

Now I would arrive with a huge electric blue piece of Yuletide news that got fifty-four miles per gallon, carrying a trunk completely full of ambivalence.

On the one hand, I loved the car. Sincerely. I breathed in gulps of the new-car smell, intentionally backed all the way down Lyle's block for no purpose other than to use the rear-view camera, and started obsessing on how I could use as little fuel as possible. No more rideshares, I told myself. No more making sure I could afford to go here or there toward the end of the month. No reliance on someone else for basic transport.

But on the other hand, guilt consumed me. Tommy wrote the story that helped the police find out what happened to our kidnappers. Why shouldn't he get the car? Yes, I did some basic reporting on a story that fell into my lap, but how did that make me the paper's best journalist of the year? All I had done was almost get myself killed, and I wasn't sure that deserved a reward from people who were glad it hadn't happened.

I had worked myself into enough of a funk that I arrived at Tommy's a growling, dissatisfied mess.

"Happy Thanksgiving," Tommy said, beaming at me when he opened the door to have me brush past his holiday hug.

"What's so happy about it?"

"Um…it's a day to remember our blessings and give thanks for what we have," Tommy said as he closed the door.

"That's the rub, isn't it?" I growled. "Blessings aren't exactly divided up according to merit."

"If you say so," Tommy responded cautiously. "What would you like to drink? We have beer, wine, or something stronger as long as its recipe isn't too complicated."

"Nothing. I'm driving," I said with a snarl.

"You are? Where's Lyle?"

"He said he might not make it because of a complicated A/C job, but he likely didn't want to hear me bitch anymore. Why don't you step outside, and you can see the source of ill feelings."

Tommy got up and pulled on his jacket, going outside for about thirty seconds before he was back inside and shouting up the stairs. "Danny! Come see Manny's new car!"

In a flash, Danny thudded down the stairs and out the front door, then silence. After about five minutes, they returned.

"Oh my God, Manny, it's beautiful." Tommy gasped. "And a Prius! That's like perfect."

"I'm not a big Prius fan," Danny said. "But you definitely got one of the prettier ones out there. And it looks like you got all the bells and whistles too, cool."

"But what's wrong?" Tommy said. "You're over there looking like a pastor in a strip bar."

"Would the car still look as good to you both, particularly you, Tommy, if you learned I won it for allegedly being the best reporter at the *South Georgia Press* last year?"

"What?" Tommy said.

"What difference would that make?" asked Danny.

"That's why I have this great car. Because my dad told me all the other editors and reporters at the *South Georgia Record* voted me as the best journalist at the paper. My problem is that I don't feel I deserve it."

"God! Out of my admittedly few friends, you take the cake," Tommy said. "Get over yourself. For your information, I'm not shocked you won. When they sent around that silly ballot, I voted for you. As did every other reporter I asked on my floor."

"But I'm not that good a reporter. Half the time my notes are for shit, I lead off interviews with stupid questions, and that whole story fell into my lap."

"Who cares?" he replied. "I didn't base my vote on how well you report, but how much I admired what you did. I know *I* couldn't have done it. And almost everyone's stories drop into their laps. I voted for you because I imagined myself in your situation, and that made me appreciate you that much more."

"I don't want to say the wrong thing, because I know next to nothing about what you and Tommy do all day," Danny said. "But it sounds to me like you don't feel comfortable accepting what other people say or think about your efforts."

I nodded. "That's more or less right."

"You need to get past that," Danny said. "I had a football coach in high school who was all about the honest self-assessment. That was all that mattered to him. Look candidly at what you did right and what you did wrong and learn from it for next time—because if we're still walking the earth, there's going to be another challenge. When we do that," he concluded, "what other people say or think doesn't amount to a whole lot."

"What he said," Tommy said. "I mean, I get it. You look at what happened and your role in it and part of you might think, fuck, I could have done so much better. Those are the observations you need to pull from when you face the next challenge. And in the meantime, enjoy the damn car and enjoy taking your friends places in it," he said, narrowly missing my head with a pillow.

I conceded they had a point. Everyone who creates or writes or builds something must be able to appreciate the whole of what they did and not merely focus on whether this or that step or word or rivet was exactly the right one. Or, at my dad often says, anything worth doing remains worthy, no matter our proficiency in it.

We passed the rest of our time together joyfully. We ate turkey fricassee, potato pancakes made from mashed spuds, a casserole Tommy created from leftover rice and veggies, and all that remained of a sweet potato pie. After the meal, Danny phoned a special request for Lyle to come over so they could discuss Tommy's plans to renovate the carriage house for their eventual bed-and-breakfast. Lyle, ever the good sport, announced he had drained his last Freon line for the day and came over. The pair of them vanished to look at rafters together.

That left me and Tommy to cover the remaining leftovers with plastic wrap and load the dishwasher.

"A bed-and-breakfast, huh?" I asked.

"That's the plan," Tommy replied.

"Have you two given a thought into how much work that is? I get that hospitality, cooking, and looking after people is your thing, but it's also a twelve hours a day, seven days a week job."

"We know. But we both want to do something where we work for ourselves and can build over time," he said as he covered the remaining apple and pecan pies. "I enjoy being a reporter. It's an interesting job that keeps me talking to dynamic and engaging people. But I don't love journalism the way you do. I'm not always imagining the next big story or the future market I want to cover. I can see a time when I leave the *South Georgia Record* to work with Danny full-time on this place. Besides, we're gonna have five bedrooms and four baths at most. It's not like we're gonna try to be two people running the Ritz."

I could see his point, but I didn't want to look too closely at it either. Neither Lyle nor I had brought up the future much, as in what would we do if I got the opportunity to join the staff at the *Wall Street Journal* or *New York Times*. When I considered the question honestly, I couldn't see Lyle leaving Bonne Chance Motors either. It had become such a part of his life.

Instead of having that conversation, we had fallen into focusing on a narrow horizon. What were our plans in ninety days or six months? This felt easy because Lyle had always lived his life that way, and I hadn't wanted to raise the question, finding such a warm home in his arms that I didn't have any desire to be anywhere else. But I wondered how long I would be able to discover enough of the sorts of stories I liked to report in our bucolic hometown.

❖

I stood at the center of a mat in the center of Lyle's workout space. Its surface felt cool and soft under my bare feet. I wore a light gi with a helmet and blindfold. Tension raised the hair on the back of my neck and on my arms as I awaited the assault I knew would come but could not predict.

Lyle attacked from behind me on my right, trying to tug me from my feet and defeat me by pulling me off the mat. But I remembered the training we'd practiced for months and bent from the waist to lower my center of gravity and make myself harder to move. I stomped on his feet at the same time I reached through his legs to strike repeatedly at his groin.

He grunted and his grip slipped for a second, leaving me enough time to twist in his hands and attack his ears and face with my elbows until he let me go and I retreated back to the mat's center. I won that round. I pulled off my helmet and blindfold and found him with his eyes watering from where my elbow connected with his nose.

"You get better every time we work out," he said. "I'm going to have to start wearing a face guard."

"Well, I've had a good teacher." I hoped the compliment would get me an easier workout, but he shot me a hard look.

After I'd recovered from the kidnapping last year, Lyle had decided I needed to have some training in a self-defense discipline called Krav Maga, which teaches its practitioners to focus on attackers' weak points. Today was one of our twice-weekly training sessions.

"Sparring," he said. We each got into our light pad suits and took our positions on the mat.

Lyle came at me hard, with everything. His goal, again, was to get me off the mat and onto the floor. Mine was to remain on the mat.

Today, I was in trouble from the start as a flurry of blows made my head spin. As he knocked me off balance, I was forced to step backward off the mat.

"You're thinking too much," he declared. "With the blindfold on, you react by instinct and you're lots faster. No thinking, doing. As soon as the eye sees, the hand or foot should respond."

He pointed me back onto the pads and returned, this time wearing the big, cushioned gloves.

"Punch and kick drill," he said. "Go."

In this exercise, he moved the gloves up and down, left and right, and I tried to hit or kick them depending on where they were. I got one point for each successful strike, and the drill ended when I reached fifty.

"No thinking, no thinking," he almost chanted. "Now, now, now," he said, meaning I should strike at each word. At first it was impossible, but gradually I found a place where my brain remained in neutral and I moved on instinct alone. When I finally reached fifty, I collapsed, panting, onto the mat. He dropped down beside me.

"Terrific ending, Papito," he said. "It still takes you too long to get there, but we can keep working on that."

"Goody," I gasped.

I sensed his grin and felt his calloused hand making its way up the inside leg of my light pad suit.

"Join me for a shower," I panted.

"I thought you'd never ask."

Afterward, we shared some time on the big master bed. Lyle lay stretched out on his stomach while I straddled him, working my hands up and down his back and shoulders. I bent to kiss that little place behind his right ear, making him shiver.

"Stop," he said. "That tickles."

I returned to rubbing his back, which drew a satisfied groan.

"I have a question."

"Okaaaaay."

"I'm not asking because I'm thinking about anything specific, but have you ever considered living anywhere else?"

"Hmm, what?"

"Living someplace else. Anyplace. Somewhere different than here."

"Like where?"

"I don't know. Anywhere. California. Vermont. Montreal. Miami. The Yucatán?"

"Papito, what? Are you looking to move? You only just got here," he pointed out.

"I know. And I don't want to live anywhere else, right now. I'm just thinking about the future. Our future. That's all."

He turned to his side, making me fall back onto the mattress. We lay facing each other.

"Does this have anything to do with your mystery funk from yesterday?"

"I don't know. That's what I'm trying to figure out." I traced my finger up his chest, through his small forest of hair.

"I thought I had a pretty clear reason for moving back home. I wanted to join my dad's paper and make a point with him about my skills or worth or something. Earn his pride."

"Okay, that makes sense."

"But then I met you. And you were at the heart of this huge fight that also happened to be this huge story. Now it's a few months later…"

"And you're wondering whether you've achieved everything you set out to do here?"

"A little bit," I admitted. "But then I look at what happened from my point of view, the ultimate insider's perspective I guess, and I think I'm nowhere near close to doing that. I mean almost everything took place accidentally, at least as far as I was concerned. You, Lucinda, Oscar, and Eva were the principals. I helped out, and I was glad to do it but didn't do much in the end—and I recognize that's not the way you or my dad or Tommy or a bunch of other people look at it."

He kissed my nose.

"God, Papito, what goes on in that head of yours! I believe you think too much. But for what it's worth, here is the answer to your question. No, I've never desired to live somewhere else. I've traveled to different places. Atlanta. Washington, DC. New York City. Chicago. Los Angeles. I had fun there, and they were great to visit, but home has always been here for me."

"And that's the way it will always be?"

"Not necessarily. I mean, I would never say I would on no occasion consider living somewhere else. But so far, I haven't found anything or anyone who made a compelling case to move."

"And visiting other places?"

"Oh, Papito, I will always be up to travel. In fact, you might be the one to get me to make a trip outside the US. I've always been too intimidated to go to all the trouble of getting a passport and all that stuff." He kissed me again and slapped my butt.

"But now I have to stop lazing around up here and go see if that tailor has finished altering that tux for me," he said. "Danny and I agreed there was no way we were going to our first holiday party together without all of us being dressed to impress."

I laughed. "Do I get to see it first?"

"Not until the morning of," he said.

He ducked into the walk-in closet to start pulling on clothes while I cast my mind on what I had to wear. I felt confident my current tux remained stylish and fit for the event, but the AthenaLibre annual holiday cocktail party dominated the St. Michael's Harbor holiday social calendar and might require a new shirt. I resolved to get to Henry & Mechum first thing Monday morning.

CHAPTER 2

Deck the Halls?

AthenaLibre started in St. Michael's Harbor in the year 2000, when two local boys, Derek Fuller and Andrew Blanc, got together in a foreclosed warehouse to program better video games. Their early success led to more computer coding, the steady hiring of employees, and, finally, the purchase of the nearly empty industrial park surrounding their depot.

That space became the AthenaLibre campus, and when I pulled the Electric Blue Gumdrop onto Innovation Avenue, the property's perimeter fences shone in a series of white, red, and green holiday lights. Santa drove his sleigh past a sky-colored menorah on each side of the main gate, while winter scenes, Christmas trees, dreidels, and Kwanzaa symbols stretched along the rest of the fence.

"Wow, they went allllll out," I crowed as we joined the line of cars and limos slowly moving up to the gate.

"Yeah, it's pretty." Tristan spoke up from the back seat. "We've been watching them set it up, but I haven't seen it all lit."

"It probably costs a lot to light all that," said Lyle.

"Naw, man," Tristan said. "All those lights are LEDs, so not much at all."

"Looks like a pretty good turnout," I said, watching the number of cars.

Eventually, we arrived at the gate, where a young woman in a security uniform wrote down my license plate information and checked us in.

"Jose Porter, Lyle James, and Tristan DeJesus," I said.

She consulted her clipboard. "You're in parking lot number one, Mr. Porter. Drive straight through two blocks, turn left, continue past the headquarters building, and make the first left. Take any space available. Happy holidays."

I followed her instructions, driving slowly past blocks of one-story brick and wooden structures. This was my first time visiting the company's campus, and its size surprised me.

"Wow, Tristan, this place is huge."

"Yeah, it's kind of like a little town," he said. "It can take half an hour to walk from one side all the way to the other, and a lot of people have those electric scooters to get around faster."

"Where do you work?" I asked.

"Two places. Mondays, I do admin stuff in an office down that way." He indicated somewhere behind us. "But on Wednesdays and Fridays, I help out with Dr. Nikolaidis in Lab 5."

"Where is Lab 5?"

"It's in the HQ building, the place we're going for the party."

I made the left, and a large structure loomed in front of us.

"Right there," he added.

I had seen a photo of the AthenaLibre headquarters on its website, but it hadn't prepared me for the reality of a building built in the shapes of globes and tubes. The architect had been inspired by a three-dimensional model of a water molecule. A large ball representing the hydrogen atom stood in the center, connected by two tubes to smaller globes that depicted the two oxygen particles.

"The big ball is admin," Tristan said. "And those windows and balcony way up at the top are the offices for Mr. Fuller and Mr. Blanc. The smaller globe to the right is for chemistry labs, and the one on the left is for computers and robotics."

We pulled into the first lot and took the first spot we saw that wasn't reserved for people with disabilities. We got out, locked up, and started for headquarters, passing several signs that directed parents with children to one of the large buildings about a hundred yards away.

"Do parents with tykes get their own party?" Lyle asked, looking at the small groups of adults and youngsters headed for the other location.

"I don't think so," Tristan said. "But I believe they set up a Santa's Playland for the kids in one of the warehouses."

We arrived at the front door, where two young people in jeans and AthenaLibre jackets were busily checking in guests waiting to enter. A young Black woman immediately came over to Tristan.

"Hey, Tristan," she said.

"Hey, Marie. Are you working during the party?"

"The first part. After we get the guests checked in, we can join the party too. You're looking fine," she said, looking him up and down. "Prom tux?"

"No. My two uncles helped me pull this together," he said.

"Well, good job."

"You want our names?"

"Oh yeah," she said, tapping on the tablet she carried. "I know you're Tristan DeJesus. Are you Mr. James or Mr. Porter?" she asked Lyle.

"James," Lyle replied.

"And that makes you Mr. Porter," she said to me. She dug into a bag I hadn't noticed before and pulled out three red plastic wristbands, each with a small, metallic square.

"Put those on your wrists," she said. "You need them to get into the main party room as well as to get drinks. We have open drink counters but a five alcoholic beverage limit on the night. Have fun, gentlemen, and come find me later for a dance, okay, Tristan?"

"Okay, sure," he said, suddenly appearing awkward.

Marie turned to the next group of guests as we found the door. It opened when Tristan flashed his wristband in front of a solid black plate on the wall.

"Wow, security is pretty tight," I murmured to Lyle after Tristan went off to find us some refreshments. The AthenaLibre lobby felt a bit like a space-age art gallery. Several modernistic sculptures in plastic, different metals, and cement dotted the room, and several modern canvases hung on the walls, including one I thought I recognized as by Jackson Pollock.

Tristan returned with Lyle's beer, my White Russian, and a brew for himself.

"Hey, since when do you get to drink alcohol?" Lyle said.

Tristan blushed. "It's Christmas," he said, "but if you guys object, I'll go trade it for a Coke."

"Hell, I don't care. You're not driving, and I've been drinking since age eighteen."

"I agree with Lyle," I said. "But you won't live it down quickly if you embarrass us here tonight. I'm a little surprised they served it to you."

"It's all computerized," Tristan said. "You choose what you want from a screen and then hold your wristband over one of those metal plates. Your order comes up, and the team of people behind the bar make it and leave it where you can pick it up."

"I wonder if this spells the end of the friendly barkeep," Lyle said.

"I hope not. Friendly barkeeps are among the few truly good things about bars."

"Let's go up to where the music is," Tristan said.

We got on the escalator and rode to the next level, where we heard a band doing a reasonably good version of "Rockin' Around the Christmas Tree." Our wristbands opened the main party room door, leading into a huge space dominated by a dance floor and a Christmas tree over twenty feet tall.

"Look," Tristan said, "there's Dr. Nikolaidis," and he rushed off to greet him. Lyle and I waited until he brought back a lean man in his mid to late thirties with well-trimmed curly brown hair and beard, dark eyes, and a shiny smile. Despite the holiday venue, he wore a three-quarter lab jacket and carried a small tablet.

"Mr. Jose Porter and Mr. Lyle James, please let me introduce Dr. Phillip Nikolaidis, my immediate supervisor during the AthenaLibre internship," Tristan said in a rush. "Niko, please meet my friends and mentors, Jose Porter and Lyle James."

"Delighted to meet you both," Nikolaidis said. "Tristan is an extraordinary young man. Your mentoring him is clearly having a good effect."

Tristan stood up straighter, smiled shyly at Nikolaidis's words, and took a small step closer as the older man threw his arm around his shoulders. "I've found Tristan takes his responsibilities with me very seriously. In fact, my team has made more progress so far this year because we've had an intern like Tristan to help us."

"Of course, we're pleased and proud to hear that," I said, "but we don't take any credit for Tristan's skills or character traits. He had those before we began helping him find his feet going forward and build some confidence along the way."

"Well, he certainly talks about you both a great deal," he said as he played with the hair at the base of Tristan's neck.

I shot Lyle a look, hoping he noticed. Tristan spied a diminutive Asian woman nearby and excused himself to greet her.

"He's expressed satisfaction with his duties working for you, Doctor, but he's mentioned he hasn't found them challenging," I said.

"I'm not surprised. We often struggle with keeping our work interesting to young people," Nikolaidis said. "That's partly the nature of our industry."

"How do you mean?" Lyle asked.

"Making a scientific discovery is often the result of patiently conducting experiments that can often be repetitive and, well, boring," Nikolaidis said. "To use a common metaphor, the forest can be exciting but the individual trees much less so. Sadly, Tristan has been learning about how bleak this scientific work can be at times."

"What areas of research are you working in now, Doctor?" I said.

"Flavorings," he replied with a smile. "Specifically, how we might make plant-based proteins fool the human palate into thinking they are animal-based."

Tristan returned with the Asian woman.

"Dr. Nikolaidis," she said.

"Ms. Fin Chow," he replied.

"Jose and Lyle, this is Ms. Fin Chow, the intern program coordinator," Tristan said. "Ms. Fin Chow, these are my mentors, Mr. Jose Porter and Mr. Lyle James."

"Pleased to meet you both, I'm sure. I hope you've been enjoying our little holiday soirée."

"Absolutely," Lyle said. "The building, the decorations, everything has been grand."

"Thank you. As you may know, AthenaLibre got its start in St. Michael's Harbor, and we've begun to realize how important a role we could have as we begin to give back to the community."

"Was that some of the motivation behind the internship program?" I asked.

"A bit. Although we look upon that as a bit of enlightened self-interest as well. We need to keep cultivating our source for the next generation of coders and researchers."

"Is coordinating the internship program your sole duty, Ms. Fin Chow?"

"No, and that was astute of you, Mr. Porter. I'm vice president for public engagement for the firm. What do you do?"

I chuckled. "I sensed there was a broader portfolio there. I'm the chief business reporter for the *South Georgia Record*."

"Of course! I thought your name was familiar. And Lyle James! You were part of the team that won the Tinker Creek battle last year."

"Guilty as charged, ma'am," Lyle said.

"Well, I'm truly honored you came," she said, "since my grandmother owns one of the properties you helped save. Now I get to thank you both personally."

"And I want to ask you for an interview about the internship program," I said. "We've noticed a trend among corporations to be more thoughtful about their engagement with their surrounding communities."

"I think that's a fine idea. Tell me, would I do as an interviewee, or would you want to talk to either of our CEOs, Mr. Fuller or Mr. Blanc? My schedule is relatively flexible, but theirs are not."

"Actually, I think it would be fine just to speak with you. If we could throw in a couple of short interviews with two of three of the interns, that would be great too."

She reached in her small bag, brought out a card, and handed it to me as I passed her one of mine. "Excellent, Mr. Porter. I'll be in touch. Let's try to get this done during holiday time when it's quieter and easier to schedule."

I gave her a thumbs-up in response as she headed off to greet her next guest.

"Enough of this gabbing," Lyle complained. "Where do we go to get some of the big shrimp I see all these people eating? I'm about to starve."

Having introduced us to his two bosses at AthenaLibre, Tristan excused himself to see if he couldn't find some of the other interns. I told him to be out in front of the building no later than eleven thirty if he wanted to be sure of a ride home.

Lyle and I started to look around for the source of the crustaceans when our attention was arrested by the arrival of a muscular woman wearing an enormous blond beehive that was last in fashion in 1966. In addition to glitter and what appeared to be rhinestones scattered through her hair, she wore a slinky red cocktail dress, white fur stole, jade earrings, and gold lamé shoes.

Her outfit shocked us enough that neither of us of spoke a word until she said, "Excuse me," in a voice that belonged on a 1930s sound stage. "My name is Nadia Elena Reznikov, and I am looking for my fiancé." She extended her hand, the occasion demanding I take it and introduce myself and Lyle.

"And who would he be, ma'am?" asked Lyle, after the introductions.

"Dr. Phillip Nikolaidis," she said. "Dynamic, young, good looking. Usually wearing a lab coat."

"Really? We were just talking to him, but I don't know where he went after he left us. Maybe that woman there might know." I pointed to Ms. Fin Chow across the room. "She works here."

"Thank you. You are very kind," she said, sailing off.

Then we followed a trail of shrimp-eating people to find two big food lines. We had joined the one that looked like it moved faster when I heard a bass voice speak slowly from behind me. “Merry… Merry…Merry Christmas, Manny!”

I turned around. “Pierre! This is truly a surprise. Merry Christmas! What are you doing here?” An old friend from school, Pierre Chamel now served as St. Michael’s Harbor’s city clerk. When I first arrived back in town, he had been an assistant in the office, and he’d played a key role in helping me and Lyle fight to defend his home and business. Pierre had grown up with a significant stutter that he overcame as an adult by slowing his speech much of the time.

He stepped aside to bring up a petite, elegantly dressed woman with a shy smile. “May I present Emily Powers, my girlfriend and ticket to this fantastic party because she works here. Emily, this is my friend from school I was telling you about, Manny Porter.”

“Very nice to meet you,” I said. “I don’t know where Pierre has been hiding you.”

“That’s easy,” she replied. “New York. He wanted to hold off getting together full-time until he finally got a promotion. When he was made city clerk a year ago and a job opened up here, we decided to take the plunge.”

“Well, it’s been wonderful to meet you both. Let’s get together soon,” I said. “Now, I better get going or Lyle is going to eat my arm.” I laughed.

❖

Nobody spoke on the way back from the party. A long work-week combined with good food and choice booze had left us all sleepy. I felt relieved I had stopped at one cocktail and kept to the protein all night, or we might not have made it home.

Sunday morning, I asked Lyle what he thought of Tristan’s boss, Dr. Phil. “Did it seem to you Dr. Nikolaidis acted a little touchy-feely with Tristan at the party?” I asked, holding his feet while he crunched his abs.

"Sixty-eight, sixty-nine, seventy." He stopped for some water. "How so?"

"I don't know. Touchy-feely. The arm over the shoulder, playing with his hair. All that shit."

"Well, I noticed, but I'm not sure I'd call it touchy-feely."

"Why not? It was like they were a couple or something," I said, a little startled by his response.

"Whoa, hold on a second," Lyle said. "Is that a little green homophobic goblin that's popped up on your shoulder? Men can touch each other, even their hair, without having sex or even flirting, you know."

"I'm not homophobic," I said. "I thought I made that clear earlier this morning. I merely wondered if Nikolaidis acted a little forward when it came to Tristan, that's all."

"I don't know that I share your concern," Lyle said, starting the first set of pull-ups.

"Why not?"

"A couple of reasons, actually," Lyle said. "First, when Nikolaidis touched him, Tristan didn't flinch or move away. That suggests he's done it before and Tristan is okay with it. Second, Nikolaidis is from a culture where men are more tactile with each other generally. When I visited a Greek friend's family about a decade ago, I saw a lot of physicality among men who were definitely not sleeping together." He resumed his pull-ups.

"That makes sense," I acknowledged. "But there's a pretty big power differential that might discourage Tristan from rejecting those touches if he doesn't like or want them. And the physicality you saw in your friend's family was between men of equal position, right? Tristan being an intern and Nikolaidis being his scientific director/boss doesn't put them on the same level, does it?"

Lyle kicked his feet to start his body swaying, the prelude for moving to the next rung. "I don't know. Those are good questions. He's your mentee, why don't you ask him?"

I should do that, I thought later as I got dressed. But that was the rub. I, the guy who loves asking questions, had no idea how to ask this one.

I pondered different approaches I might use as I drove the Electric Blue Gumdrop through holiday traffic on the way to Jardin Divin to find an elegant Christmas ornament to give Lyle for the tree this year.

From March through October, Jardin Divin provided St. Michael's Harbor plant lovers with everything they needed to keep their indoor and outdoor gardens growing fantastically. Then, come November, the entire two-acre retail facility switched into holiday mode, with Christmas trees, festive lighting, ornaments, home decorations, yuletide plants, gift wrapping, and seasonal cooking classes.

The goal was to create a one-stop holiday wonderland, and they succeeded enough that I felt a little overwhelmed. Fortunately, a few minutes in front of a map of the yuletide kingdom helped me narrow down where I needed to go. Within a relatively short time, I found two charming ornaments I hoped Lyle would enjoy.

I had positioned myself in a long checkout line when a small female voice got my attention.

"Excuse me, but aren't you Manny Porter?"

I turned to find Emily Powers, Pierre Chamel's girlfriend, looking quizzically at me from off to the side with a shopping basket over her arm.

"I certainly am, Ms. Powers. And how fun to meet you again so soon after the party." I stepped out of the line, allowing us to speak without blocking anyone else.

"It is nice, and particularly lucky since I wanted more time to chat with you. Would you like to share a hot chocolate with me? Pierre says it's pretty special."

"Of course. Lead the way."

I followed her through what felt like a small forest of pine, yew, and fir trees to the garden shop's snack bar, which had been done up as a gingerbread house. After ordering two large hot chocolates and a small plate of madeleines to split, she regarded me from under her long lashes and stylish Tyrolean hat.

"You're every bit as handsome now as you were beneath the lights at AthenaLibre," she said.

"And you're a good deal more forward." I chuckled.

"Oh, I apologize. I forgot myself," she said. "But Pierre has talked about you enough that I feel I know you, at least a little bit."

"Really?"

"Oh yes. He thinks very highly of you. For example, he says you were the one person he felt confident to turn to about his old boss, the late and not lamented Mr. O'Hara."

I paused. "At the risk of undermining your confidence in him, I'm afraid I don't know what you're talking about," I said.

"Didn't he confidentially slip you a drive with city data about the Tinker Creek eminent domain filings on it?"

"Ms. Powers, I can't answer that question. It was a confidential informant whose identity I promised to protect."

"Of course," she said. "Foolish of me to ask. He said you were old-fashioned about some things."

I laughed dryly. "I'm not sure how old-fashioned I might be, but guarding confidentiality is about the only way I can do a proper job as a reporter. If it got out that I shared the identities of sources, I soon wouldn't have any—and then how would I find out what's going on?"

A cute young woman in an elf costume stopped at our table to deliver two bowls of steaming hot milk, two diminutive stainless steel pitchers, and a plate of the lemony French favorites. Seeing our confused faces, she picked up the pitchers, poured their melted chocolaty goodness into each milky bowl, and handed us two spoons.

"Voilà," she said and moved on.

The chocolate aroma wafting up from each bowl as we stirred made both our stomachs growl.

"My goodness, it appears neither one of us had breakfast this morning," she said.

"I've never been much for breakfast, and this morning it was toast and coffee. But enough about my job, what's it like working for AthenaLibre? And I'm not asking as a reporter, but as a curious friend."

"After the first ten months, it's been grand," she replied. "Way ahead of my old job."

"How so?"

"My old job had a lot of micromanagement. Let's just say it was very frustrating."

"And AthenaLibre is different?"

"One hundred percent. Not only could I go to the coders for a program to suit what I needed to do, but I also implemented that program, hired the staff I needed, and set it up with a minimum of interference from administration."

"What do you do for AthenaLibre again?"

"Procurement, more or less. I've implemented a shop model where we have five supply depots on the campus. Everything coming in gets a tracking barcode, and everyone who comes in for supplies has to have a barcoded employee ID to track what they take."

"That sounds very efficient. Who determines how much of something an employee can have?"

"Someone other than me," she said, laughing. "We, meaning my little supply depots, operate on the honor system. We never say no. Now, if you walk out with twenty-five ounces of something but were budgeted for only five, admin may come down on you, but we won't."

"How about socially? What's it like working there? I mean the company seems to have a lot of support in the community. It's a major local employer. Teachers like having AL researchers address science or math classes. What's it like working there if you're not one hundred percent math- or science-focused?"

"It's pretty nerdy," she said. "I mean, I'm pretty math-oriented, but I still don't get half of the math jokes they put up on the humor bulletin board. And there can be some arrogance about that too, but overall it's a pretty sane place to work. And they're very good on work-life balance."

"My mentee is currently an intern there, so I admit I'm especially curious about his boss."

"Oh? What's your mentee's name? I might know him since the interns usually get stuck coming into the supply centers for coffee for their labs."

"Tristan DeJesus."

"Oh, yeah. I know Tristan. He stops by the chem/bio shop pretty regularly."

"So, you probably know his direct supervisor then, a doctor named Phillip Nikolaidis?"

"Ah, the mystery man. I'm a little surprised he even has an intern."

"Nikolaidis is a mystery man?" I asked.

"That's what some of us call him, mostly because very few people know a lot about him. He definitely keeps to himself, works major amounts of time, and doesn't usually go in for social events. In fact, this year was the first we've seen him at a holiday party, and he's been here almost eight years."

"What's he working on?"

She paused and looked a little uncomfortable. "Now we're coming into an area I don't know enough about to give you a proper answer," she said. "If I can use a forest and tree metaphor?"

I nodded.

"His area of research has a lot to do with the physical structures of chemical compounds and the impacts of those architectures on their effects," she said. "So if a compound has a given molecule in a certain position and that position was to be changed somehow, would the compound react or act differently and how."

"Got it," I said.

"Back to my metaphor. That is the section of the forest he works in," she said. "I don't know which particular trees he's working on or what he's trying to do with them, but that's the general idea."

"Interesting," I said. "And important. I expect his work touches on a number of different areas, everything from vaccine and drug development to diverse types of biosciences. Tell me, are all the AthenaLibre projects this secretive?"

"Not at all," she replied. "In fact, most researchers working in similar areas often link up to share their findings and brainstorm strategies. Nikolaidis never joins any such association, partly because he's the only investigator working in precisely that area."

"You said you were surprised Nikolaidis has an intern, yet you know Tristan. That suggests Tristan is pretty close-mouthed about who he works for and what he does."

"I suppose so," she said. "Come to think about it, mostly Tristan and I talk about video games, not what he's working on or for who."

We both neared the end of our hot chocolates, and one lone madeleine sat in the middle of the plate.

"Want the last cookie?" she asked.

"Chivalry precludes. It's yours."

"But feminism counters." Her eyes sparkled with amusement. "Let's split it." A quick flash of her table knife settled the question before I could respond, and the cookie tasted lovely with the last of the drink. We started to gather our things.

"You've been very good about keeping to sensible questions and avoiding gossip," she said in a low voice. "But I have a bit I've been burning to share with someone else besides Pierre."

"Go on," I said, intrigued.

"Well, Nikolaidis has this extraordinary fiancée—"

"I've met her. And I agree, extraordinary is an apt word to describe her."

"Well, at the end of the party, Pierre went to get the car, leaving me in the HQ lobby with that big glass wall, remember?"

"Yes."

"Through the windows, I saw Nikolaidis and his fiancée having a tremendous argument," she said. "Other people didn't appear to notice, so I think it was one of those whisper arguments where couples don't want anyone to know they're arguing. But I could see their facial expressions were terribly fierce."

"What happened?" I felt a twinge of distaste at the eagerness in my voice.

"Right at the moment their taxi pulled up, she drew back and slapped him across the face. Hard!"

"How hard?"

"With enough force that he dropped his phone and staggered a bit."

"My God."

"Then she got in the taxi, and it drove away."

"But how did he get home?"

"I presume he called another cab or a rideshare," she said. "I didn't see the very end because Pierre brought the car, and I had to go." She stood to gather her coat and shopping basket. "I think this has been occupying my mind because it solidified what I found odd about the relationship as soon as I met her."

"Which was?"

"How odd that someone as discreet, retiring, and private as Phillip Nikolaidis would be engaged to someone with the exact opposite of those qualities," she said.

❖

Discussing AthenaLibre with Emily Powers and then getting through the holiday checkout lines made me late to meet Tristan at Baldwin House. My Prius clock had changed to three when I pulled up on the refuge's quiet street. I went around to the back to find Arundhati Dass in the house garden, picking winter squash for dinner.

"You just missed him," she called to me as I entered the yard. "He wanted to make sure he got a court so you two could shoot hoops together."

"How are you doing, Ms. Dass?"

"Doing well," she replied. "My hip still gives me grief when I get up in the morning, but I try not to complain. There's no one to listen anyway," she said, laughing with a dry cackle that made me think of walking through leaves in the fall.

"How's Tristan doing?"

"My champion!" she replied. "Letting him stay on as a renter was such a good suggestion of yours. His rent helps with the house finances month to month, and his presence helps stabilize the house, especially with the younger ones."

As the foster home of last resort for LGBTQ youth from three states, Baldwin House tended to have a floating, impermanent population. Last year at this time, for example, its residents were mostly older teens, and Arundhati luxuriated in a house that almost ran itself. Now Tristan was the sole occupant over age fifteen and had become a natural leader among the others.

She leaned over to me. “There’s something up with him, though,” she said in a low voice, although the yard remained empty except for us. “He’s spending a lot of time on the house computer, and he carefully deletes the history before he gets off it. Plus, he’s missed dinner twice this week as well, which is really unusual.”

“Has he said why?”

“No. And of course, I can’t ask him. He’s not one of my residents anymore. If he obeys his modified set of rules, it’s none of my business. But I think our boy may be in love.”

“Well, I’d better get down to the community center,” I said, pressing my palms together in front of my chest and bowing. “Namaste, and thanks for everything you do, as usual.”

“Namaste,” she replied, picking up her basket of vegetables.

The two-story Tinker Creek Community Center was in the shape of a crescent moon, most of its windows facing an interior common produce and flower garden. Two-thirds of the building, one-third on each end of the moon, were allotted to activities involving the neighborhood’s oldest and most junior residents. The middle of the crescent contained the space provided for more mature children and young adults and held the gym’s basketball courts. I entered through the middle door.

Once inside, I followed the rhythmic sound of Tristan warming up and sat on the visitors’ bench, where I changed my street shoes. He acknowledged me with a nod as I took the court, then shot me a bounce pass when I made a run for the basket. The laid-up ball danced and spun briefly on the rim before falling the right way with a swish.

“Damn! I already see who’s gonna have lady luck today,” he declared.

“Hey, no luck, no luck. All skill.”

“Uh-huh, yeah, right,” he replied. “Horse?”

I nodded. “You got a coin?”

He dug into the pocket of his gym shorts and pulled out a quarter. I was pretty sure it was the same coin as last time.

"Heads I go first, tails you go second," he said.

"Yeah, right. Heads you go first, tails *you* go second."

He flipped the coin. It arced high and caught the sun from the skylight for a few silvery seconds before falling back the court. Heads. He went first.

"Handicap?" he offered.

"Naw, you saw me make that layup."

"Okay," he said. "I just hate humiliating my elders."

"Just keep talking."

He surprised me then, moving not to the foul line where he usually starts but to the right. He positioned himself, took aim, and sent up a ball that found nothing but net. It barely made a swish as it fell through.

"H," he said, passing me the ball.

I moved to the same place and made my stance. He was right to feel confident. He had executed this shot dozens of times, while I didn't as often. But I remembered what Lyle had been teaching me about controlling my breathing. Swish, the ball dropped through.

"H," I replied with a grin.

"Ooooh-wee, lucky again! You better not use up all that magic on the first round. You might need some later."

"Yeah, yeah, just shoot the ball, Jesus."

He moved to the three-quarter position. "Bank shot," he said. The ball spun high, almost too lofty at first, but then it kissed the backboard at the right place and rebounded in. "H-O," he announced, sending me the ball as I moved into position.

"Bank shot," I called. "What's goin' on with you at work?" I sent the ball in a sweet arc right against the backboard. It dropped cleanly through the net. "H-O."

He moved to the foul line.

"Jump shot," he called, then positioned himself, leaped, and released. I could tell the shot was too wide. Sure enough, it hit the rim and bounced clear. "H-O," he said as he chased the ball down and then walked it back. "It's probably nothing, but I got an admirer at work," he said.

"Really? Who?"

"I don't know yet. We've only talked over the computer."

"Your work computer?"

"Of course not. I'm not stupid." He passed me the ball. "His home computer and the Baldwin House computer."

"Foul shot, swish," I called, then took my position and let it fly. I knew it was on target as soon as it left my hands, and it went through the net with a quiet swish. "H-O-R," I said with a grin.

"Yeah, yeah."

"How do you know he's at work?" I asked, passing him the ball.

"Because he contacted me through Knock Knock using my work email. Plus, he knows what I wear to work and tells me when he thinks I'm looking, you know, hot."

"Ooh la la," I said. "What's Knock Knock?"

He sent me a look before he positioned himself at the foul line. "Foul shot, swish," he announced prior to sending the ball through the net with ease. "You need to keep up with shit," he said. "Knock Knock is a new dating app that lets one or both people stay anonymous if they want. The thing is, he's not out." He threw me the ball. "H-O-R."

I moved to the first quarter position.

"Jump shot, bank," I called before sending the ball up. From the outset, I could tell it was a weak attempt, but I held my breath as it barely bounced in. "H-O-R-S. So, what do you know about him?" I asked as I threw him the ball.

"He's older, he's got a cute profile, he's educated. He looks hot in his underwear."

"You've seen him in his underwear?"

It spoke well of Tristan that he blushed a little. "I sent him a photo of me in my gym gear without a shirt and that's what he sent back, but he put a big green dot over his face."

"How much older?" I asked.

"I don't know exactly, but a bit older than you. Maybe like Lyle's age."

"Lyle's age? Dude, that's old."

"No, it's not. You two are like older brother older, not like dad old."

"Except this is where experience comes in. I'm too old to be dating someone barely nineteen. How long has then been going on, anyway?"

Tristan looked uncomfortable. "Like two months."

"Two months!" I felt my head spin.

Tristan moved to the first position. "Jump shot, bank," he said, sending the ball perfectly against the backboard and into the basket. "H-O-R-S."

"How come you never mentioned this before?" I asked. He grabbed the ball and came back dribbling it slowly.

"We were both pretty busy, and I felt a little embarrassed about it," Tristan said. "For real, I decided to break it off like twice already, but each time he talked me out of it."

"So, why tell me now?"

"He wants to meet face-to-face," Tristan said. "Since that feels like a big step, I thought I should let you know what's going on." He bounced me the ball.

I moved to the basket's left side, my head reeling with everything he had said so far. He was nineteen. It wasn't reasonable to demand to go with him to meet this dude. What was prudent for keeping him safe? "For the game," I said, "calling swish."

I moved into position and took my stance before sending the ball arcing toward the basket. Sadly, it hit the rim as it fell in. "Fault. H-O-R-S." I went for the ball and brought it back slowly, dribbling as he had done. "Congratulations, I guess. You haven't really had a boyfriend before, right?"

"Not really, no," he replied. "And for real, I'm not sure I want one now. But I really want to see him finally and figure out what's up."

"I guess it's impossible for me and you to meet him together."

He looked hard at me. "Dude, it's not like I need a chaperone," he said. "Plus, he's not out yet. How am I going to bring a reporter to our first meeting?"

"I know. That wouldn't make sense. Can you do me a favor, though?"

"What?"

I passed him the ball. "Meet him in a public place. Badda-Bean or here or outside L&F. Somewhere with people around. It's just so much safer."

"I'll try, but not likely," he said. "He's pretty paranoid about the whole thing. On the up side, I'm thinking it's unlikely someone who works at AthenaLibre is gonna turn out to be a dangerous sex maniac. I mean, they did a pretty long background check on me, and I'm just an intern."

He positioned himself on the basket's left side. "For the game," he said. "I call swish." Then he sent the ball up and through cleanly, it barely made a sound. "Game. HORSE."

"Thanks for telling me," I said. "You know I'm always gonna be on your side and just want you to stay safe."

"I know," he said. "Thanks for not freaking out about it."

"Well, you're not fourteen anymore," I said with a shrug. "You've got to make and live with your own decisions. Just listen to your gut and be careful. Any time your little voice tells you 'This is a stupid idea,' listen."

He laughed. "Yes, sir."

"Now, on another topic, you ready for the college bus tour on Tuesday?"

"All packed. They know I'm off at work. I'm ready to be here at six thirty Tuesday morning, ugh."

"You got the names of the people you're going to look up at each place?"

"It's on my phone, Dad."

"Don't Dad me. Failing to plan is just planning to fail, but you know that already. Where are you hitting first?"

"UNC Chapel Hill is Tuesday night and Wednesday morning. Duke is Wednesday afternoon, evening, and Thursday morning.

NC State is Thursday afternoon and evening, and we drive back on Friday."

"Sheesh, you'll be tired," I said.

"Yeah, but right now I'm interested in five schools. After this trip, I hope I can shorten that list to two or three."

We hugged then and circled back for another game. He returned later to Baldwin House, where he promised to help one of the younger residents with her algebra homework while I returned to Lyle at BCM. Little did I know it would be weeks before we would experience this sort of time together again.

❖

Anna Fin Chow and I had set 8:00 for the interview about AthenaLibre's intern program. I pulled up to the campus gate at 7:50 and found I was expected.

"Good morning, Mr. Porter. You can use the A parking lot beside HQ," said a young woman in a green uniform and cap at the gate.

"You don't want to see my identification?"

"I saw your name on the daily visitor log," she replied. "And I checked you in at the holiday party. Hard to forget a car this color."

I nodded. That it was. If I had been allowed to choose the car, I would have picked one that was a little more forgettable.

Anna Fin Chow waited for me with coffee at a table near the front of the glassy lobby.

"Good morning, Mr. Porter. Thank you for coming," she cooed. "Given the hour, I took the liberty of bringing you a cup."

She had replaced the husky, wise elder quality from her holiday party voice with a professional girlishness I associated with stereotypes of 1950s secretaries. I hoped this wouldn't signal a retreat into canned public relations answers, because I suspected the holiday party Ms. Fin Chow would make for a much better interview.

"Thank you." I sniffed the brew in the mug she handed me. It smelled delicious. "I've already had coffee, but yours smells too good to resist."

"Thank you." She beamed like a University of Georgia sorority girl.

"I decided to start us off here because human resources wanted to use my office for one of their advanced hiring interviews. It's inconvenient, but I had to agree my office would make a much better impression on a candidate than their shabby old cubicles."

I nodded to signal my compliance.

"Excellent. I thought we would do the intern interviews first, so they can get back to work, and afterward you and I can chat about the program. How does that sound?" She tilted her head and fluttered her eyelashes at me.

Dear God. I wondered when and why she decided she needed to adopt this flirty caricature of the woman I had met at the holiday party. That professional had come across as someone who could answer questions with provocatively thoughtful replies. But this corporate flack made me fear she might not have any newsworthy responses at all.

She pulled a file folder from the large bag hung across the back of the chair.

"Here are bio sheets for the three interns I thought you would want to interview today," she said, sliding it over to me. "They cover all their basic information, so you won't have to waste time with those questions," she said, still in the flirty voice. "Digital copies of those photos can also be sent to you if you need them."

This, at least, was a little more like it and reassured me the professional from the party still lurked somewhere underneath the makeup and saccharine voice. I opened the folder and examined my subjects.

Alison Cassidy, Vernon Baxter, and Jennifer Ayadi looked like they would be fine interviewees. The first two were local kids who planned to attend college next year, and based on his address, it looked like Vernon Baxter lived in Tinker Creek. Jennifer Ayadi came from Atlanta and was on track to graduate from Spelman College.

I drained my coffee mug. "Shall we go?"

We walked over to the far set of elevators, and she used her ID card to summon one. Once inside, she punched the third-floor button.

"The first two interns work in labs belonging to our chemistry and life sciences wing," Ms. Fin Chow explained as we walked into the third-floor hall. "Ms. Ayadi works in a lab on the computer science and robotics side of the building."

We passed a hallway that had a sign for restrooms.

"Excuse me, but that last coffee was maybe a cup too far," I said. "Would you please excuse me briefly to visit the facilities?"

"Of course."

I walked down a hallway of darkened windows on either side and came upon the restroom door after about thirty feet. I had finished my business and stepped back out into the hall, flicking water from my fingers, when the overhead lights began flashing and a siren's unearthly wail filled the air. I paused, stunned, but before I could think to do anything sensible like get back to Ms. Fin Chow, a wall panel dropped from the ceiling to block my way.

Instinctively, I hurried down the hall in the other direction but discovered that blocked as well. I was effectively a prisoner.

Then the wailing stopped. When I walked back to the restroom door, all the lights in the previously darkened hallway were on. Instead of standing between walls of dark windows, I now viewed a couple of sophisticated and elaborate laboratories. The one on my right contained a short bank of computers; a table filled with burners, beakers, and tubes; several other empty pieces of furniture; and a whiteboard on which a complicated chemical formula had been drawn. No people were in the room.

The laboratory on the left had a larger bank of computers and two doors, both shut. It had a table full of chemistry equipment too, but the other pieces of furniture held laptops or different machines. And this workspace was empty of people too, or almost.

At the far end of the room, from the corner of the last window, I spied the figure of a man. He was about medium height with short hair, wearing a white, three-quarter lab coat, and he wasn't moving.

In fact, his stance struck me as odd, almost the attitude of someone beginning to dive from a board into a pool. Torso inclined, arms slightly out in front, legs and feet behind. But nobody could hold that position without falling.

At that point a door opened and two green uniformed security guards stepped into the room. They spent a few moments looking at the man in the lab coat before one left in a hurry and the other whipped out a notebook and started writing things down.

I moved to the barrier that had dropped into the hall and listened. Nothing. I thought about pounding on it to let someone know where I was but remembered that Ms. Fin Chow knew. I hoped I could count on her to alert somebody they needed to lift the barricade.

I wished I could get into the room. But the window glass felt thick, and I couldn't break in without letting the whole floor I was doing it.

Finally, the barricade blocking my hallway slid back up, revealing a green-uniformed security guard and St. Michael's Harbor's Officer Pistou, according to his name tag.

"Mr. Jose Porter?" the guard asked.

"As of this morning," I replied. He didn't smile.

"You need to come with us, sir."

They escorted me out of the building by way of the emergency stairs. The elevators were apparently still not over the effects of whatever the wailing siren meant for them.

"What happened?" I asked.

Neither the guard nor Officer Pistou answered.

We stepped from the stairway at the lobby level into chaos. Crowds of employees, police, firefighters, and EMTs clustered and shifted through the sunlit space. No one appeared to know what was going on, and the sound of radios on different frequencies filled the air.

The pair led me through the front doors and out into the chilly but sunny day. I felt grateful for my pullover and my jacket, which I hadn't removed inside. We crossed the roundabout driveway and halted at what appeared to be a bus stop. A sign on a pole read HQ, and three colorfully painted park benches faced it in a semicircle. Pistou indicated I should take a seat on one. I did.

"Don't move," Pistou said before heading back inside, leaving the guard to stand by the pole and make sure I didn't go anywhere.

I watched as things gradually became more organized. The numbers of AthenaLibre employees milling around dropped. Police cordoned off part of the front drive to park their cars. I watched the medical examiner's black van arrive and deliver a half dozen crime scene technicians who disappeared inside.

Finally, Pistou returned. "Come with me," he said.

I followed him back inside and into a taped-off area where I noticed the police had appropriated one of the company's fine coffeemakers. A familiar figure sat at a table beside it, looking like a rumpled partygoer after the drinks had gone.

"Good morning, Chief Detective Walker," I said in my most cheerful voice. He looked up.

"Manny Porter," he growled. "Have a seat. I might as well take your statement now."

"Of course. Anything to help the police."

"Can it," he snarled.

I sat down.

"As soon as I thought a body at the city's number one employer was shitty enough, they told me the only non-corporate person in the whole building when the body was found was one Jose Porter. Then I knew the day was gonna be special." He pulled out a small digital recorder and turned it on. "Interview with Mr. Manny Porter at AthenaLibre HQ, seven December at ten thirty-five a.m. So, what are you doing here?"

"I'm the guest of Ms. Anna Fin Chow, the company's VP of public relations, and I came to interview interns."

"Interns?"

I told him about meeting Fin Chow at the holiday party, scheduling an appointment, arriving and getting started until everything went pear-shaped in the building.

"Where is Ms. Fin Chow now?"

"I haven't a clue," I said. "But here are the bios of the three interviewees she had lined up." I slid my folder across the table to him. He glanced at the sheets inside and passed it back to me.

"Let me get this straight," he said. "After the building's panic button got pushed, you were trapped in a hallway next to my potential crime scene?"

"I was stuck in a third-floor corridor between two labs," I said. "When I entered the corridor on the way to the restroom, the lights were off in the labs. But when I returned from checking to see if I had a way out, both spaces had their lights on. That's when I saw the body."

"Did you see anybody else?"

"No."

"How long were you there?"

"I don't know. It felt like a long time, but it was probably only twenty minutes or so. I saw the two corporate security officers arrive, and then the police arrived later."

"What did you think?"

"Excuse me?"

"You were standing there looking at a dead guy for almost half an hour. You're a civilian. This isn't usual for you. What did you notice or think about it?"

"I could only see him from the side, so I couldn't recognize him. I thought he looked suspended, but I couldn't see any ropes or wires."

"Suspended?"

"Like he was frozen at the moment he was diving down to the floor, but something had to be holding him up there. His head was down at his chest and his hands looked swollen or puffy, like when people have circulatory issues."

"For what it's worth, he was held up by thin stainless steel wire," Walker said. "It was looped at least a dozen times around his neck. They have a big spool of it in the space."

"So, a suicide." My voice carried my doubts.

"No comment," he said. "And anything I tell you is off the record anyway. Until we get a report from the medical examiner and crime scene guys, this is an unexplained death. But no, my money's not on suicide either, even though someone made a half-hearted attempt to have it look that way."

"Why not?"

"C'mon, Mr. Smart Reporter. How many people hang themselves while their feet touch the floor? And the reason they reached that far was that he supposedly hung himself from the aluminum frame that holds the ceiling tiles in place. Those wouldn't carry the weight of a small child, much less a full-grown man."

I was about to ask if they had a name yet when we were interrupted by a belligerent voice that crossed the sun-filled space like a cannonball.

"What are you doing here, asshole?"

Walker leaned forward and turned off the recorder.

I looked around to find the short, balding, combative Abner Smalls, the *Record*'s lone police reporter, pushing past a protesting officer to enter the taped-off space and stand, glaring, in khaki pants and incorrectly buttoned blue shirt about ten feet from us.

"Good morning, Abner," I said, deliberately pitching my voice lower. "I'm just having a conversation with Chief Detective Walker here."

"Conversation my ass," he said. "You're reporting a crime scene and jumping my beat. Just because you're Daddy Porter's golden boy, that doesn't mean you get to walk all over everyone else. I'm the shop steward, you know!"

Chief Detective Walker chimed in. "Relax, Mr. Smalls," he said in a reassuring tone. "Mr. Porter is actually a witness in this matter, and I was just taking his statement. We were about to wrap up. Mr. Porter, we'll need you to come by the station sometime today to read and sign a hard copy."

"Of course."

"The department knows which reporters are assigned to cover us and which ones have done so for a long time," he said, looking directly at Smalls.

"Thank you, Chief Detective," Smalls said in a calmer, mollified tone. "I know the department values loyalty, and so do I.

But maintaining our internal boundaries is not the job of the people we cover. Believe me, this is not over!"

I gathered my jacket back around me and zipped it up.

"In that case," I said, "you might want to check yourself in a mirror before you leave the house. Improperly dressed people are often not taken seriously. Good day."

I felt his eyes burning into the space between my shoulder blades as I walked out the door.

CHAPTER 3

Enter the Grinch

Though Chief Detective Walker hadn't revealed the name of the deceased to me, he did disclose it later to Abner, who wrote a serviceable story based on the little bit the police were willing to give him at the time. The dead guy was none other than Tristan's boss, the mysterious loner, Dr. Phillip Nikolaidis. The police had still not determined a cause of Nikolaidis's death but had not ruled anything out, including suicide.

Susan Owen, the newspaper's business editor, waited in my office when I walked in the next morning.

"Good morning, Susan," I said breezily as I hung up my jacket. "This is a surprise, but not a big one."

"You and I are going to slowly walk to your father's office, and you're going to give me your side of what happened, so I can be prepared when I get there," she said.

"That bad, huh?" I raised my eyebrows at her.

"Abner Smalls might have the reporting skills of a cockroach, but he's been around for a long time and is popular, particularly with other employees who have been around for a long time, like printers and truck drivers. Plus, he's shop steward, so he automatically has the union members."

"Is he going to be there with us?"

"No, he opted to make his complaint a formal union grievance, which means he got to present it to the publisher alone, without interruption, first thing this morning."

I winced. Few things irritate my father more than starting a day off with conflict.

We set out, and as we strolled, I told her about arriving at AthenaLibre, the promising cast for the interviews, the building shutdown, seeing the body, being found and escorted out and giving Walker a statement.

"I really don't see how there are any grounds for complaint," I said. "I couldn't have jumped his beat because I couldn't have known there would be a death. Plus, I didn't seek an interview with Chief Detective Walker. He pulled me in to make a statement."

She agreed. Presently we arrived at my father's office and Rosa waved us through. "He's waiting for you," she said.

We entered to find him finishing up a phone call. As soon as he hung up, he motioned us to the triad of chairs set up in front of his office's big bay window. Sunlight danced off the red leather.

"All right, let's cut to the chase," he said as soon as we sat down. "Jose, Ms. Owen tells me you were supposed to be at the AthenaLibre headquarters yesterday morning, is that right?"

"Yes, sir."

"And you had no forewarning of the building shutdown?"

"No, sir."

"In fact, he had no choice about meeting and speaking with the police officials," Susan said. "He was escorted out of the building to the police officials without anyone inquiring whether he wanted to be or not."

"When did Smalls arrive on the scene?"

"At the very end," I said. "I had finished my statement, and the chief detective and I were wrapping up my interview."

"I understand there were some aspersions cast?"

"Yes, sir. He called me an asshole and a golden boy of yours, sir, with the implication that I could get away with anything because we are father and son."

"And on your part?"

"I referred to the way he was dressed, sir, calling attention to his misbuttoned shirt and implying he should not be taken seriously because of it."

Dad winced. "There's no other way to say it, Mr. Porter, but Abner Smalls predates either one of us at this paper and cannot be ignored. He came to see me this morning full of flash and vinegar, accusing me of having sent you into the biggest crime story of the year to shake him off that long-term beat. Of course, that was nonsense for the reasons you and Ms. Owen have laid out, but nonetheless, it took me the better part of an hour to get him off that theme and to hammer out a resolution, so here it is."

He slid a memo addressed to me with a copy to Ms. Owen across the desk to us. "First, you're both going to get reprimands in your personnel files for the insults you've leveled at one another."

"But—"

"No buts." He glared at me. "Staff collegiality is essential on this paper, and you wouldn't have gotten a reprimand at all if it hadn't been for your shirt comment. Actions have consequences, so maybe you can learn to better control that impetuous tongue."

"Yes, sir."

"Second, going forward, the AthenaLibre unexplained death, or whatever it is, as a crime and investigation is Smalls's story. Is that understood? That means anything involved with the investigation, its progress, or lack of it is his concern, not yours."

"Yes, sir."

"This, however, is the third part. Anything having to do with the death or investigation's impact on the company, its organization, its operations, its competitiveness, and its morale is your story. We want it covered because the company is the second-largest employer in the area after Bethlehem Baby Food. Any questions?"

"I will be able to use facts from the investigation as they come to light, correct? For example, today we're carrying Smalls's story that the dead employee is Phillip Nikolaidis. I didn't report that, but I can still go forward using it in my reporting?"

"Of course, but if any news is being broken about the investigation, I want Smalls to break it."

"Yes, sir."

"Now, policy aside, what's your gut tell you about this story? Does it have legs or not?"

I paused. “Since we have two reporters, I’m going to answer on two tracks,” I stated. “As far as an investigation, I believe it does have legs. The police have no doubt concealed this from Smalls or made him promise to sit on it, but I don’t think Nikolaidis’s death is unexplained. I think they’re going to call it a murder as soon as they get the results from the medical examiner’s office. From there, we’re talking investigation, suspects, possible arrests, and trials, all with legs.”

“And the second track?”

“That’s harder to measure. From the little reporting I’ve done so far, Nikolaidis was a loner, a solitary figure. He didn’t join the research cliques a source told me often form to share data and strategy. Does anyone give a damn if he’s dead? Do people care that one of their own is murdered? I don’t know. I suspect the initial corporate impact is going to center on his research subject, so that’s where I’ll probably start.”

“All right. As usual, keep Ms. Owen briefed, and she will keep me in the loop. And please steer clear of Smalls. He’s not worth it, and I need you focused on your work.”

“Yes, Mr. Porter,” I replied, feeling like a sixth grader who’d had his hand slapped.

Then he waved us out.

Susan flashed a grin. “A reprimand was the lowest possible grade of disciplinary action. I think you lucked out that he launched the insults first,” she said.

“I know, but it’s still frustrating. Smalls is a dinosaur. I mean, I looked at the way he and Walker gazed at each other yesterday. Talk about a love fest. I bet there’s a lot that doesn’t get reported about the cops in this town, going back to when the best predictor of being arrested in St. Michael’s Harbor was the color of your skin.”

“I agree with you,” she said as the elevator stopped on my floor. “But it’s not your beat. Pick your battles, Manny, please. I’ve already got enough headaches without having to defend you.”

❖

I returned to my office determined to erase the experience of Abner Smalls from my day with a parade of reporting successes. I sat down and started through the voice mails. One of the oldest was from Anna Fin Chow, sounding suitably stressed and apologetic. I called her back first.

"Anna Fin Chow."

"Ms. Fin Chow, this is Jose Porter."

"Mr. Porter, I am so, so very sorry," she said in an abject tone. "After you came out here and everything."

"It's okay. We can reschedule the interviews. My editor still wants the story. But what happened?"

She sighed. "AthenaLibre built this building with an eye to the future. That meant constructing it with tomorrow's needs in mind. The ability to conduct a wide variety of research was one of those requirements."

"And that meant the building had to have a comprehensive emergency shutdown system?"

"That's right," she said. "In case of dire emergency, the program seals off areas of headquarters, automatically deploys sprinklers and anticontaminants if needed, and summons emergency services, including hazmat teams."

"Wow," I said. "Has it ever deployed before?"

"Only in testing and then only once or twice a year, at night, because the tests are so disruptive."

"That explains why so few people seemed to know what was going on."

"Sadly, yes. Administration has already announced it will review its policy on training for the emergency system."

"Why did it deploy this time?"

"One of Dr. Nikolaidis's lab assistants came in and found the lights off. She turned them on, and there was the body. She panicked and hit the big red 'in case of emergency' button."

"Who usually opens that space?"

"Generally, one of the interns," she said. "Hold on, I have the name here."

"No need. Tristan DeJesus, right?"

"That's right." Then, as she remembered I had recommended Tristan, she lowered her voice. "For what it's worth, I'm glad he wasn't the one who found the body."

"So am I. Look, I need to let you know I'm working on a story about the impact Nikolaidis's death might have on the company and its operations, so I have a couple of questions."

"Go ahead," she said, and I heard the clicks of a keyboard.

"At the holiday party, Nikolaidis told us he was researching improved flavorings, but other sources at the same event implied he was working on species-specific pesticides. Which one was it? Or was it both?"

"The only research topic I knew about involved pesticides," she said. "But I don't know every investigator's complete portfolio."

"Could you find out, please?"

"Of course."

"And will the company have any statement about his death regarding its product and research agenda? Will someone else be taking up his work where he left off, for example?"

"I'll check, but we may not have an answer yet. This has only just happened."

"I understand. Thank you."

"And Mr. Porter?"

"Yes?"

"I'll follow up with you about the intern story. I get the feeling we're going to need some good stories in the next few weeks."

"I'm looking forward to it."

Of course, just because Nikolaidis might have been researching something, that didn't mean the company had products or customers ready to go based on that. I needed to talk to someone who could give me a better idea of where AthenaLibre fit in the broader tech and research industries.

I stopped by the employee café, got their biggest latte with extra sugar, and headed down to the basement, where I stood on a big red X in a corridor and pushed the button on the wall.

"What do you want?" came a grumpy, vaguely accusatory voice from the poorly mounted wall speaker.

"I need your expertise, please," I said, trying my best to sound friendly. "I brought your favorite salted caramel latte, extra-large, extra sugar." I lifted the takeout cup to where he could see it. I heard a trumpet blast, and Bernie's heavy, reinforced security door opened wide. I darted in before it began to close again, standing inside the metallic-smelling space, facing a wall of stacked keyboards and towers of old hard drives.

"Where are you?" I called out.

"To your left," he said from somewhere.

I saw a small trail between the piles of computer shells and innards filling the space. I followed the path about a dozen feet until it opened into a remarkably empty work area. Bernie sat at a terminal in the middle, looking noticeably paler and thinner.

"Every few years I decide to clear out," he said. "Maxine's Recycle will send their big truck this Friday, and all that"—he waved his arm to encompass the half of the room I had come from—"is gonna be gone. What can I do you for?"

"I know you keep your ear close to the tech world," I said. "I wondered what you're hearing about a company."

"Ha!" His cackle echoed like a cracking whip. "I bet I know which one—AthenaLibre. The fight for the white castle is about to go public."

"What do you mean?"

"Ground rules first," he said. "You can't quote me, but you can use my shit on background as a source familiar with the industry. I can't give you any documents to back up what I say, but I can send you to other people you can quote who will tell you the same thing. Are we good?"

"We're good."

"Great, now gimme the latte."

I passed over the cup like I was paying for an oracle to read the insides of a frog and got out my notebook. Bernie took the lid off the coffee and swigged.

"Ahh," he said, then indicated a battered chair nearby. "Might as well sit, this could take a bit."

For the next ninety minutes, Bernie told me the story of Derek

Fuller and Andrew Blanc, two hotshot community college coders who spurned matriculating at prestigious technical universities and instead founded a company they called AthenaLibre.

At first, they set modest goals, toying with developing new video games to capture a share of what became an exploding market. But as the games began to become more like movies, they determined they could earn better and easier money by consulting with other game developers. They expanded the company and its research portfolio, adding labs specializing in chemistry, biology, pharmaceutical compounds, and robotics—again with a focus on innovations to improve current products. But as they piled up victories in every area, a crack in the company's foundation became more apparent.

"They're two extremely different guys," Bernie said, adding that he had been their classmate for a year in community college.

"Fuller is a deeply introverted man who comes from a little bit of money. His dad was a US ambassador, and his mother is the daughter of a noted French fashion designer. His childhood included things like summer vacations in Nice. Fuller is the one who is happiest on a computer or in a lab, as well as the one whose ambitions are mostly scientific and less commercial."

Bernie sipped from his coffee. "Blanc is entirely different. The son of a Merchant Marine and a waitress, his summers didn't include vacations at all, much less on a foreign beach. But while Blanc is Fuller's equal when it comes to scientific intelligence, he surpasses his partner in his interest in commercial goals, as well as being the better looking of the two.

"Essentially, once AthenaLibre became successful, Fuller had found his home. He had a lab filled with projects and someone else to sell his discoveries to the outside world. What more could he need? But Blanc had always seen AthenaLibre as a stepping stone to bigger and better things. Further manufacturing, maybe a career in politics. Hollywood and producing movies also interested him. Who knew? All he needed would be to cash in on the AthenaLibre goose and her golden eggs and move on. They argued about it for a year before they finally compromised."

"But it wasn't a perfect compromise?"

"Tut, tut—no running ahead. But you're right. Nobody was really happy with the outcome."

"Could you speed it up a little? I'm running out of coffee."

"Last year they privately sold forty-nine percent of the company to Cogitare, a New York- and London-based scientific investment fund, with a charismatic CEO named Jasper Billings," Bernie said. "Blanc agreed to stay on as marketing president for two years to maintain continuity and help integrate the two business cultures. But the techie rumors suggested it had not gone smoothly.

"The conventional wisdom is that Billings and Fuller haven't gotten along, but the truth is they can't stand each other. Like oil and water. Fuller thinks Billings has all of Blanc's negative commercialism but without any appreciation for the science. Billings thinks Fuller is a weakling too wrapped up in his science to run a company in the real world, and that's where it stood yesterday morning when someone walked in on their dead researcher."

"Wow. Where does that leave operations?"

"Not as bad as you might have thought. Blanc is acting as a buffer between his former partner and Billings. And if you think about it, it's in no one's interest to drive the company down. But they have lost some researchers in the last six months. I can point you to a place where you can probably find some to talk to."

"Yeah, thanks," I said. "That sounds like the next step."

❖

The address Bernie provided was in the city's older warehouse zone north of downtown. Lyle warned me that parking my new car in the neighborhood might not be a good idea, and my taxi driver, a cheerful young Iraqi refugee named Tariq, stopped in front of the address, then turned around to look back at me.

"You certain this is the place you want? I can switch off the meter while you check your phone to make sure."

"No, thank you. I'm confident this is the right building. But the door I want is down on the side," I said.

"Uh-huh." He looked doubtful.

I paid him the fare, adding a healthy tip to reward his consideration for my well-being, and left the car. Number 14, Dock 3 slouched in the evening mist like a seaman down on his luck. Its front window spaces were filled with the sort of glass tiles popular in some 1970s bathrooms, but these were grimy enough that they hadn't admitted light in over a decade.

I thought about using my fingertip to draw "wash me" in the dirt covering one of the larger ones near the entrance, but I refrained. What had been a reinforced red door looked like it had been painted shut. The wall above it bore a faint sign, emblazoned in the same red against the white boards, that read "Smoke only Montecristo cigars! Cuba's best." I wondered briefly if my mother's family had sent any of their harvests here.

Bernie had told me the door I wanted would be down the side of the warehouse with a large "F" painted in white. He also said I wouldn't need the label because it would be the sole portal that had been opened in the last year. He was right. Door F lacked the piles of junk blocking the rest of the stoops, and its short wooden stairs and porch looked sturdy and had non-slip treads on them.

I climbed the brief staircase to the deck and tried to knock on the door with authority.

"Who?" came a gruff inquiry from within.

"My name's Porter," I replied. "I'm expected."

The door buzzed and opened to reveal a giant sitting on a medium stool in front of a wall of small lockers. He had to have been three inches taller than Lyle, and Lyle had two on me, thus he towered over my five-ten. In addition, he stuffed at least 225 pounds into his khaki pants and tight shirt. Muscle strained his seams everywhere. I wanted to ask where he found his clothes, but his expression didn't invite pleasantries. He studied a piece of paper on a clipboard.

"Porter, Jose?" he asked.

I nodded. He put a checkmark on the sheet beside my name.

"Guns?" he inquired.

"Not for me, thanks," I replied quickly, a bit shocked at the question.

"No, smart guy," he muttered. "Guns? As in do you have any guns on your person?"

"Never. Not a one."

"There's a detector at the bottom of the stairs that's gonna scream like a motherfucker if you try to take one upstairs, so it would be better for everyone, but especially you, if you turned it over now."

"Nope. Not a gun on me at all," I said quickly.

"Cell phones?"

"Yes, of course."

"Turn it off and pass it over," he said.

"What?"

He sighed. "Turn your phone off and hand it to me," he said slowly, enunciating each word as though he was speaking to a small child.

I took out my phone, powered it down, and handed it to him. He put it into a locker, did something else in there that I couldn't see, and closed the door. Then he handed me a piece of plastic carrying the number 7.

"Collect it when you leave. Go straight up the stairs. First landing, bar's to the right, game room to the left. Have fun."

I climbed to the first landing. A velvet rope prevented me from going any farther, and the room to the left had no lights burning. Then I stepped into the space on the right to find myself in in a room that Toulouse-Lautrec could have painted, all dark wood and velvet with gilded mirrors reflecting the dim lights.

A large horseshoe-shaped bar, complete with a central mirrored backsplash and side walls of tiered liquor bottles, dominated about a third of the space, while the rest was made up of café tables seating two or three arranged around the room. A small candle danced on each table, and a dim spotlight from somewhere above lit each one as well as every barstool.

No bartender was in sight, but I recognized the room's one

customer seated on a stool. Albert Cross looked to be about forty and had dressed as dapper as Bernie had predicted he would, with a tailored pale gray shirt, formal charcoal-colored pants, and well-polished shoes. A dark blue tie with a gold clip and matching shiny cufflinks completed his outfit. I felt wholly underdressed when he waved me over and offered me his hand.

"You must be Jose Porter."

"And you must be Albert Cross."

"Guilty as charged. Take a seat," he said, motioning to the barstool next to his.

"Thanks for meeting me," I said, looking around. "Where is everybody?"

"Oh, it's early yet for a Thursday." He sipped his cocktail. "What are you drinking?"

"Oh, nothing for me, thanks."

He shook his head. "Rules of the house are that everybody has a drink. It doesn't have to be alcoholic, but everybody has something."

"Then I'll have a kir," I replied. "But there's no bartender."

"Horatio's gone downstairs to bring up some bottles. He'll be back soon."

I looked around more closely. I realized the central mirrored backsplash would let me effectively study any of the other bar patrons without their knowing it. Then I looked more closely at the parade of golden figures running along the glass's bottom edge. At first glance they looked like gilded cherubim, adding to the place's rococo atmosphere. But when I looked more closely, I realized they were small tableaux, representing fornicating couples in about every configuration.

"What is this place?" I asked Cross.

"This is a private bar and club," he replied, "catering to those over twenty-one years of age who enjoy well-made cocktails and/or testing their luck and skill at various games of chance."

"Why meet me here?"

"Why not? I'm a member here. It's familiar and safe. And there are no rules against inviting visitors. Why did you want to interview me?"

"I'm working on a story about AthenaLibre and the impact, if any, of Dr. Nikolaidis's death."

"Ah, yes. Poor Niko. I read about it in your paper. He was a member here, you know."

I reached into my back pocket and brought out my notebook. "May I? They took my cell phone downstairs."

"Of course. If you spell my name correctly, you may quote me too. But," he said, narrowing his eyes, "you can't write anything about this place, understood? This is a private club, and the members want to keep it that way."

"I understand. So, Dr. Nikolaidis was a member here?" I sought to move the conversation back on topic.

Cross drained his glass and set it down. "In general circumstances, we have a rule against revealing anyone's membership, but as Niko's passed on to the celestial speakeasy in the sky, I doubt he would be harmed if you knew."

"I guess I'm surprised. The little I have learned about him made him seem like a very dry, serious sort of person. Not someone I would have easily imagined in a poker game."

"People have many different sides," he said. "Niko in particular. I know he was particularly dedicated to his work, but he could be a demon at the poker table too. The two don't cancel each other out."

"How long did you work for AthenaLibre?"

"About a decade."

"And what did you actually do?"

"I worked in almost every section at one time or another," he said. "I can't tell you what I did exactly because I signed one of those pernicious nondisclosure agreements, but at different points I've been both a hands-on researcher and a research administrator. I really liked it there. Ah, here's Horatio."

A dark-skinned Latino man wearing white gloves and dressed in a tuxedo arrived carrying a box that clinked as he set it down.

"I apologize, Mr. Cross. Some of today's delivery was not where it was supposed to be, and I had to find it," he said.

"No matter, my friend," Cross replied. "Another Maker's old-fashioned for me and a kir for my young visitor."

As Horatio set about making the drinks, I picked up the thread of my questions.

"Then why'd you leave?"

He sighed. "I presume you heard about the Cogitare sale?"

"I have."

"Let's just say the lack of unified direction from the top after the sale began to make the job less fun," Cross said. "When you get put on and pulled off a project six times in six weeks, as I was toward the end, it gets to be more frustrating than enjoyable. Plus, I had this," he said, waving his hand.

"This?"

"Poker, of course." He lowered his voice and leaned over to me. "I can make more playing poker here on a Friday or Saturday night than I could in a month before."

"Really?"

"Of course. There's no house, so no one fixes the games. Members organize and call all games."

"Are you playing tonight?"

"Oh no. Just watching tonight. If I were playing, this would be a club soda with lime in my hand," he said with a chuckle.

"One last question, Mr. Cross. Would you be surprised to learn anything at AthenaLibre had an impact on Niko's death?"

"You mean, was there anything at work that could drive him to suicide? Oh, I highly doubt it. Niko was far too focused on his objectives to pay much attention to any surrounding difficulty."

"How about here?"

"Here?" he sounded surprised. "Oh, I see. No, the club doesn't loan money, so it's impossible to fall into debt here. And anyway, Niko didn't play regularly enough for the bug to really grab him," Cross said.

❖

Lyle muttered and jerked as I slipped away early from my side of the bed. The bus returning Tristan and the other college hopefuls from their tour was scheduled to pull in at two p.m. I wanted to be on hand to meet him. That meant getting into the office early.

I had a job at age nineteen too. It wasn't an internship at an exciting tech company, but it was five days per week employment with responsibilities. Every summer weekday, a crowd of about fifty children and ten retirees counted on me to open the Surfside Swimming Pool promptly at ten a.m. and then watch over their lives for the rest of my shift as lifeguard.

The older adults also depended on me to clear the water at noon so they could swim laps. I took my job seriously, and I saved the money I earned to help meet later college expenses. I wondered what I would have felt then if my supervisor died. I resolved to be on hand to help answer Tristan's questions and headed into the office.

AthenaLibre's statement about selling Andrew Blanc's share in the firm awaited me in my email when I sat down at my desk. The announcement deployed the usual doublespeak corporations roll out when they want to sound confident without saying much of anything.

Translated: *One of our two founders has sold almost half the company to a private equity fund none of us like. We don't expect this to screw us up too badly, but we haven't any certainty that it won't. Check with us later.*

But as much as I disliked the obfuscation, my other research bore out the firm's announcement. Andrew Blanc's cashing in hadn't hurt the company in its existing business, and it was too soon to tell what effect it would have on its future commerce. And while departures like Albert Cross's couldn't help the situation, it was far too early to measure how much damage, if any, their leaving caused.

Nikolaidis's death didn't have a lot of impact on the company either, and I felt peeved. It offended me that a scientist in charge of a significant laboratory could have killed himself or been murdered without the company missing a beat. The passing of someone working to serve an enterprise should have an impact, I thought, no matter if he or she was as much of a loner and outsider as Nikolaidis.

But the facts remained as I had found them. I put away my

curiosity for now and filed the article I had at deadline rather than the one I wished I had.

A cluster of parents or older siblings had gathered in the shelter of a covered bus stop in front of the community center when I arrived. A bank of clouds had shut out the sun from earlier and brought a bit of a wind as well. For the first time this month, it felt like winter.

I joined the edge of the small group and wondered if the trip had helped Tristan move closer to any decisions about his future. Narrowing the world of possible schools down to the five that were relatively nearby had been comparatively easy. Shrinking that list to two or three had proved more difficult.

"I could spend five hundred dollars just applying to colleges," he had said. "I need to get this list down to something realistic."

I hoped this trip helped do that since it wasn't clear what might happen to his internship now that his boss had died.

Almost precisely on schedule, the Fleetwood bus turned off Washington Street and started the slow roll up the community center drive. The crowd became a little more animated, with younger siblings jumping up and down or demanding to be held where they could see. The bus rolled to a stop with a long diesel groan.

Tristan was the fifth one off, stepping slightly away from the stairs to where he could stretch.

"Oh, damn," he said, shaking himself all over. "I don't think I'm going to want to ride a bus ever again. Or at least not very soon."

"Rough trip?"

"Naw, not really. Just long. And I'm just a little bit too tall for the seats," he said. "Lemme grab my bag, and we can talk on the way home."

He found his bag quickly, and I debated whether to offer a ride, but he set off walking toward Baldwin House, which wasn't too far away.

"So, how was the trip?" I said, following him.

"Good, man. Eye opening. I can't wait to go to school. All the different schools were a little scary, but they were mostly amazing."

"Do you think you narrowed down the list any?"

He stopped and looked at me. “Don’t tell nobody yet, especially Ms. Dass, but yeah.”

“So, don’t keep me in suspense, which one is it?”

“UNC Chapel Hill. That’s the one. They were all great—better than great. But that school had the people that made me feel confident I can succeed there.”

“Congratulations!” I said, hugging him. “That’s fantastic. Be sure to tell me if you need a recommendation for the application and where I’m supposed to send it. I’m curious, though, why didn’t you want me to tell Ms. Dass?”

“She won’t ever say it, like, out in the open, but I’m pretty sure she wants me to go Duke,” he said. “And Duke is my second choice, but it’s a pretty distant second.”

We started walking again, but slowly. I despised what I was about to have to do. I saw a bench coming up.

“I have some news too,” I said. “but it’s the kind of news you sit down to hear. Let’s park it on that bench up there.”

“Uh-oh, that doesn’t sound good,” he said, and I hated the worry in his voice.

We sat for a moment.

“So, what’s up?”

“Man, there’s no easy way to say this, so I’ll just say it. On Tuesday, the morning you left on your trip, the woman who opened the lab found Dr. Nikolaidis dead.”

He sat for a moment, looking stunned. Then he shouted, “What the fuck?”

“Tristan, I’m sorry. I hated having to tell you, but it’s true. It happened.”

“What are you talking about? This can’t be right. He just reviewed my work a few days ago.” He got up and paced rapidly back and forth in front of the bench. “Manny, this is bad. This is my job, man. Are they still going to need me? I was counting on that money. I won’t be able to find anything else. How could this happen? Was it a heart attack? He wasn’t that old.”

“They haven’t said definitively yet,” I said in a deliberately low voice. “But they’re thinking now that he was murdered.”

"What? Like a break-in? We didn't keep anything in that lab except the laptops." Then the energy seemed to leave him all at once and he sat down heavily. "Manny, what am I going to do?" he asked in a lost voice totally unlike his usual confident tone.

"Well, right now, we're gonna walk you home and get you fed, cleaned up, and rested," I said. "We can start figuring out what to do tomorrow morning, because we won't have any answers today."

We got up from the bench and started moving again. Then I spied a familiar car that made me uneasy, driving toward us slowly.

"Tristan," I told him in a low voice, "I need you to follow my lead here, okay? Let me do the talking for the next few minutes, and if you get spoken to, you are all about polite, okay?"

"What?"

"Okay?"

"Yeah, fine. Okay."

By then Detective Walker had come upon us, stopping the vehicle on the other side of the drive, getting out, and crossing over to us.

"Well, well, if it isn't Jose Porter, out on a December day. How was I so certain that we were going to cross paths today, Mr. Porter?"

"I can't say I know, Detective Walker. Maybe you got an extra dose of that detective sixth sense in your coffee this morning," I said. Tristan stiffened up slightly beside me.

"And who might this be, then?" Walker asked.

"Senior Detective Walker, may I present Tristan DeJesus, my mentee who is working at AthenaLibre this summer. He's just back from a college tour. Tristan, this is Senior Detective Walker with the Saint Michael's Harbor Police Department."

Walker snapped his fingers. "That's why I knew," he said. "It turns out that this young man right here is the one I am looking for."

"What?" Tristan and I said simultaneously.

"That's right. As part of an ongoing investigation, I need Mr. DeJesus here to accompany me down to headquarters."

"Why?" I said.

"Nothing serious," Walker said. "Just some routine questions.

I'm confident we can get him back to Baldwin House within a couple of hours."

"Questions about what?" Stress forced Tristan's voice into a higher-than-normal range.

"I'm afraid I'm not at liberty to say."

"Then I'm afraid I'm not at liberty to go anywhere with you."

"Tristan," I started to say.

"Then we do this the harder way," Walker said. "Tristan DeJesus, I am formally taking you into custody as a person of interest in the unexplained death of Phillip Stefan Nikolaidis." He grabbed Tristan by the shoulder and had him in handcuffs in what seemed like a second.

"Wait! Don't, you can't do this," I yelled.

Walker glared at me. "I can and I have to. It's my job, Mr. Porter."

"What are you doing? I haven't done anything," Tristan shouted. "Manny, you know this dude! Tell him. Tell him I haven't done anything!"

"C'mon, Detective Walker, you know me. I can make sure he's at HQ for you bright and early tomorrow morning…"

"Let me go, please!" Tristan was almost crying. "I haven't done anything, I swear."

"Mr. DeJesus lives in transient accommodation. He has no family in the area and no full-time job. He's coming in now." Walker began pulling Tristan toward the car.

"Manny!" Tristan shouted. "Manny, man, help me."

"Can I come with him?"

"You can come to headquarters if you like, but not in the car."

Walker opened the car door and pushed Tristan in, with his head down.

"What the fuck, Manny, I didn't do nothing," he said.

Walker got into the car.

"Don't worry, man. I'll get you a lawyer," I shouted through the closed car window. "Don't say anything until she gets there!"

And then they were gone.

Chapter 4

Making a List

I stood in the driveway a few precious moments, watching the car pull out into traffic, before I dashed back to the bench, my jacket, and my phone.

My first call was to Carolyn Mondial, the attorney who helped me and Lyle fight off the eminent domain attack. She picked up immediately. I could hear holiday music playing softly in the background.

"Manny," she said. "What a surprise. I was just thinking this morning that I don't see you and Lyle often enough."

"Carolyn, I wish I could chat, but I really can't," I said, aware of my breathlessness. "My mentee, Tristan DeJesus, really needs your help."

"Manny, calm down," Carolyn said. "I remember Tristan. What's happened?"

"I can't go into all the details, but Tristan's been arrested and taken in for questioning. He needs a lawyer, and you're the only attorney I know. They won't let me be with him in the interrogation room. Can you please go down there and represent him?"

"Oh, Manny, how horrible! But it's been a while since I've done any criminal—"

"Please. You've met him. I'm confident he trusts you. He doesn't know the first thing about the process or anything. They didn't even read him his rights."

"Okay," she replied. "I can at least represent him through the interrogation. Now, where did they say they were taking him?"

My next stop was the St. Michael's Harbor Police Department, which stood across the street from the St. Michael's Harbor jail. I wasn't sure how long they would take asking Tristan questions, but when he was released, I wanted to be there. Once I arrived at the station, I settled into one of the uncomfortable chairs in the front waiting area and plugged in my phone so it could charge. Then I picked it back up and started dialing.

My first call was to Baldwin House. The last Ms. Dass had heard, I was to meet Tristan's bus at two o'clock and walk or drive him back from there. Now it was almost four and she hadn't a clue where any of us were.

"Oh, Manny, thank God," she said as soon as she picked up the call. "The police have been here looking for Tristan. They really were rude and bullying, you know? They demanded I show them Tristan's room, but I refused. Then they said they would be back with a warrant, and they were very mean about it. The other residents were very upset. Police are triggers for two of them, you know. We've never had the police here officially before. Manny, what's going on?"

I told her what happened, which alarmed her more. But I told her I was at the police station too and recounted my call to Carolyn Mondial. She felt relieved but confused.

"I don't know what I should do," she said. "Part of me feels like I should go up and make sure Tristan's room is clean, in case they come back with a warrant. I'd hate to have strangers in his space if he has dirty laundry strewn about."

"No, Ms. Dass, don't do that," I replied more sharply than I intended. "You and I know you only mean well, but the police might misconstrue your cleaning as an attempt to cover up something."

"Then we should just do nothing?"

"Ms. Dass, do you believe Tristan has done anything wrong?"

"Of course not."

"Good. Neither do I. So, the best thing we can do for Tristan now is make sure his rights are protected and help the investigation move as quickly as possible. Since we know he didn't do anything, I expect the police inquiry will find that out as well."

"That makes sense," she said, "but I'll be frank. Sometimes I don't believe the police are on our side."

"I understand."

I called Lyle next to let him know I was going to be late and not to hold dinner. When he asked me why, I felt myself let go of the stress and worry, and I laid out what had happened in as straightforward a manner as possible.

"That's rough," he said. "So, you're at the police station now?"

"Yeah."

"All right, come on home when you're done. I won't hold dinner, but I'll have something for you to eat when you get in."

"Thanks, Lyle, I love you."

"I love you back, and Manny?"

"Yeah."

"Try not to worry. Walker is a good man. He'll get to the bottom of this."

"I'll see you at home."

There was nothing more to do but wait. At almost eight o'clock, I caught sight of Carolyn collecting her phone from the front desk, and a few minutes later she was by my side. But she was by herself.

"Where's Tristan?"

"Shh, let's talk outside as we walk to our cars."

As we stepped out of the overly warm room, both of us gasped slightly at the chill. Carolyn zipped up her jacket, and I pulled my coat closer around me. We set off slowly toward the parking garage.

"They're holding him over for arraignment," Carolyn said. "Most likely he will see a judge on Monday."

"*What?*" My question echoed from the hard concrete surfaces around us.

Carolyn stopped. "Look, Manny, something's going on. I don't know what yet. Tristan and I still haven't had any time to talk alone."

"But how can they move for arraignment? I'm confused."

"They say they have Tristan's fingerprints from inside Nikolaidis's cottage," she said. "And Nikolaidis had a shrine to Tristan in a bedroom closet. A *lot* of photographs, Manny. And

Tristan's not answering any questions except to maintain he didn't kill Nikolaidis and he knows nothing about how his body came to be in the lab."

I slumped against the garage wall, my head reeling at the news. "When we got together right before the college trip, he told me he had a secret admirer at work, and he was thinking of meeting him."

"Really? Did he say who it was?"

"No. But he was sure it was someone at AthenaLibre because the admirer contacted him at his work email address soon after he started the internship."

Carolyn whipped out her phone and spoke into it. "Reminder for 13 December. Motion to preserve all email at AthenaLibre to or from Tristan DeJesus." She turned back to me. "I knew there had to be more to this, Manny. But Tristan must start talking. He's the only one who can give us his side of what happened."

By the time I pulled away from the station, it was close to nine o'clock. I meant to head straight back to Bonne Chance and Lyle but instead found myself taking an earlier exit into the western part of Tinker Creek. I parked the car off Madison and walked up the side alley until I reached the gate that read 416 1/2. I opened it and stepped inside. From the shadowed and wintry yard, I could see that Detective Walker's apartment was dark. I bundled myself down at a picnic table to wait.

I must have drowsed, because the next thing I felt and heard was the cold, metallic clank of a partially crushed beer can bouncing off my head onto the table. Walker stood about ten feet away in his rumpled coat, downing another brew to have a second can to throw.

"Doesn't a man get to cross his own front yard without encountering Jose Porter yet one more blessed time in less than twenty-four hours?"

"He might. If he wasn't heading up an investigation that interested me and my readers."

"Your readers? Harrumph. Mr. Abner Smalls, a colleague at the paper, I believe, warned me I should never talk to you. And we both know he'd keel over with a stroke right now if he saw you were sitting in my front yard like this."

"This is not an interview," I said. "I just wanted to hear some things."

"Damn it, Porter, you know I can't discuss the inquiry."

"I'm not here to ask about the investigation. I know the prosecutor is seeking an arraignment on Monday. I'm here to ask about you."

"Me? Why?"

I got up and walked over to him, close enough that I could look into his eyes for any answers that might show themselves. He stood stock still.

"I wanted to ask whether you're the kind of detective for whom an arraignment of a poor Hispanic kid ends a case, or are you the kind of detective who will keep after the truth until he's satisfied he knows all there is to know?"

His eyes grew flinty. "If you're asking whether I'm prejudiced enough to decide 'the Hispanic kid did it' and drop any interest past that point, I'm going to consider that an honest mistake brought on by a lack of familiarity and not a deliberate insult that demands I lay you out flat. But if you must know, man to man and entirely off the record, I still have way more questions than answers and haven't come anywhere near close to making up my mind, arraignment be damned."

A light went on over the door at the end of the yard.

I smiled up at him. "That's what I hoped to hear, Chief Detective."

"Now, I suggest you get that cute little ass on home to your man before my landlady sends her German shepherd out here to take a bite out of it," he said.

❖

I awoke with a jerk as a ten-foot-tall jail guard loomed above Tristan, about to strike his head with a thick baton. Beside me, Lyle pulled me in closer with his muscular arm. His unshaven cheek moved like soft sandpaper against the back of my neck as he gently kissed me.

"Hmmm, you slept badly," he murmured into my ear.

I nodded. Nightmares had tormented me all night, but that didn't mean I felt like talking about any of them.

He found and traced one of my nipples and I sensed it harden. Lower down, below the sheets I felt another stirring.

"Lyyllle, sleepy," I whispered with a hint of whine in my voice before I dropped into the darkness again. The next time I awoke, light streamed in from the skylight over the bed and the rich smell of brewing coffee wafted in from the kitchen.

I groaned as I stretched one arm up to reach for the window, but before I knew it, a mighty force seized me by the shoulder and pulled me on my back again. I looked up into Lyle's bright eyes and smile.

"Hey…" I started to protest before he gave me a long, passionate kiss. "No fair," I gasped when we came up for air. "You've brushed your teeth. Kissing me must be like kissing one of those horrid vending machines in the waiting room at police headquarters."

"What do I care?" he said. "If stale Cheetos be the taste of love, let me but savor more. But that's not all, my prince. You shall find me burnished, scrubbed, perfumed, and anointed in every crevice, crack, and opening of my person."

"You're crazy," I said, gazing into his eyes again.

"Like a fox," he growled, pulling my mouth against his for another long kiss where, this time, he handed me the reins and I became both initiator and driver. I finally broke off for a check-in.

"You ready?"

"Never readier," he said, his voice husky with desire. "And don't hold back. I want everything you got and then some."

With that, we put Lyle's lovely, custom-made Swedish mattress through its most vigorous workout ever as I mixed my passion for him with my current anxiety about Tristan to blend an emotional fuel that took us to Jupiter and back. Afterward, as we lay entangled, panting and laughing and feeling the pulse of our life together, I kissed his cheek.

"Thank you," I whispered. "That wasn't in the usual playbook."

He purred contentedly. "What do the French say? Vive le différence. Feel better?"

"Only about one thousand percent," I replied as we lay on our sides, facing each other. "How'd you know I needed that?"

"It didn't take rocket science to figure out what happened yesterday might create a need to seize command today. Besides, sometimes I like a good pummeling."

I sat up. "I didn't hurt you, did I?"

"No, because I took some common-sense precautions. But I would enjoy one of your outstanding back rubs later today."

"Agreed."

"Now, let's get cleaned up and have some breakfast. Cannibalism is on the horizon if I don't get some food in me."

Later, over a meal of eggs Benedict, hash browns, and more coffee, we discussed Tristan's dilemma and its impact on our life together.

"When I heard about the opportunity to join the mentoring program, it presented itself as such an obvious decision. Why wouldn't I take on a role of modeling responsibility and other positive traits to a younger person who may not have had much exposure to them?"

"And yet, here it is getting really serious, really fast."

"Exactly. My presence in Tristan's life now is more important than ever before. But because we're together, I've dragged you into it—and it's not like you don't already have plenty to do."

Lyle added some more cream to his coffee before finishing it off. "Chill," he said in his take-command voice. "You're so impetuous. For the record, you might not have foreseen this possible outcome when you signed on to the mentoring program, but I did. And I agreed anyway."

"You did?"

"Of course. But now that the arrest has happened, the important question that needs to be asked is whether you think he did it."

"Of course not."

Lyle raised his eyebrows at me. "We won't do Tristan or

ourselves any good if we don't keep an open mind about everything and not just rush to acquittal as fast as others might rush to condemnation. Now, has he made a statement to the police?"

"Not as far as I know."

"Since that hasn't happened, he obviously can't have established an alibi. How about motive? Did he get along with his boss?"

"It sure looked that way. Nikolaidis sang Tristan's praises at the holiday party."

"But you were disturbed enough about how Nikolaidis interacted with him physically that you brought it up two days later. And didn't the police find practically a shrine to Tristan in one of Nikolaidis's closets?"

"But you were the one who pointed out that Tristan didn't shirk or pull away when Nikolaidis interacted with him an overly friendly manner. I don't have any answer for you about the shrine, except that we don't know Tristan knew about it."

"How about means," Lyle asked.

"Nikolaidis was garroted with an extremely fine steel wire of a type that isn't readily available outside scientific supply houses. And which was formed into a noose to display the body. If anything, Nikolaidis stood a bit taller than Tristan, and I don't see Tristan overcoming his boss, strangling him with wire, then forming a wire into a noose. I don't think he even knows how."

"Tristan really needs to make a statement," Lyle said. "We're past the point where he does himself any good by staying silent. What does Carolyn think?"

"The last I heard, her strategy is to try for a moderate judge for arraignment and argue for no bail or low bail, to get him out of jail. If I can just talk to him one-on-one someplace other than jail, I can get him to open up."

"How realistic is it that he can make bail?"

"I don't know. I don't even know how bail works."

"Tristan can get out of jail if he promises to appear on a future date for trial and can put up a certain amount of money as a guarantee."

"How much money?"

"That depends on the crime, the person, and the judge."

"What if Tristan doesn't have it?"

"He stays in jail unless someone on the outside, whether family, friend, or bail bondsman, can come up with the cash."

"The bail bondsman?"

"That's a business that will put up the bail for Tristan provided Tristan pays them a fee. The catch is that while the bail bond firm will get their money back when Tristan shows up for court, Tristan will never get his fee back. That's gone."

I stared down at my plate, suddenly having lost my appetite.

"What?"

"Tristan's basically fucked," I said. "He doesn't have any family or friends who can put up bail money, and I'd be surprised if he even has enough in savings to pay a bail bond fee."

"BCM could pay a bail bond fee out of our emergency capital fund, provided it wasn't too high."

I looked up at him. "You'd do that?"

"No, but *we* could do that. Both of us will sign the form."

"Thank you," I cried, getting up and going to him for a hug.

"Don't thank me yet. There are still a lot of things that have to happen first."

"One thing more," I said.

"What?"

"If Tristan gets out of jail, he won't qualify any longer to remain at Baldwin House. He may have to move in here with us."

"Let's concentrate on one problem at a time," Lyle replied.

❖

Lyle's suggestion that we take on one challenge at a time rang in my ears Monday morning when I arrived to find a note commanding I come to the publisher's office at nine o'clock, or in about ten minutes.

I arrived right at nine to find my father at his desk across from Susan and an empty chair. Susan signaled with her eyes that I was to take the vacant seat. I sat down.

"Good," my father said. "With everyone here, we can begin. Derek Fuller, AthenaLibre's current director of research and former shared CEO, saw our early edition and called me at home about your story, Jose."

"Okay," I said, uncertainly.

"Since I do not, generally, discuss business over breakfast, Mr. Fuller agreed to call me back here." A phone rang in Rosa's office. "That would be him now. Put him through, Rosa."

His desk set chirped, and he picked up.

"Good morning, Mr. Fuller," he said in his round, ringmaster's voice that he usually reserved for accountants or tax officials. "May I put you on speakerphone? My business editor, Ms. Susan Owen, is here and would like her to share our conversation…excellent. Now, Mr. Fuller, what part of our story didn't you feel we got correct?"

"I don't suppose there were any errors of fact in the article," he said. "But it was the way the facts were laid out that concerned me. Someone could read the article and conclude we are having trouble competing for new research contracts because of our deal with Cogitare, which isn't true."

Susan spoke up. "Excuse me, sir. Are you disputing that your company has the lowest level of new business for next year than it's had at this time in the previous five years?"

"No."

"Nor did we state that the sale to Cogitare caused the slowdown," she pointed out.

"But you did quote some former employees who implied that."

"Yes, but we included their reasoning and used their names wherever possible. What else could we have done? We weren't in the position to dispute their opinions."

"Look, I didn't call to be combative. I'm mostly concerned about our relationship going forward," Fuller said. "What can we do to help shape the next story about us?"

"We're not going to be able to draw you a map, Mr. Fuller," my dad chimed in. "But the next time the company has some major piece of news, I suggest you alert us in a more timely manner."

"I understand," Fuller said.

"Also," Susan said, "We printed your company's statement on the Cogitare deal verbatim, and it didn't say anything about its impact on future business. You're always welcome to provide us your firm's perspective on something so that can appear in the story as well."

"We haven't traditionally considered media communications an executive level responsibility, but it sounds like we might need to do that going forward," Fuller said. "Thank you for your time, Ms. Owen and Mr. Porter."

"You're welcome," they both said, and Fuller rang off.

Dad hung up the phone and looked at us. "For the record, I consider that story well reported and edited, and I think we were right to run it," he said. "But with that understood, we're now on notice that AthenaLibre is sensitive to its coverage, and I want all articles about them double fact-checked. Understood?"

We nodded.

"Thanks for coming up here," he said. "Susan, you can go. Jose, please stay."

We waited until Susan left the room.

"I understand you had a bit of a confrontation with Chief Detective Walker on Friday."

"I happened to be present when he arrested a suspect in the Nikolaidis killing, yes."

"What did we agree about keeping out of Smalls's stories?"

"I wasn't *in* Smalls's story, sir. I happened to be there during the arrest. I didn't report the arrest, seek any interviews, or do any reporting."

"Why were you there?"

"One of the young people coming back from the college tour the community center sponsored was one of the interns from the AthenaLibre story that is on hold. I'm keeping up my contacts for when it becomes active again."

"Okay, but just keep it cool, please. He sent me a hot email over the weekend about it."

I felt grateful the paper had stood behind my story, but as I left his office, I resolved to try harder for an interview with Fuller or

Billings or at least someone in an executive office. Then I wondered how Anna Fin Chow had fared in the fallout from the story.

But a text from Carolyn Mondial knocked all the AthenaLibre concerns out of my mind. The judge had set Tristan's bail at an eye-popping hundred thousand dollars. I texted thanks to Carolyn for letting me know, then told Lyle.

Judge set price of Tristan bail at $100,000, I messaged him. *What are we going to do*?

Meet me at the corner of 6th and Monroe at 12:30. he wrote back.

I sped through returning more calls so that I could make it to the intersection on time. Sixth and Monroe was one of the underdeveloped Tinker Creek crossings, with a wig shop and nail salon on two corners, and a burger joint and office building on the other two. I spied Lyle waiting in the BCM truck and parked behind him.

"Here, put this on," he said when I approached, handing me a shoulder holster.

"What the fuck? I don't own a gun."

"I know. But he doesn't know that. And let me do the talking inside, but try to look mean, like you do sometimes when we practice self-defense moves."

I tried to remember the menacing sneer I perfected while on the mats.

"Yeah, that's the one," Lyle said. "Let's go."

Lyle entered the building first and climbed up the stairs to the right of the small lobby while I followed. We went about halfway down the corridor to 216 where a wooden door with a frosted window proclaimed in large letters "Opportunity Nox, Licensed Bail Bonds."

Lyle opened the door, and a bell rang as we entered what looked like a small bank lobby with a wooden counter, cashier's cage, and some chairs for waiting. A silver front desk bell sat before the teller station. Lyle tapped it authoritatively.

"All right. No need to ring twice," came a whiny voice from the back. "I'm on my way up."

I got a brief glimpse of an older, puffy face and gray hair sliding into view behind the bars when a wooden shutter suddenly dropped over the opening.

"Go away! We're closed."

"No you're not, Howard," Lyle said in a patient tone. "Your hours are on the door, and we're well inside them."

"It's my business, and if I say we're closed, we're closed. Now go away. I'm…I'm not feeling well. I might be contagious."

"Ha!" Lyle's laugh echoed across the room like a gunshot. "Howard, who do you think you're fooling? If you're not feeling well, it's because you had too many martinis at lunch. Now lift that shutter and talk to me, or you're gonna make me come back around there to have a more personal conversation."

The shutter rose, and we encountered the older round face again, but this time I saw his cheeks carried a rosy hue as though he might have had some alcohol at lunch. His red and white polka-dot bow tie was askew.

"Oh God, what do you want now, Mr. James? I don't owe you any more money."

"That's true. My associate Jose and I are here for your services," he said, pointing to me. I tried to look meaner.

"What?"

"That's right. We want you to post bond for a young man we know who has been unfairly charged with a crime he did not commit."

"What's the name?" Nox sounded interested.

"Tristan DeJesus, arraigned this morning in St. Michael's Harbor."

We heard tapping at a computer keyboard. "Oh my God, that's a murder case," he said, "and the bail is one hundred thousand."

"So?"

"I don't do many of those—mostly because that amount will take my capital down to nothing, and if he skips, I'm out of business."

"He's not going to skip."

"Who says?"

"We say," Lyle replied. "Jose here is making it his personal goal to guarantee Mr. DeJesus shows up bright and shiny for his trial date so you get your money back."

"I can't get out of this, can I?" He looked at Lyle with pleading eyes.

"Nope."

He gave a long sigh. "Okay," he said. "Fifteen thousand."

"Seven," said Lyle.

"You're joking!" Nox almost screamed. "This is a murder trial. I'm putting up a hundred thousand."

Lyle shook his head.

"Okay, twelve," Nox said.

"Eight."

"Eleven."

"Ten, and I continue to keep quiet about certain inflated accident claims on a brand-new Cadillac with Georgia plates 3XY—"

"All right! What are you, an elephant? Ten it is."

"Excellent." Lyle smiled for the first time since he arrived. "It's always interesting to come see you, Mr. Nox."

"Yeah, yeah. Just remember, you hold my whole world in your hands. That little bastard better damn well show up for trial."

"Text me your bank information, and I'll send it along as soon as DeJesus walks into the sunshine."

"It's supposed to be the other way around," Nox said.

"But, Howard, we know each other so well. Of course you can trust me. By the way, how's that Caddy running, anyway?"

"It gets me around."

"Just to show no hard feelings, bring it around later this week and I'll tune it up and change the oil for free."

Nox perked up considerably. "You'd do that?"

"Small businesses got to look out for each other," Lyle said.

Emily Powers texted me the time and location of Nikolaidis's funeral. Given the fact that I was practically in the room when they found his body, I decided to go.

The first thing I noticed about the service was how well attended it was. Certainly, Nikolaidis didn't care about the number of people who came to his funeral, but I imagined any of his family or friends might have been comforted to see the crowd.

Second, the collection of mourners remained standing. I arrived a couple of minutes late and stood beside the attendees in a back pew, waiting for the signal to be seated that never came. Fortunately, I decided against wearing my truly formal shoes or I might not have been able to walk out under my own power at the end.

Finally, Nikolaidis was in an open casket. I had been under the impression this practice had fallen out of favor and felt shocked to see the subject of the service propped up in his white coffin looking suspiciously like the guest of honor at a party.

At first, I imagined this would be his body's entire role in the affair, seeming to reign from his coffin as though he sat on an odd sort of couch. But then it became clear we were expected to show our sorrow at his passing to Nikolaidis personally.

As soon as this dawned on me, I started looking for a way out of doing it, short of getting up and walking out. I didn't know what to do. I hoped my back-pew neighbors would not wish to see the man up close either, so I could join them to avoid approaching the corpse. But no, they wanted to go up, and that meant I had to go up too, unless I fancied standing in the aisle like a stump, blocking their progress.

Slowly, we went, one after the other, through the small chapel to the front. There we either kissed a large wooden crucifix propped like a strange tree branch on his chest or genuflected and paused a moment. Then we moved on to express our condolences to the family before winding back to where we started.

I didn't see anyone in the queue ahead of me that I recognized as an AthenaLibre executive, but Emily Powers was there. Anna Fin Chow was in the line, too, and I acknowledged Albert Cross from the back as well as two of my former sources for the article.

When I arrived at the coffin, I slowly made the sign of the cross and took a moment to examine the corpse. I had no frame of reference, of course, but the mortician had done a good job on Nikolaidis. He didn't look dead but asleep, and someone had performed an artful job with a high-collared shirt and some makeup to hide any of the bruising around his neck.

Then I moved on to the first family member, who wore a severely angular black dress that Queen Victoria might have favored, white gloves, and an enormous hat and veil that covered her entire head almost as a basket.

"My sincere condolences on your loss," I said to her. She raised her white gloved hand and grasped mine.

"Too kind," she replied in a heavy Russian accent.

"Ms. Reznikov?"

"Yes, that is who I am."

"You probably don't remember, but I'm Jose Porter. We met at the AthenaLibre Christmas party just a couple of weeks ago."

"Of course I remember," she said. "That party is where it all began to go to shit."

"I'm sorry, I didn't realize."

"No, it's nothing," she said, clamping down on her previous outburst. "Everything happens because it happens." Turning slightly, she said, "May I present my brother, Gregor, and Pyotr, an old and loyal friend of my family."

"My condolences to you both," I said.

Pyotr narrowed his eyes at me. "Jose Porter," he said. "You were the reporter who was in the corridor when they found Nikolaidis's body, weren't you?"

"Well, yes, that was me," I said while marveling at the man's memory and wondering where that fact had been reported. I hadn't written it, and I doubted Smalls had put it in any of his articles. But Pyotr began whispering to Gregor in a language I didn't understand.

"Nice to have met you both," I said, moving a couple steps to my left, where the priest introduced a thin, young brunette woman who looked like she needed to lean on him to stand.

"Niko's half sister Melissa Nikolaidis," the priest said, "and her boyfriend, Joseph."

"My condolences to you both."

This drew nothing but a sad smile from Melissa and a low-level fist bump from Joseph. "Thanks, man," he said, in a way that meant *thanks, man, for being here so I'm not the only Brown man in this room*.

After we all went through the receiving line, the funeral came to an end swiftly. The priest led the congregation, still standing, in another set of prayers, and then blessed and dismissed us. The Nikolaidis party left first, with the Reznikovs striding quickly outside while Melissa, Joseph, and the rest of us followed.

But I didn't leave. As the line of mourners snaked from the chapel and broke into clumps to head for cars, I reentered the sanctuary. I wanted to take a closer look at the icons that crowded the walls almost like faces from outside, converging in front of windows.

I had been contemplating the eyes of two icons when I heard a slight cough behind me and turned to find the priest looking at me with interest.

"May I help you?"

"Oh, no, Father," I said. "I haven't ever been in a Greek Orthodox church and thought I would look around before I had to leave. Are you locking up?"

"No," he said. "We don't lock the church until after evening vespers. So you can feel free to look all you want."

"Thank you."

"If I might ask, how did you know the deceased?"

"I didn't. At least not really. I'm a reporter for the *South Georgia Record* and I met him for the first time at AthenaLibre's holiday party a couple of weeks ago."

"Ah," he said. "Niko had invited me to that party as well, and I regretted missing it. I understand they served some truly enormous shrimp."

I laughed. "That they did."

"Let me apologize. I have you at a bit of a disadvantage. I know your name, but you don't know mine. I'm Father Christian Ampleforth, at your service." He bowed slightly from the waist.

"Correct me if I'm mistaken, but that's not a very Greek or Orthodox sounding name."

"You wouldn't be wrong. The water they splashed on my infant head was completely Anglican. I came over to become an Orthodox priest when I was about twenty."

"That was quite young to decide for a life of God, wasn't it?"

"In my case, no," he said with a laugh. "But as it was, I think my parents found my conversion rather a relief because it meant I wouldn't become a Roman Catholic."

He started to walk slowly back up toward the altar, and I joined him. "How well did you know Niko?" I asked.

"Quite well. Niko was among my most faithful and regular congregants. He came to me regularly for confession, and I gave him mental and emotional support from time to time."

"So, you may not have been surprised to learn of his possible death by suicide?"

"Au contraire. When I first heard it, I was shocked. Suicide is one of the sins that still bars you from a burial in the blessed ground, you know. And nothing I saw or heard from Niko since I met him five years ago made me imagine him as suicidal. But this isn't an interview, is it?"

"Oh no, sir. I'm not taking any notes. Anything we talk about is off the record unless and until we decide otherwise."

"That's a relief," he said. "I don't mind talking with you, but my bishop does not look kindly on his priests' names in newspapers."

"I understand. I'm curious about how you can be so certain suicide was out of the question as a means of Niko's death. Other sources have identified him as down and a bit depressed. They said he felt trapped by something."

We stopped walking and he turned to me. "Niko and Melissa's upbringing was unstable, tumultuous," he said. "And in my opinion, that left them with some vulnerabilities. In Niko, one of those weaknesses was an inability to confront challenges head-on in real time."

"What do you mean?"

"Faced with an immediate and difficult problem, Niko, with assistance, would always figure out how to handle it. But when first finding out about the difficulty, Niko considered it overwhelming and despaired of a solution even though he would always come upon one in the end."

"For example?"

"Two days before he was found dead, Niko came to tell me he was thinking about calling off his marriage."

"Oh, wow. Did he say why?"

"No, only that things were not as they seemed. I convinced him to go on retreat about it and see if that might help him resolve whatever conflict he faced."

"And did he do that?"

"He made reservations at a retreat center outside Atlanta on the morning before he was found dead. So, I believe he was far from suicidal. He was reaching for tools that had helped him previously."

We resumed walking.

"I see. I agree that doesn't square easily with a man who supposedly committed suicide."

"But hasn't the suicide theory been put to rest?" he asked. "I understood the police have a suspect in custody."

"Yes, that's true. A very young man who worked for Niko as an intern."

"Oh. I hadn't heard who it was. That sounds possibly very sad."

We stopped at the door to the room where priests change in and out of their robes for services.

"If I may ask you one last question. How well did Niko know his fiancée, Ms. Reznikov? I ask because I met them both at the party, and I thought they might have been an odd couple."

"I don't know, exactly, but my impression was that it hadn't been very long. Ms. Reznikov is possessed of a forceful and somewhat demanding personality, and I'm not sure Niko had figured out how best to interact with her," he said. "Now, if you'll excuse me, I have a meeting and I need to prepare," he said before entering the vesting room and leaving me behind.

Chapter 5

Double Check Everything

I began to suspect Pierre's girlfriend had superpowers. Though she hadn't been in St. Michael's Harbor long, she knew a wide variety of people, and those individuals both recognized and championed her.

I thought about that as I arrived at the Langston Café, a popular Tinker Creek lunch spot, and was swiftly whisked inside by a slim Black girl who showed me to arguably the best table in the coveted second-floor dining room.

Emily arrived about five minutes later, looking radiant in a burgundy coat, pearl gray blouse, blue skirt, and short white pumps.

I stood as she walked up and pulled out the chair opposite mine. "Ms. Powers."

"Such a gentleman, especially when the lady is late," she said with a smile as she took off her coat and hung it on the hook beside mine. We sat down.

"I wish I had your pull," I said.

"What do you mean?"

"I mean that if I called up the Langston Café and asked for the best two-top on the second floor, they would have told me it was available in about six weeks. You made your request yesterday."

A young Hispanic man arrived with water glasses, a full carafe, and menus, departing as quickly as he came.

"Ah," she replied. "I can't claim any of that power. Pierre has the pull. Not I. I think your paper's popular culture reporter should do a story on him, the very first city clerk rock star," she said as she opened the menu. "I mean it. You should drop by at one of the town hall meetings the mayor's office holds every once in a while. His sessions are full."

A cute, dark-haired lad of about twenty appeared at our table.

"Hi, my name is Mario. I'll be looking after you today. May I bring you something to drink?"

I looked over my menu to find Emily regarding me mischie-vously.

"Do you trust me?"

I nodded.

"The gentleman and I will begin with a glass of the Mama Cass Cider," she began, "to accompany the fried chicken lunch, both with dark meat, and the collard greens as sides. And we'll finish with a slice of key lime pie."

"Yes, ma'am. All excellent today. They served us the fried chicken for family lunch today, and it was awesome," he said before he left.

"Why would I have to trust you with any of that? It sounded delicious."

"Because I wasn't sure if you would appreciate hard cider at lunch. And I was late for our meal, so I wanted to streamline the process," she said. "Also, because I feel a little guilty that I really don't have many details to fill in the space around this big thing I have to tell you."

"No need to feel guilty. Just spill."

"Okay. I can't give you any details yet, but I'm certain Nikolaidis was working off the books."

"Off the books?"

"On a private research project—something he did not pitch to the new contract committee," she said. "Or maybe he did pitch it, but they passed. In any case, something that doesn't appear in the company's research portfolio."

"Someone can do that?"

"Sure. It's not that unusual on a small scale, but it's pretty rare to have an investigator take over a whole lab for a pet project."

"Oh wow. Which one?"

"Lab 5C," she said. "It's the one right behind the space he used for his declared research."

"What did he use it for?"

She shook her head. "I don't know yet," she said, "but I'm almost positive Tristan knows something about it."

"Tristan?"

"Every week, Tristan made two runs to the supply store that served Nikolaidis's declared labs," she said. "Not unusual. In fact, that's the sort of job interns often do. But then later in the same week, Tristan goes on another supply run, this time to a supply room where he's not known. He picks up all that stuff for the 5C lab."

"How do you know all this?"

"I can't go into a lot of details without boring you to tears," she said, "but basically I looked at data I see every day from a different perspective, and this time, what he was doing showed up as clearly as fluorescent writing in a dark room."

My mind reeled. I knew Carolyn Mondial would pick Tristan up from jail and bring him to Lyle's later today. I wondered how I could ask him about this new angle.

"One more thing," she said.

"What?"

"If you go to the AthenaLibre loading dock and walk past the truck bays all the way to the left, you'll come to a door."

"So?"

"My AthenaLibre ID key card will open it, but so will this standard closet key," she said, holding up a thick, industrial-looking key. "Most everyone knows about this door, and almost everyone will either have one of the closet keys or be able to get one easily. And when the closet key is used, it doesn't show up on the building security log."

"So, the bottom line is that almost anyone could have been in the building on Monday night when Nikolaidis was killed?"

She nodded. "Probably including Tristan."

❖

After our delicious lunch, I parted ways with Emily and headed back to Lyle's place to be there when Carolyn dropped Tristan off. I had stepped off the elevator into the living room when its chime sounded. I returned to the intercom and called down.

"Hello?"

"Hello? Manny? It's Carolyn and Tristan."

In the background, I heard Tristan's disbelieving voice. "This is it?"

I punched the elevator button to send the cab clanking down. Lyle got up from the couch and walked over to the lift as we heard it start to climb again. I suddenly realized how nervous I felt and instinctively moved closer to him.

The cab stopped, the bell chimed, and the doors opened. They both stepped off. Carolyn appeared more tired than I had ever seen her. Tristan looked down at the floor.

I felt shocked. The upstanding, energetic, focused young man I knew, bursting with expectation and delight, had vanished. In his place, I found a boy with shoulders slumped, hair unkempt, looking mostly at his feet, silent.

"Welcome to you both," Lyle sang out, breaking into the moment with a saccharine cheerfulness. Carolyn stepped forward with a sigh into one of Lyle's deep, healing hugs while I moved closer to Tristan.

"Hey, bro," I said, my arms outstretched. "Welcome home."

He took one step into my embrace, and it was like a dam broke. Suddenly, with his head on my shoulder and his face at my neck, he poured forth tears with a power that felt as though they came from his deepest soul.

"There, there," I whispered to him as I began to rock slightly and pat him on the back. "It's okay. No worries. I got you. You're okay. Let it out, let it out. You're okay."

I wanted to help him feel better, but as we rocked together, he held me tighter and cried harder. I signaled to Lyle that he and Carolyn might want to split a coffee in the kitchen or his office or anywhere else. Thankfully, he picked up on it and began to walk

Carolyn toward the rest of the apartment while I maneuvered Tristan to the huge leather sofa.

"Let's just sit here a minute and kind of pull some things together," I said, easing him down against the cool surface. He nodded and let go of me. I sat close beside him and held on to one of his hands. "First things first," I said. "Are you hurt at all? Anything cut or bleeding or bruised?"

He shook his head. Thank God for that, I thought.

His crying had diminished to gasps and gulps, and he began to catch his breath.

"I…I don't know what you might think," he gasped after a few minutes. "But I'm not crazy, and I'm not on drugs."

I shook my head. "Of course not. You've had a terrible few days. I'd be more concerned if you walked in and acted like nothing was wrong."

He took a deep breath. "The first thing I want to do is tell you I'm sorry," Tristan said, his eyes starting to glisten again.

I began to shake my head, but he continued immediately.

"Hear me out. Back on Sunday before the college trip, you gave me very good advice about meeting my secret admirer," he said, "but I was stupid. I didn't listen and I should have."

"What happened?"

He sighed again and looked down, but then lifted his head and began to tell his story in something of a monotone.

"Me and this secret admirer dude had been flirting back and forth online like all day until, for real, I could tell we were both pretty worked up. So, when he texted me again about coming over to his place because he was all alone, I figured let's do it. Let's see what's up. He texted me the address, and it was in the TC. I could ride my bike over there. So, I showered up, pulled on this old basketball jersey I have that I think looks sexy on me and some basketball shorts with no underwear, got on my bike, and went."

"When you arrived, were you surprised at how it looked?"

"Yeah. It was really small, but it was like a house. I mean it had a fence and a yard and flowers and shit. And the house had a little porch area too. I was wondering how does this dude have all this? But I remembered him talking about a landlord, so I thought he must just be renting it."

"So, you went up to the door?"

"Well, I rode around the block a couple of times first. But then I locked my bike on a parking meter and went up there. Door didn't have a doorbell, just a knocker, so I knocked."

"And when Dr. Nikolaidis answered the door, how did you feel?"

Tristan jumped to his feet and started pacing. "To tell the truth, I didn't know how to feel. I mean, out of all the shit I imagined going down with this dude, having my boss opening the door just was never in the picture, you know?"

"What did you say?"

"I don't even remember. I must've asked him what he was doing there. He said, 'Because I already know all about it. I think you better come inside.' "

"How did that make you feel, and did you go in?"

"Shocked and scared. But I went in."

"What happened next?"

Tristan sat down again. "He takes me to the living room and tells me sit on the couch while he goes and gets us some Cokes. So, I sat there in this room and I figured this place had to belong to his granny or something because it just sort of had this old lady feel about it, you know?"

"Then?"

"He came back with a tray with two Cokes in glasses on it. As soon as I sipped mine, I knew he'd put something in it. I think rum."

"What did you talk about?"

Tristan got up again. "He told me he loved me. That he first saw me way back on our first day, when Ms. Fin Chow took us on the intern tour. He said he went to Ms. Chow to make sure I was assigned to his lab. He also said he hoped I could love him too because I'd find him a caring and passionate man."

"What did you say?"

"I told him I was sorry but what he wanted was impossible. It wasn't about age or looks or anything, but it was about him and me. He was my boss. I didn't, couldn't think about him like that. Then he wanted me to stay over that night, but I told him I couldn't because I had to be on the college tour bus the next morning. He said he could drive me to the colleges instead and we could say he was my uncle helping me find a school." Tristan stopped and looked down again.

"What happened next, Tristan?"

"He said I would be crazy to pass up such a valuable opportunity, but I said he was just plain crazy and I was going home. He started yelling then, calling me names and telling me to get out of his house, but when I went back to the front door, he ran up and tried to pull me back and keep it shut. I told him to get off me but he wouldn't. So I hit him."

"You hit him?"

Tristan nodded.

"Where?"

"I don't know. I gave him a jab to his face, so maybe his eye or his nose. Something like that because he started bleeding and yelling at me, and then I think he fell down."

"You didn't see him fall?"

Tristan shook his head. "I got the door open and I was gone."

By then Carolyn Mondial and Lyle had walked back into the living room.

"Tristan, why didn't you tell me any of this before the arraignment?" Carolyn said. "It might have made a difference."

"I had to tell Manny first. He was the one who tried to help me, and I ignored him. I had to set it right between us first," he said. "Plus, how was it going to change anything? It was Dr. Nikolaidis. I saw how other researchers acted around him, how they addressed him. They didn't know he was gay. Or that he was a perv. Why would anyone want to listen to me?"

"What happened when you got out of the house?" I asked.

"I almost blacked out the combo to my lock, but then I remembered it, thank God. As soon as I got the bike free, I was out of there. I was afraid he'd come out of the house after me. Then I rode home. I put the bike where I usually do and went in through the kitchen door. I could hear Ms. Dass on the phone in her office. I kept quiet and headed to my room."

"So, nobody saw you come home?" Carolyn asked.

He shook his head. "Not as far as I know."

"What time was all this?" I asked. "What time did you get to his place and what time did you leave?"

"I think it must have been nine forty-five by the time I actually went in," Tristan said, "And it was just past eleven when I left."

"How do you know that?" Carolyn again.

"Because the bank clock rang while I was fooling with my bike lock."

"Do you remember how you got home? What streets you took?"

"No, but I went the fastest way I knew. I didn't stop anywhere."

"I'm ahead of you," Lyle said to Carolyn. "The businesses that I know have CC cameras in that part of the TC are the 7-Eleven on Jackson and Taggert Hardware's lumberyard on Sixth Avenue, but I bet others might have them too."

"And I can check with the city to see if there might be any traffic cameras," she said.

We paused while we all thought about the possibilities. Finally, Tristan spoke up. "What happens now?"

"Now we'll show you to your room here, and you can take a shower and clean up some. Get some rest if you want," Lyle said.

"I have one more question," I said.

"Okay."

"There's been some confusion about what Dr. Nikolaidis was working on in the 5C lab," I said. "Can you tell us anything about that? What did Dr. Nikolaidis have you pick up on your third supply run each week?"

Tristan shrugged. "Different chemicals, usually," he said. "Sometimes other stuff. And I didn't make that extra run each week, more like every third week."

"Did he tell you what he was working on?"

"Nope. All he said once was that when it was finally finished, it would save a lot of lives and make him a lot of money, but I only heard him say that once, when he had something to drink."

"It's been a long day," Lyle cut in. "Let's let Tristan get cleaned up and get some rest. There's time for more questions tomorrow."

❖

The recent information from Father Ampleforth, Emily, and now Tristan did nothing to quench my curiosity about Dr. Phillip Nikolaidis. If anything, I felt thirstier for knowledge now than I had been the day after his murder. I thought this might be the right time to approach his grieving fiancée.

The St. George Hotel broods over the southern part of St. Michael's Harbor like a gargoyle. Built in the 1920s from western Georgia's gray stone in the French Second Empire style, the building's architects tried to use columns, cornices, and statues to distract from its dark, massive bulk, but despite their best efforts, the resulting structure cast a sinister profile on the horizon.

The interior was not much better, I thought. Lots of red and gold fabric and dark wood failed to hide a shabby atmosphere. But the main lobby and front desk maintained a regal air, and the manager, dressed in a dark suit with the hotel's trademark red tie, pocket square, and boutonniere, kept to a formal standard.

"How may I help you, sir?" he asked smoothly.

"Jose Porter for Ms. Nadia Reznikov. We have an appointment."

"Very good, sir. If you just wait in the day lounge, I'll let her know you've arrived," he said, indicating a curtain-draped door to the right of the front desk.

I had turned away from him and toward the opening when he stopped me, pointing to his screen.

"According to this note, the lady requests you join her in the Peacock Suite, sir. Ninth floor and to the right off the elevator." I resolved to research the lodging rate per night when I got back to the office and headed up.

I knocked, and the door was opened by Gregor, the man I'd met briefly at the funeral. Tall, muscular, and blond-haired, he wore a sharply tailored suit and an almost severe crew cut. I straightened up slightly as he studied me with his cool gray stare.

"Yes?" he said.

I reached in my pocket and retrieved one of my cards. "Jose Porter, *South Georgia Record*. Ms. Reznikov and I have an appointment."

"Wait, please," he replied, shutting the door with a small slam. But he returned after a minute. He stood aside from the doorway and bowed slightly from the waist. "My sister will see you now."

"Come in, Mr. Porter, please, and stop rewarding my brother's overprotective formality," came a husky female voice from within. I stepped through to find her curled into one of the room's deep leather armchairs.

She had pulled her darker blond hair into a ponytail, and she wore a white blouse, green ankle-length skirt, and slippers on her feet peeping out from beneath her. Her face was clean of makeup and looked like she'd been crying.

"I keep reminding him we are in the US now and no longer in Minsk, but he rarely listens," she said, pronouncing the US as "oos." "Please have a seat."

I sat in one of the more conventional chairs. "First, please accept my condolences again for the loss of your fiancé," I said. "I can't imagine what you're going through."

"Thank you for remembering," she replied with a tight smile. "One of the challenges with which I have been struggling has been that I have no formal role in all of this."

"I'm sorry, what do you mean?"

"When a woman loses her husband, she is called a widow," Reznikov said. "She wears black, and there is a list of things she has to do. Everyone recognizes her for her loss. But when a woman's fiancé dies, who is she? Where is she? Do I put on mourning clothes too, like a widow? Do I go out again to find a new man? What am I supposed to do? You are one of the rare ones who recognize this."

I nodded to accept her comment but didn't offer my own. I preferred to move on to the topic at hand. "If it isn't too painful, I wanted to speak with you about your fiancé. We're considering doing a profile of him and want to find out more. For example, how did you meet?"

She chuckled and drew a small vaping device from a black box on a table beside her. "We met at my grandfather's funeral when we were both twelve years old," she said, watching my face. "Please don't be shocked. Our families are quite traditional, and ours was an arranged meeting. An agreement between our elders set our marriage in motion just after we were born." She drew a deep breath through the device, then blew a marvelous ring with the fine mist. "Our meeting in the church garden was the first step."

"Arranged marriages are rare these days. How did you feel about the families' agreement?"

She shrugged. "It helped that I liked him and found him attractive, along with smart and ambitious. I don't take a romantic view of marriage, Mr. Porter. Neither did Niko. It's a contract—an agreement of respect between two adults who share the same goals. That is all."

"What were those goals?"

"Wealth," she said, "and the things it gets you. Security. Comfort. Status. Power."

"No children?"

"We agreed to delay that decision until later."

"That seems very...efficient," I said. "And not really in line with the way Christianity sees marriage."

She blew another smoke ring. "I agree, but this was an area of compromise between us. I take a pragmatic view of religious faith. Niko did too. After he survived an accident, he took a more romantic, serious view. But we both believed our marriage must be founded on mutual respect."

"Was a lack of respect the cause of the fight between you and Niko on the night of the AthenaLibre party?"

"You heard about that? I'm not surprised. People will always talk." She blew a ring of vapor directly at me. "Even a woman who looks at marriage pragmatically dislikes coming second to her fiancé's work."

"Several witnesses have described the dispute in almost violent terms. Did you really make him drop his phone?"

"I might have." She blew one last ring and began to return her device to its black box. "You need to understand, Mr. Porter, I have a temper like a thunderstorm. It comes up fast and terrible but blows over quickly. I don't believe in resentment."

"What do you know about the work you said came first with Niko?"

"That was one of our issues. I always craved more knowledge about his lab, but he never wanted to share with me. All I was able to figure out was that it had to with sleep. And he said it would make us a lot of money."

"How did you learn of his death?"

"Father Christian. Niko had a folded-up copy of a church program in his pocket, so the police contacted him. He brought me the news."

"So, you weren't listed with AthenaLibre as Niko's emergency contact?"

"Apparently not."

"What did you think had happened to Niko when you learned he had died? Did you believe it could have been suicide?"

"Never. Niko was a very strong man. Not so much physically, but in terms of determination, in terms of the will. I don't believe suicide would have ever occurred to him."

"What do you think happened to him?"

"To tell the truth, I don't know yet. I heard they have arrested a young man—a Latino—but they haven't said anything about motive. Why would that young man have killed him? Niko never had cash. He never mentioned working with any drugs in his lab."

She looked tired and sad. She tucked the vaping device back into the wooden box.

"On a more pleasant topic, how are you finding the rest of your stay in our city?" I said.

"Extremely lovely people and climate. The architecture is pretty good but not perfect," she said as she glanced around us.

"I take it you don't approve of the hotel?"

"Oh please, don't misunderstand. I like the St. George. But its appearance is a little bit like the big hotels in the old USSR. They were meant to impress but too often merely loomed. But we do truly appreciate the Dragon Bar here! Isn't that right, Gregor?"

From his parade rest position by the door, the brother gave an almost imperceptible nod.

"What do you like about it?"

"Oh my God, the drinks! Have you had one of their Dragon's Blood cocktails?"

"Not in many years."

"You must have one again. I am convinced if I drank one a day I would probably live forever, but I could never drink more than two in one night."

"Well, thanks for your time, Ms. Reznikov. I don't want to intrude on you anymore."

She looked up and smiled.

"Not at all, Mr. Porter. I hope I was able to help you with your story. I enjoyed remembering Niko at a happier time."

❖

After the Reznikov interview, I had enough information to risk checking in with Chief Detective Walker. Smalls wouldn't be happy and would try for my scalp if he found out. But given the stakes for Tristan, I couldn't let Walker rocket a routine investigation over to the district attorney. Besides, if I had to write some kind of article about AthenaLibre's security breach with the key or the possibility Nikolaidis had not wanted to get married after all, giving the lead officer a heads-up would help keep him on my side.

I swung by Badda-Bean for two cups of their extra-large café con leche and drove over to Walker's efficiency flat. I knocked in the available space around a prominent construction paper and marshmallow wreath. I lucked out that his door lacked a peephole, and he opened it before knowing I stood in the hall.

"Oh, Jesus H Christ on a raft," he said with a groan when he saw me. "It's eight o'clock in the goddamn morning. Don't you ever rest?"

I had caught him at the end of his shave, wearing a white T-shirt, khaki trousers, and socks. No shoes.

"Peace offering," I said, holding up the takeout Badda-Bean cups.

He stood aside to let me pass. "You're already here, so you might as well come in, but I don't have much time. I'm not going to let you make me late."

"Understood," I replied. "Nice wreath, by the way."

"My niece made it for me. What'd you bring, anyway?"

"A large café con leche for both of us," I said, cracking open one of the lids to release a rush of humid, slightly salty air suffused with the aromas of creamy coffee and cinnamon.

He sniffed appreciatively. "Of course, it's not Edmonds." He walked back into the bathroom, referring to the freeze-dried concoction that usually passed for his coffee in the HQ canteen.

"Damn right. I've brought you an elixir from the Elysian Fields, where coffee is worth paying for."

"The question is what do you want for it?" he said from the bathroom.

"Nothing at all, really," I almost purred. "Except maybe an update on where you are on the Nikolaidis case."

He bolted out of the bathroom and glared at me, still wiping his face with a hand towel. "You know I can't talk about that."

"So don't talk, just listen as I update you on what you have so industriously discovered while the rest of the world thought you were pushing papers and eating doughnuts."

He shot me an angry look but came closer to the table while putting on his shirt.

"For example, earlier this week you found out Nikolaidis was *not* happily betrothed but had discussed breaking the engagement and canceling the wedding only two days before he was killed."

"What?"

"Send one of your more sophisticated and well-spoken men—or go yourself—to Father Christian at St. Photius Greek Orthodox Church and ask about it. I expect the conversation will prove enlightening."

Walker didn't respond verbally, but he nodded.

"Also, did you know about the loading dock door that lets anybody with a physical key enter the building without recording the action in the security system?"

"Yeah, that we did know about."

"And?"

"And nothing. It's a wash. As far as we can tell, everyone who worked in the building knew about the damn door, including your little pal Tristan, by the way. That could have been how he got in, killed his boss, and got out again without being seen."

"Yeah, right." I didn't bother to keep the sarcasm out of my voice. "So, given this marriage angle, will you guys check out Ms. Reznikov?"

"The grieving fiancée? Really?"

I shook my head. "Call it reporter's instinct, but all was not how it seemed in that relationship."

"If your account checks out with the preacher, I'll consider it."

He finished combing his hair and returned to the table to drink the last of the coffee. I had to admit he looked good in the morning cool, before confronting the day's tragedies and disappointments.

"You clean up well, you know," I quietly remarked.

"So do you." He smirked. "When you first started bugging me about this case, I wondered if you might be campaigning to get into that twink's pants, but then I remembered the sort of man who really gets you going." He smirked again and slid his hand down his trousers to outline the bulge.

"Now you're just being crude."

"Nope. I'm the one being honest. We both know what turns you on."

"So?"

"So, if it's not sex, what is it? Why are you working so hard for this kid?"

"I don't know. Justice, I guess. What kind of person would I be if I stood by while an innocent person was convicted of a crime? And actually, I'm sort of responsible for all this happening to him."

"How so?"

"I suggested he apply for the internship in the first place. None of the previous winners I'd met were as bright or interesting, so I thought he'd make a good candidate. I told him he could use me as a reference and took it upon myself to sing his praises when the company called, so I had a role in him going to work at AthenaLibre."

"So, you feel a little responsibility. I can see that," he said.

"And really, he's just a cool kid. He's like the version of myself I wished I could have been so long ago, so I'm a little invested, yeah."

He walked back over to the fridge and pulled out a bottled coffee drink. "Want one?"

"I thought you were heading out to work?"

"Interviewing a knowledgeable source is work."

"I'm a knowledgeable source now?"

"Since it doesn't seem likely you're going to stop inserting yourself into this case, yes. And as much as part of me wants to rat you out to the paranoid Mr. Smalls, I won't spill to him either—provided you answer my questions."

"Provided they don't compromise my own sources, I don't mind helping the boys in blue."

"Deal?" He extended his hand, and I shook it.

"Deal."

"Why are you so convinced he didn't do it? Leave off all the good character crap. I believe in good character too, but sometimes that's all they *let* us see."

"Okay, fair question. Let's look at the physical evidence."

"Sure, if you want. But that's not running in your kid's favor. We have his fingerprints at the scene and on a roll of wire that we can show was the source of the murder weapon. We have his prints in the victim's house, which proves they knew each other outside work, and he had a key for access to the building without registering on the security system. Finally, as far as I know, the kid doesn't have an alibi."

"But you can't place him at the scene on the night of the crime because he wasn't there," I said. "Besides, you said yourself half the company had one of those keys, and you still don't have anything like a whisper of a motive."

"True, but a jury doesn't need an eyewitness to convict, especially in a high-profile murder. As for alibi, I dunno. Maybe the good scientist was backing off marrying the blond bombshell because he had a thing for the kid. Maybe he tried it on with him, the kid said no, and Dr. Niko threatened blackmail. Put out or get out. A bit melodramatic for contemporary times but who knows? I expect we'll find it eventually. We usually do."

I froze the smile on my face in response to this latest speculation, made without having read a statement from Tristan. Instead, I returned with a new line of attack.

"But your scenario doesn't account for size differences. Tristan is tall, but he's a lightweight. I would be shocked if he weighed a buck and a half soaking wet. Nikolaidis would have had an inch or two and about thirty pounds on him. How was this kid supposed to immobilize a man that much bigger and stronger, then strangle him and string him up? I just don't see it."

"So, who looks good to you for the deed?" he said, tossing his coffee bottle perfectly into the recycling can.

"I don't know yet, but I'm still really curious about Reznikov and her brother."

Walker grunted but didn't counter, so we dropped the conversation to let him get dressed and me back to the *Record*. As I pulled away in the car, I felt good about our conversation but not positive about whether Walker would check up on the Reznikovs. What if Ampleforth felt more guarded about talking to the cops than he did talking to me, and didn't verify my account? I put the thought aside. It's no use worrying about what you can't control, I thought.

CHAPTER 6

Gonna Discover

When I got home after my deadline on Friday, I stuck my head into Lyle's guest room to check on Tristan but was surprised to find him not there. I came back to the living room as Lyle stepped off the elevator. I paused to welcome him home.

"No hugs," he said, trying to stop me. "The guys and I spent all afternoon on a broken-down transmission. God only knows what I smell like."

"Only the most potent perfume ever," I joked. "Transmission fluid, sweat, and frustration. You could name the scent Friday Five O'Clock and sell it for fifty bucks an ounce in bottles with your photo on them."

"Get out," he replied with a grin as he fell into one of the living room chairs.

"Do you know where Tristan is? I wanted to check in and see how his day went."

"Nope," Lyle said. "Not that that's unusual. I appreciate him helping around here to pay for room and board, but it would be nice to see more of him too."

"He's probably over at Baldwin House. I think he tries to keep in touch with the kids even if he doesn't live there any longer." I told my smartphone to call Ms. Dass. She picked up on the first ring.

"Oh yeah, he's here," she told me. "I glanced in from the kitchen about fifteen minutes ago, and I think he and Terry were wrestling with algebra. Do you want to speak to him?"

"No, it's okay. I would never want to interrupt algebra," I replied with a chuckle. "He's been out a couple of days now, and I wanted to check in with him and see how he's doing."

"Good," she said. "I was going to call you and suggest that if I hadn't heard differently."

"How come?"

She paused before replying. "I don't know. He's never been an easy one to read. On the surface, he's the usual Tristan. He's cheerful, good with the younger ones, and willing to help with whatever's going on. But he's much quieter now and seems sad a lot. Before, when he helped the youngers with their homework, it sounded almost like a party. He laughed, they laughed. But when I checked on what was going on a few minutes ago, I had to go to the kitchen doorway and look because I didn't hear anything. That's not like him."

"Hmm, I'll try to get some time with him this weekend," I replied.

"You might try the community center tomorrow morning. I overheard him on his phone, reserving one of the basketball courts for nine."

"Thanks, Arundhati, I'll do that."

The next morning, I enjoyed a leisurely breakfast with Lyle, then walked up to the community center to see if I could find Tristan. I timed my arrival for 9:10, after he would have gotten there, claimed the court, and started taking shots.

The front desk stood empty when I arrived, but the electronic scanner recognized my card and let me in. When I went back to the men's locker room to change into shorts and a tee, I noticed that number 19, Tristan's usual cabinet, was closed and locked.

Since the front desk remained empty when I returned from the lockers, I flipped the reservation book around and had a look for myself. Tristan had booked one of the older uncovered courts at the back of the property. I set out.

On the way, I ran into Alfred, the old man who worked as the weekend porter at the center. His determined stride and wrathful face signaled he was not in a good mood. I waved to him and he stopped, but without his trademark smile.

"Morning, Alfred," I said in a cheerful voice. "What's going on?"

"Damn kids. They think because they all have phones it's all right to use them to make other people's lives more difficult."

"What do you mean?"

"I mean twenty minutes ago someone called—a woman or a boy, I don't know which—singing me a song about how a pipe had burst in the ladies' restroom and water was pouring out into the volleyball court and how I better hurry down there."

"And did you?"

"Of course. I know what water can do to those floors. I hurried down there so fast I thought my heart would just about jump out of my chest when I got there."

"And what did you find?"

"Nothing," he almost roared. "No water, no flood. The room's dry as a bone. Nothing on either volleyball court. The whole thing was a stupid hoax."

"Well, I'm glad it was only a false alarm," I said. "Think how bad it would be if it had been true!"

"There is that," he admitted. "And it's not like I had all that much on now anyway."

"Exactly."

"What are you doing down here this morning?" he asked.

"I hoped for some one-on-one with Tristan DeJesus. Seen him?"

"Court twelve."

I arrived to find him making shots, and I leaned against the opponent's basket and watched him. When he finally noticed me, he came over and passed me the ball. I dribbled it out, turned, and hooked one up for two points.

"Nice," he said. "You've been practicing."

"Not really. I just got lucky. Horse?"

"I don't know. I beat you pretty good last time."

"You won by one basket!"

"A win's a win. Besides, I try to respect my elders."

I decided to try another tack. "C'mon, man, I've missed you."

He stopped dribbling. "I missed you too," he said, heading for the foul line. "Shoot for first."

He stopped at the painted stripe, braced, and sent a beautiful shot arcing to take all net with a swish. I caught the ball and headed out to the line.

"Match that," he said, laughing.

"It just needs to go in," I reminded him.

"So, get it in."

I took a stance, aimed for the safest off-the-backboard shot, and let it fly. It struck with a clunk and dropped immediately through the net.

"Another lucky shot?" Tristan said.

"Naw, man, I just been watching you."

"Flattery won't get me to throw the game," he said with a grunt, sending another ball arcing through the net.

"I watched you to see what *not* to do." I sent my next one up, and it rolled around the rim twice before finally dropping in.

"Almost lost that one," he said.

"But didn't."

He dropped two paces back from the foul line, frowned, and sent one curling toward the basket. I held my breath. If he made it, I would have to match it with my next shot. But he didn't. The ball hit the backboard at an angle and bounced off the rim without going in.

"You first," he said.

I chose to start on the right side. These were among the most difficult for me to make, without a backboard. I braced myself and sent it up in a high arc that looked like it would drop the ball right into the basket. But it hit the rim, bounced straight up, and came back down through the net. I dashed after it as it rolled away.

He whistled. "Wish some of your damn luck would rub off on me. It's not fair."

I came back dribbling the ball. "So, what's going on?"

"With what?"

"Like there's anything else?"

"You're friendly with Ms. Mondial. I figured she was keeping you up to date."

"Dude, it doesn't work like that. She's *your* lawyer, not mine. She'll only tell me stuff you say is okay to tell me, and I'd rather hear it from you." I passed him the ball.

"Now we see what skill, practice, and discipline brings versus luck," he said before sending up a perfect side shot that fell through the basket almost making no sound. I rolled my eyes as he chased down the ball.

"So, what's happened?" I asked again.

"She took me back down to police headquarters yesterday morning, and I gave my statement on video and on paper for the steno lady," he said. "Ms. Mondial was in the room with me, and I kept my focus on her. That was the only way I made it through."

"Were there any cops there?"

"Yeah, the big red-haired dude. A detective. He was there, but he didn't ask any questions."

That was interesting, I thought. "What else?"

"The detective told us the security camera at the burger place on Jackson Avenue caught me cutting through their parking lot on the way home that night, but then he said it wasn't a pure alibi because the camera's timer wasn't working correctly and had the wrong day."

"Damn."

"I know, right?" He passed me the ball. "Your turn."

I moved to the next spot. "So, what's next?"

"The police keep investigating, and I keep waiting," he said. "Ms. Mondial said she thinks the prosecutor will take it to the grand jury next week."

"H-O," I said, sending the ball up to glance sharply off the backboard into the net.

"You *have* been practicing," he said, stepping up to the same spot. "H-O," he called before launching a perfect shot that caught only net as it dropped through.

I ran after the ball and dribbled it back. "Do you understand what the grand jury thing means?"

"I think so," he replied. "She laid it out pretty clearly. Grand juries have twenty-three jurors, and sixteen need to be present to conduct business. The prosecutor has to convince twelve of them that I most likely did the crime for me to go to trial. If they don't have the votes, then they don't indict, and there is no trial. But the prosecutor can try again with a new grand jury, especially if she has more evidence."

"Did she think the prosecutor can get the twelve?"

"She thinks the case against me now is weak, but she told me not to get my hopes up. She said prosecutors can almost always get an indictment if they want one, because the process is so one-sided. For example, she can't be there to stand up for me or cross-examine any witnesses."

I moved to the foul line. "H-O-R," I called, sending up my standard shot. It sank through the net cleanly. He ran after the ball and dribbled it back.

"I'm glad you came today," he said. "I've been thinking a lot about something, and I wanted to ask you about it. H-O-R," he called and made the foul shot too. But when I brought the ball back and passed it to him, he picked it up.

"Can we just call this one a tie?" he asked.

I shrugged. "Of course." We walked over to the bleachers and sat down. "So, what's the decision?"

"Ms. Mondial thinks the case against me is so weak that even if the prosecutor gets the indictment, they'll offer me a deal."

"What sort of deal?"

"They would drop any murder counts and instead charge me with something less serious. In return, I'd plead guilty to that less serious accusation."

I looked at him in shock. "But you didn't do anything."

"I know, man, but look at me." He stood up suddenly. "I'm the age, color, and ethnicity I am. And now, thanks to my statement, the jury's gonna know I'm queer too. Ms. Mondial said taking a plea would be a way to keep a racist jury or prejudiced judge from sending me to prison for a long time." He sat down again. "And I think she might be right."

"Wait," I said. "Did she definitely say to take the deal?"

"No. There is no deal offered yet, but she wanted me to be aware of the chance."

"Okay, I get that. But isn't this the sort of question that you can't really answer hypothetically?"

"Yes, about the details. But not about the basics. No matter the details of any deal, I'm not sure I'm ready to stand up in public and say I did something that I didn't do."

"Well, that's still a decision you don't have to make yet. Let's see if we can gather more facts and more evidence so you don't have to make it."

He grinned. "You had the luck today, but it was sure with me the day we met. I can't thank you or Lyle enough."

"Don't mention it. I saw where Ms. Dass brought home a pile of lemons from the store. Let's go see if she made some lemonade."

We got up and walked back to the locker room, where another shock awaited.

"Damn, dog, look at my locker!"

The door of number 19 swung loosely from its hinges, with a big chunk out of it where the lock had been.

"Don't touch anything," I said, running to the front to get Alfred. He came back with me and delivered another round of curses in both English and Spanish.

"That damn hoax in the morning and now this," he groaned. "And these new lockers not even a year old."

"It looks like they used a crowbar," I said, pointing to the set of notches behind where the lock should have been. "They didn't use any finesse to beat the mechanism, just a plain brute force break-in."

None of the remaining cabinets, including mine, had been attacked.

"You probably came back too quick to let them hit any of the others," Tristan said.

Alfred let him empty the locker of his possessions since he didn't believe the police would make it a priority. "This gets classified as a nuisance infraction and not really investigated," he said.

Tristan quickly looked through his things and found a twenty dollar bill he had planned go out with later had been stolen, along with a sentimental item. "Damn, man, my Pride pendant is gone. I've worn it every day since you gave it to me last year."

"That seems like a weird thing to take. Are you sure it's gone?"

"Yes, it was hanging on a hook, the same as always."

This made little sense. The twenty dollars I could see, but the pendant wasn't valuable in and of itself. It was the size of a dog tag and crafted from polished black enamel with a rainbow flag on the front. I paid ten dollars for it at the Pride parade where I and Tristan had met. I felt touched he had worn it often, but sentimental value usually didn't translate into hard cash.

I looked up and Tristan was dressed and ready to go while I was still in my shorts and tee.

"Be only a second," I said, heading back to my locker.

"Late as usual," Tristan said.

❖

After sharing some of Ms. Dass's mouth-puckering fresh lemonade, I returned to Bonne Chance Motors to help Lyle get the eight-foot-tall Douglas fir set up in the main room.

"Remember, you promised to come back this evening in time to help us find a way to decorate this monster," I reminded Tristan before I left. "I understand that a big space needs something of size, but Lyle forgets we don't have the ornaments for much more than a five-foot tree."

"Don't worry, I'll be there."

When I stepped off the clunky elevator, I saw Lyle had gotten the tree established in its base and watered it. The branches, released from their traveling bindings, had gracefully lowered to more natural positions, and the entire apartment smelled like a Pine-Sol commercial.

I looked up to the top, roughly a foot from the ceiling. "Wow, that is a lot of tree."

"I know," Lyle said, a little self-consciously. "I didn't really understand what you meant until I got it up in the stand. My ambitions were almost too big for the room."

"Almost is the key word. Fortunately, it's a thin tree instead of a fat one. That means it only really dominates the room in height. There's still plenty of space to move around in here."

"That's true."

I bent down to try to peer through the branches to the trunk. "I don't suppose you considered—"

"I'm way ahead of you. We can't cut the trunk to make the tree shorter without either creating a huge hole on one side of it or removing many pretty lower branches."

"Okay, then. It looks like we're going to have a big tree this Christmas. How are we going to decorate it?"

He pointed to a box beside the couch that contained neat coils of lights. "A few years ago I thought I might go ahead and have a tree, so I bought those at the King's Kastle Health Salon's moving sale. We could start with those."

I looked at the lines of brown bulbs and twisted wires in the box. "What about ornaments?"

"I have a box of forty-eight silver balls and another one of forty-eight gold balls. And I got two containers of that ropey tinsel stuff and some packages of icicle things."

"Okay, all those are positive."

"And I think we have one other crate of decorations, but I have to go check."

I nodded as he got on the elevator and it began to descend.

Meanwhile, I got started on the lights. Four strands appeared to be a useful length. I found the plug in the first loop, tugged it out a bit, and put it into the socket. The good news was they all lit up. But the less welcome observation was that they were all red. Not the jolly, ho-ho-ho kind of red, but the why-don't-you-come-up-and-see-me type. I sat on the couch and gazed at the four loops at my feet. They all worked. And they all looked like they could decorate the red light district in Amsterdam. I wondered whether we could have harlotry as our Christmas tree theme this year.

Downstairs, the elevator restarted, and soon both Lyle and Tristan got off.

"Look who caught a ride up with me," Lyle said happily.

"Wow. You weren't fronting," Tristan said. "That is a seriously big tree."

"Yes, and it's going to be interesting too," I replied. "Lyle, the lights all lit up, so yay, but the color is an unusual one for Christmas. What kind of establishment was this health salon?"

"Is," he said. "It's still in business. They just moved off Jackson around the corner onto Twelfth Street. I bought those at their relocation sale. Twelve bucks for four big strands of lights, pretty good deal, huh?"

I inserted the one of the plugs into the wall. The string lit up the color of a bordello couch pillow.

"It is if you think more than kissing should happen under the mistletoe," I replied, trying hard to keep from breaking into laughter.

"Oh my God," Lyle said.

Tristan howled. "Oh, that's great!"

"We have a choice," I said. "We can use the streetwalker red lights on the tree and gradually replace them as needed, or we could go out and get whole new strands in less controversial colors?"

"Keep them," Lyle said. "They won't be the only thing on the tree, and Jesus was a friend of prostitutes anyway."

"I agree," Tristan said. "Besides, remember the St. Michael's Harbor motto this Christmas: 'Recycle, Repair, Reuse.' I can't see throwing away four strands of working lights just because some people might not like the color."

"The city has a Christmas motto?"

"Baldwin House is a city agency, so we get all the circulars," Tristan said. "I bet you didn't know last month was Leaf Collection Month, either."

"So, it's decided. Lyle, any luck with those other ornaments?"

"Yes, if Tristan will give me a hand with this crate. It's not heavy, but it's too big for one person to carry."

Together they went into the elevator and reappeared bearing a large, secure-looking wooden box stamped Fragile and Handle with

Care. They set it down gently beside the tree. Lyle disappeared into the lift again and came out with a crowbar.

"These ornaments have a backstory," he said. "Years ago, when I had recently taken over BCM, I launched a package deal to build the customer base. I don't remember exactly what we charged, but we offered an oil change and tune-up for one low price plus a gift, and the gift was one of these ornaments."

He went to the side of the box and inserted the bar between the wall and the top and gently pried it up. Then he moved a foot down and did it again and kept working as he spoke.

"You probably don't know this, but St. Michael's Harbor has a large community of vintage automobile enthusiasts. They sponsor a show every spring, and they are willing to spend good money on their cars. Well, I wanted a piece of that market, so I chose to give away these ornaments."

With a final protesting shriek, the lid came off the crate to reveal an expanse of old newsprint, peppered with occasional metallic gleams and flashes. Lyle carefully reached in, removed a clump of newspaper, and drew out a lovely Model-T Ford ornament, complete with starter crank. He also pulled out a blue 1924 Duesenberg, a 1954 pink Cadillac, a 1938 red Mercedes-Benz, and a lemon yellow 1957 Chevrolet.

"Oh wow," Tristan said. "They're really pretty."

"Yeah," I agreed. "And the detail is great. How come you still have them?"

"This crate arrived after the promotion ended, and the marketing was so good, we didn't have to do it again," Lyle said. "Some of the people who took us up on the offer are still our customers decades later."

"Well," I said, "since Tristan is probably the last one of us to decorate a Christmas tree, he should supervise you while I go and pull something together for us to eat?"

"Sounds like a plan," Tristan said.

"It's not like I don't know anything," Lyle objected.

I pointed to the coils of red lights. "I rest my case."

Later, as we ate dinner looking at their work, I praised them for having done such a good job. Not only had they managed to decorate a large tree with few resources, but the placement of those assets also detracted from the lights' tawdry color. Our Christmas fir looked more playful than sleazy.

"It's a beautiful tree," I said as we enjoyed it over a last glass of wine. "Well done."

"Thank you," Tristan replied, "but most of the credit belongs to Lyle. He genuinely has a talent for ornament placement. I'd be surprised if there's one ball or car I put on that tree that he didn't move to a better position."

A series of sharp beeps from the coat rack made all of us jump.

"I thought we agreed to turn off the personal cell phones after six p.m.," Lyle said.

"I did. That's the work phone I can't truly turn off. Let me see what's up."

I walked to my jacket and found the phone in my pocket. The one new message was in text-speak but exciting nonetheless. It read: *I no ur asking bout Nik. B @ MLK Skating Gazebo @ 3 PM 2morrow.*

I turned to Lyle and Tristan. "Don't get your hopes up," I cautioned. "But we may be getting someplace with this story after all."

❖

"I don't see why you won't call Detective Walker and give him the heads-up," Lyle said for about the thousandth time as I pulled on a long-sleeved T-shirt. "Or, failing that, let me come with you."

I looked at him, then leaned in to give him a deep kiss. "I love that you're worried about me, and I understand your concern. I genuinely do. But this is a source who wants to talk to me about the Nikolaidis case. They might even be a material witness. I need to hear what they have to say, not report them to Walker so he can scoop them up."

"But that's just it. We don't know who they are. They could be the murderer. You've been more than generous to the police with your information. Don't you think the killer might have caught on to that?"

I looked at him again and took a deep breath. The last time we had been involved with killers, his best friend and I had wound up in a hospital.

"Look," I said. "If whoever this is wanted to meet in an abandoned warehouse or on an isolated beach, I'd refuse and suggest we get together somewhere else. But MLK skate park on a sunny Sunday afternoon—even in December—must be among the most public places in the city."

"At least let me babysit the front gate for you," Lyle said.

"Of course I'm going to agree to that. If I said no, you'd go anyway, so why should I bother?"

The city installed the skating space at MLK after a skateboard magazine named the park one of the five most challenging places in the state for boarders to test their skills. Thousands of skaters, some international, responded. While the city appreciated the income they brought, many non-skating park users objected. The solution was to reclaim a part of the park nearest the creek and turn it into a skaters' paradise, with enough obstacles and challenges to keep them busy for a hundred years.

At its narrowest and highest point, the V-shaped skate park had a few bleachers and an attractive gazebo surrounded by lawn with its one gate situated opposite, across the obstacles and ramps.

I arrived at 2:40 and gradually made my way around the edges on my way to the gazebo. Everyone using the space appeared to be skaters, from grade school to college aged, with significantly more boys than girls. No one looked sinister, dangerous, or adult, for that matter. I found a seat about halfway up the bleachers next to the gazebo and waited to see what would happen.

After about five minutes, a slim teen who had been sitting by himself on the edge of a half pipe got up, hopped his board, and executed a perfect ride down and out of the obstacle. Then, while seeming not to be aware of me at all, he moved through the challenges until he reached the bleachers, hopped off the board, and climbed up to sit beside me.

"Jose Porter?" he asked.

"If you're Rico."

"Cool," he said, offering me his right fist to bump.

I bumped back. "Does Rico have a last name?"

"Just Rico for now. You're not a cop."

"You did your homework."

"Yeah, well, it wasn't hard."

I felt like we had done a pretty good job of establishing our bona fides and stepped it up a little. "This is your meeting, why am I here?"

"I wanted to talk."

"About…skating? Christmas? Why you got track marks down your left arm?"

His body tensed. "Hey, man, I don't use."

"But you did." I grabbed the arm to look at the marks more closely. "Two or three years ago."

"Get off me," he said, furiously. "I'm clean for more than two years."

"Congratulations," I replied a bit more gently. "I know that took something to do."

"Yeah, well, you don't have to be such a prick. Niko. I wanted to talk about Niko, or Dr. Nikolaidis, probably, to you."

"What about him?"

"I knew him."

"Knew him how?"

"I just knew him, that's all."

"Sorry, I need more than that. What would an award-winning researcher at one of the hottest companies in the country want with a fourteen-year-old skate punk?" I started gathering myself to leave.

"He was one of my clients," he said in a loud voice.

I stopped getting up. "One of your clients how?"

"How do you think?"

Gradually, in fits and starts over the next hour, Jaime "Rico" Pelado told me about Niko, the man who arrived at his room in the boardinghouse cum brothel at least once and sometimes twice or three times a week for almost a full year. He came for sex, of course, but gradually to hang out and watch movies on Rico's small television, share a takeout pizza, or merely to talk.

"Eduardo always tells us we can't get attached, but I did," Rico admitted. "In a lot of ways Niko was my first real boyfriend, even if he was paying for my time."

"Who's Eduardo?"

"My landlord. The guy who runs the house and sets the rules."

They had met at a Christmas party around this time last year, Rico told me. Eduardo regularly threw at least two or three social events a week, where potential clients met the residents and arranged rendezvous in the boys' rooms later. Most of these were low-key affairs with a two-drink limit.

Rico first saw Nikolaidis at one of these on a Thursday night, but since the researcher did not approach him or seek out Eduardo, Rico thought he wasn't interested. But Nikolaidis came back the next night and happened to catch him coming out of the hall bathroom under one of Eduardo's extravagant displays of mistletoe. To his surprise, Nikolaidis pressed him for a kiss. He agreed and told me the man's soulful smooch changed everything.

"It was amazing, to tell the truth," Rico said. "I hadn't been kissed, really kissed, hardly at all in my whole life, and that one from Niko was like he opened up his soul and poured it into me." As soon as they came up for air, Rico took Niko by the hand to go find Eduardo and let Niko pay the fee. He remembered Niko paid for the whole night, a figure totaling hundreds of dollars.

"We were just so into it," he recalled. "We didn't even have sex until like four in the morning, we were talking and laughing so much." Nikolaidis told him stories about growing up in a Belarusian town, and Rico taught Niko slang English and some Spanish. Despite Niko continually paying to see Rico, although at a lower rate he negotiated with Eduardo, Rico became aware they both began to think of their association as a relationship—albeit not always a smooth one.

"Overall, he was pretty cool. But I can't lie. He used to like it a little rough—not like rough enough to really hurt me, but slaps and dirty names and hearing me moan and shit. I mean, there started to be a lot of anger in it for him sometimes. Afterward, he'd be all nice and sorry—and sort of sad really. And then he would be generous the next time I saw him."

One of their last occasions together, Rico said Niko had given him a bracelet. He shook his arm, letting it slide down his wrist to his outstretched hands where I could study it. I felt amazed. The bracelet was articulated, allowing it to become a snake biting its own tail. It was made of gold, with what looked like jade for eyes and a cluster of jade chips marking the head. Rico showed me where the clasp connecting the head and tail was hidden in the snake's mouth.

"That's brilliant," I said.

"Yeah, it's cool. Look at this." He ran his finger along the back of the serpent's head, and the area under the small pieces of jade moved aside, revealing a little cavity.

"Niko said maybe someone used to keep a sleeping powder in that hole so they could put someone to sleep over dinner if they wanted," Rico said.

"Did Niko ever say where he got it?"

"Only that a friend who thought it was ugly had given it to him," Rico said. "It's supposed to be old and a little bit famous, but I didn't understand much about that."

"So, you've kept it ever since?"

"Absolutely. I never take it off, even in the shower or when I'm sleeping. It helps me remember him."

"When did you see Dr. Nikolaidis last?"

"Like five or six days before I found out he was killed," Rico said. "He came around, but he was sad and didn't feel like doing anything but holding me and talking. I asked him like forty times what was wrong, but all he kept saying was that the good things in his life could never remain, and we'd probably never see each other again. Of course, I thought he was leaving me. I cried a little and begged him not to, but he said it wasn't his choice and that if I ever read about him in the paper, I should know I would always be in his heart. A few days later in the papers, they said he was dead."

I looked up to find his face pale and his dark eyes swimming in unshed tears. "I didn't even have a chance to say goodbye. Or thank you. He really was worth a lot more than the credit he gave himself."

I reached out and took his hands and the bracelet in mine.

"I'm sure he realized that in the end," I lied. "If I've learned anything in the last few weeks of reporting about Niko, it's that he had a lot of layers and a lot of secrets behind the masks he showed the world. I think you were remarkable for getting through as far as you did with him."

He seemed to brighten up at this. "I think so. Or I hope so, I guess. Thank you for looking into his death."

I took a breath and a chance. "It might help if I could take some detailed pictures of the bracelet, just some close-ups with my phone. Who knows, someone might know it, or at least we could figure out how old it is."

He paused and thought for a few moments. "I guess," he said at last. "I almost didn't show it to you because people'll say I stole it. But I really didn't, I swear."

"I believe you. Let me take the pictures."

Thus, there on the bleachers of the MLK skate park, with nothing but a pair of hands and a denim-clad crotch as a backdrop, I took photos of what could be the most valuable created object I would ever hold in my life.

Afterward, I handed him my card. "You obviously have my personal number, but here's my office number, too. How did you get access to my private line, anyway?"

"Your paper needs to train its receptionists better," Rico said with a grin. Then he pitched his voice to sound younger than usual. "I'm Billy Porter, and I'm locked out and it's an emergency. I have to contact my brother Manny right away, but his business phone just rings and rings." It was entirely too convincing.

"Well, I work with the police but not for them. If you ever need me, you can reach me on either line. Now how do I reach you? I assumed the number you used to text was of a burner phone?"

He nodded and handed me a card with a single phone number printed on it, but no name or address.

"Eduardo will answer, but he doesn't censor or screen our calls," Rico said. "I know you probably think he's just our pimp, but he doesn't own the house and does what he can to keep us safe. I think I'm lucky to have him."

I left him sitting on the bleachers, looking like one of the hundreds of other skate boys that pit skills against the park barriers every week before heading back to the rest of their lives. After dinner, I downed a double of Lyle's single malt and demanded he pummel my ass while I clung to him with everything I had, seeking absolution for all the day's sins that tore at my soul but were not mine.

❖

Monday morning brought an anxious phone call from Carolyn Mondial while Lyle and I were still drinking coffee.

"According to what I've just been told, the prosecutor barely got an indictment against Tristan on Friday," she said. "He's offering him a deal. If Tristan will plead guilty to voluntary manslaughter, the prosecutor will drop the murder charge and urge the judge to sentence him to no more than five years. With good behavior inside, that will translate to little more than three years."

"My God," I replied. "And good morning to you too." Lyle arched his eyebrows at me from across the table. "Indictment," I tried to mouth to him. He set down his coffee to listen.

"I'm sorry. This email just arrived, and I'm still wound up about it."

"Have you told Tristan?"

"Not yet. He and I already have a meeting set for nine this morning. I wanted to let you know in case he came to you for advice."

"What are you going to advise?"

She paused a long time. "I'm going to advise him to take the deal," she said, finally. "Emotionally, it's the exact opposite of what I want him to do. But from the standpoint of serving his best interests, I have to urge him to take it."

"Why? If he's innocent, and if the prosecutor barely got twelve grand jurors to agree with him about possible guilt, that signals a weak case, doesn't it?"

"On paper. On the surface, their position is frail. They have no physical smoking gun linking him to the killing or uniquely to the crime scene and will have to rely on circumstantial evidence alone. In a perfect world, that wouldn't be enough to convict anyone. But this is South Georgia, about as far from a perfect world for Tristan as you can get."

"What do you mean?"

"Elections are coming up, and I think Clark is going to run for Georgia attorney general. This case is the sort that could remain in headlines for weeks. An employee of a popular and important firm killed by immigrant kid living in a halfway house after a lovers' quarrel because, oh yeah, he's a faggot too. I won't even be able to strike potential jurors who say hateful things about gays from the stand because gay people are not a protected class."

"I see what you mean. The prosecutor could see this as an easy feather in his cap for a statewide campaign."

"Yep."

"When's the hearing?"

"That's another kicker. It's at two o'clock this afternoon. I'll barely be able to brief Tristan before he has to be in court. In case I can't get more time, can you and Lyle be there? I think your support will be important."

"We'll definitely be there."

"Great. I'm going to try to call Tristan now to see if we can move the meeting up. Is he up yet?"

"Oh yeah, I think he's out on a run now. You should be able to get him."

She rang off.

"News?"

"An indictment and a potential deal. Can you shake yourself free about two o'clock this afternoon?"

We arrived at the courthouse at one thirty and, after checking in and surrendering our phones, proceeded to courtroom number two, but the imposing leather-clad doors were locked. We sat down on a bench outside.

"Why are we so early again?" Lyle said.

"Because I wanted to make sure we got seats near the front so Tristan will know we're there. Plus, if he wanted to talk to me at all before entering the courtroom, I wanted him to have that chance."

Eventually a bailiff arrived to open the doors, and people started to flow in, but still no signs of Carolyn or Tristan. We lingered inside the door and studied the space. I knew Lyle loved the architecture of the building, but truthfully, I could take or leave this courtroom. The gazebo seal of the State of Georgia dominated the wall behind the judicial bench, flanked by the Ten Commandments to the right and the Bill of Rights to the left. I found no warmth in the white-on-white imagery.

I studied the small number of people who had come. Anna Fin Chow sat near the center aisle at about the middle of the courtroom. Emily Powers sat close to the back, and Ms. Dass took a position four rows behind the defense table.

Finally, at ten minutes to two, we went in and sat down right behind where Tristan would sit. At last, with a few moments left, they entered. I thought he looked incredibly solemn and mature and noticed he had chosen to wear the shirt Lyle and I had given him for his birthday. He turned and glanced at us but didn't speak or smile. Somewhere behind us, I heard Abner Smalls's reedy voice, so I knew he was there as well.

The bailiff said, "Please rise. The First Circuit Court for the State of Georgia, criminal division, is now in session. The Honorable Elijah Matthews presiding."

We stood as a tall, distinguished Black man entered the room from the left and climbed to his seat on the bench. He sat down. "Please be seated," he said.

We all sat.

"Okay, we have a busy docket this afternoon," the judge said. "Bailiff, call the first case."

"State of Georgia vs. Tristan Maria DeJesus, Your Honor."

The judge opened a folder on his desk and read from the papers it contained. "I see. First let's call the roll. When I announce your name or position, please signify by answering yes. Is the counsel for the state here?"

A sharply dressed middle-aged white man rose. "Yes, Your Honor. Clark Davies, state's attorney for St. Michael's County and the city of St. Michael's Harbor."

"I'm a little surprised to see you, Counselor, but welcome," the judge said. "Is counsel for the defense here?"

Carolyn rose. "Yes, Your Honor. Carolyn Mondial, defense counsel to Mr. DeJesus."

"Very good. Welcome, Ms. Mondial. I am pleased to have you in my courtroom again. Is your client present?"

"I am, Your Honor," Tristan said.

Judge Matthews glanced sharply at him. "Young man, I appreciate your attentiveness and eagerness to participate, but in the future please speak only when addressed directly, is that understood?"

Tristan looked down at his shoes. "Yes, Your Honor."

"Your Honor, may I direct your attention to the motion I filed with the clerk of court just a few moments before the session began?" Carolyn asked.

The judge scanned the small pile of papers. "I don't see any new motion from you in the file."

The bailiff approached with a single sheet of paper and handed it to the judge. "Ah, here it is," he said. He read the motion. "So, if I understand correctly, you are asking for more time to meet with your client in order to discuss his legal position?"

"That is correct, Your Honor."

"How much more time would you need?"

"Oh, three or four days, at most a week, Your Honor."

Davies stood up. "The state objects, Your Honor."

"Proceed."

"Mr. DeJesus acquired representation soon after his arrest and had counsel when he posted bail, Your Honor. This is merely the arraignment, not the start of an actual trial. Surely there has been enough time to prepare for this proceeding."

Matthews peered down at both. "I think the state has a point, Ms. Mondial. I am going to deny this motion but appreciate your bringing it." He stamped the sheet of paper and placed it with the others. "Now, I believe we have a true bill of indictment for murder that has been stepped down to voluntary manslaughter. Is that correct, Mr. Davies?"

"Yes, Your Honor."

"Ms. Mondial, have you and your client been able to review and discuss this bill?"

"We have, Your Honor."

"Is he prepared to issue a plea today?"

"He is."

"Mr. DeJesus, please stand."

Tristan stood.

"Mr. DeJesus, do you understand that you stand here today charged with voluntary manslaughter under the Criminal Code of the State of Georgia in the death of Phillip Nikolaidis and that if you are convicted of this charge, you may be liable for at least one and up to twenty years in state prison?"

"I do."

"And do you further understand that if a jury finds you had sufficient time for reflection before the killing of Phillip Nikolaidis, the jury can find you guilty of murder instead and that the possible penalties for murder include life in prison or death?"

"I do."

"In light of these allegations against you, how do you plead before this court to the charge of voluntary manslaughter in the death of Phillip Nikolaidis?"

"I plead not guilty, Your Honor."

Movie or television courtroom dramas depict what happens when all the air suddenly gets sucked from a legal proceeding by having the attendees universally gasp as uproar ensues and reporters leap for the doors in a race to be the first ones to the pay phones to call in the news. That's pretty much what happened as soon as Tristan's plea left his lips. Judge Matthews resorted to his gavel a dozen times, calling for order in the room before the noise finally subsided and everyone returned to their seats.

"May I remind everyone present that this is a court of law and not a circus," Matthews declared, directing his steely gaze to every corner of the space. "If there is so much as a hint of this sort of disruption again, I will clear this court and proceed without public observers, is that clear?"

No one said anything, but as I looked around, I noticed several people nodding.

"Now, will counsel please approach the bench."

Carolyn and Davies went up to begin a whispered, fierce-looking conversation with the judge that continued for some minutes before they finally returned to their seats.

Judge Matthews addressed Tristan again. "Mr. DeJesus, due to your youth and the gravity of the charge you face, I feel I must ask you some questions concerning your plea."

"Yes, Your Honor."

"Do you understand that the voluntary manslaughter charge is a reduced charge from the true indictment, which was for the murder of Dr. Nikolaidis, and that a plea of guilty could bring a significantly shorter sentence than you would face if you were found guilty of his murder?"

"Yes, Your Honor."

"So, I must ask you, in your own words, to explain your plea."

Tristan looked up at the judge and over at Carolyn and then around the room. "I plead innocent because I didn't kill Dr. Nikolaidis," he said in a calm, firm voice. "No finding or declaration of guilt, whether from a jury or from my own lips, can change that. If a jury finds me guilty, they will make a tragic mistake of injustice. But I would make a similar mistake if I pled guilty to a crime I did not commit. The state might make that mistake in the end, Your Honor, but it will have to do that on its own. I refuse to help by pleading guilty."

His last word echoed in the quiet courtroom until the judge cleared his throat.

"Therefore, in light of this plea, do we have suggestions for a start date for this trial," Judge Matthew asked.

"Because of the holidays, Your Honor, I don't see how we can start before February first of next year, a Tuesday," replied Mr. Davies, glancing at a small black notebook.

"Does the defense object?"

"No, Your Honor."

"Then I expect to see you both back here on February first, prepared to start impaneling a jury. I now adjourn this court for a twenty-minute break before we hear the next case."

Afterward, Carolyn brought Tristan back to Lyle's and came up with him. They both looked exhausted and as though they might have been crying.

"Come in," I said. "Carolyn, Lyle will pour you a glass of wine. Tristan, you can have a beer if you want."

"Thank you," Carolyn said. "I apologize for getting emotional, but I'm just a little overwhelmed."

"And I started because you started," Tristan said with a tight smile.

"That was quite a decision you announced, kiddo," I said to him over a hug. "When did you make it? I expect it may not have been what Carolyn advised."

"Not at all!" she said. "It's what I wanted in my heart but what I deeply feared. I strongly advised him to take the deal."

"Why?" Tristan asked.

"Because like I told you, I'm afraid they're going to come after you with everything they can now to meet their other goals. And I'm afraid I might not be able to defeat them."

"Ms. Mondial, you can forget that. You're a great lawyer, and I wouldn't want anyone else defending me. You got the judge changed, didn't you? I know you'll fight for me, and I believe we can win."

"What's all this?"

"They initially had the case before Judge Castwell, who I happen to know attends the most homophobic church in the city," Carolyn said. "I dropped him a note asking if it might be a good idea to remind the scheduling clerk he wasn't supposed to hear any more cases for at least a couple of months to let his docket clear. He shared my opinion, and the clerk's office moved the case. He would like to move up among circuit judges, and the last thing he wanted was a controversial case where his own attitudes might become a factor."

"That sounds like a great move to me," I said. "And, Tristan, when did you decide to plead not guilty, anyway?"

"For real, not until the judge told me not to speak unless spoken to," he said. "That reminded me of how my granny was always on me to tell the truth and let God sort it out. It was almost as though I could feel her with me. I mean, sticking with the truth is the simplest thing, right? It's not like I need to worry about whether I murdered Dr. Nikolaidis or killed him some other way. I just plain old didn't kill him. Not in any way. And if they're going to say I did, they'll have to prove it."

CHAPTER 7

Naughty vs. Nice

Tristan and I were in a grim mood as we traveled to Carolyn Mondial's office the next day. I felt anxiety over the scope of what we needed to investigate to clear Tristan's name, while he endured the prospect of possibly spending the rest of his life in prison.

The elevator in Carolyn's building operated slowly that morning. Tristan and I admired the holiday décor in the lobby as we waited.

"I've never really noticed how bright many Christmas decorations are," Tristan said. "Now that I might not see any for years."

"Enough of that," I said as we got on the elevator. "We need to keep our focus on getting you out from under this and supporting Carolyn's work."

He agreed. And when Carolyn opened her door to let us in, it appeared she agreed too. She had moved her desk to another wall and filled the entire free space with a number of whiteboards, chalkboards, and pegboards. One held a schedule for when briefs were due to the court. Another had photos of key pieces of evidence and key people, and the third listed unanswered questions or answered inquiries whose results she deemed unclear.

"Wow," I said. "Did you even go home last night?"

"Yes, but I admit I was up at oh-dark-thirty this morning, so I came in to do this. Welcome to the Free Tristan Command Center. We're going to beat this charge by getting and staying organized," she declared before pointing us both to a coffee station in the corner of the room. "Everything you need for a cup of joe," she said. "Briefing starts in five minutes."

We both got coffee and sat down in the comfortable chairs. Carolyn remained standing.

"Okay," she said. "Existing evidence first. Remember, under rules of evidence, the prosecutor's office has to let us know in advance whatever testimony, objects, facts, reports, or forensic data they have to support their case. Likewise, we must do the same. Understood?"

We nodded.

"Right. A forensic examination of Nikolaidis's body confirmed strangulation by wire as the cause of death. They have your fingerprints all over the lab and particularly on the roll of wire. However, they have not found your fingerprints on the wire that strangled him, nor on the wire that suspended the body.

"They also found your fingerprints in the house on several pieces of furniture downstairs, but not on any glasses, which suggests Nikolaidis cleaned the glasses you two used. Fortunately a forensic examination of the corpse confirmed that he had been in a fight in the hours before he died and that, had he lived, he would have sported a significant shiner the next day. Unfortunately, they found no definite video evidence that can prove you went back to Baldwin House that night."

"So what did the grand jury use for the indictment?" I asked. "There is nothing definite that says Tristan was even there when the killing happened."

"Remember, grand juries don't seek to prove guilt or innocence, only to answer whether there is reasonable grounds to suspect the accused committed a specific crime," Carolyn said. "In this case, I believe they made their determination using Tristan's statement, the fingerprints, and an absence of any other suspects."

I cleared my throat. "About that," I said. "I might have a line of inquiry into other possible suspects."

I told them about my meeting with Rico at the skate park, relaying everything I had learned about his relationship with

Nikolaidis, their time together, and the bracelet Nikolaidis had given him. I capped off my discourse with the photos I had on my phone.

They both sat back, stunned, but Tristan reacted first.

"That son of a bitch," he muttered. "That's a kid, for Christ's sake. A *kid*! It could have been Jeremy or Eric from Baldwin House." He got up and walked around the room. "All the time he was coming on to me and feeding me lines and shit, he was fucking a little kid."

Carolyn broke in. "How reliable do you find this Rico?"

"I was convinced as to his line of work, including Nikolaidis being a regular client, but he didn't have anything to prove it other than the bracelet. But if Nikolaidis negotiated an ongoing rate with Eduardo for seeing Rico, we need to find him."

"Exactly."

"I've asked my computer whiz to get me everything he can from the phone number Rico gave me, and I'm expecting a callback soon. Assuming what Rico told me is correct, we need to decide what we should do with the information."

"How comfortable are you with the police?" Carolyn said.

"Well, the last time I met with Chief Detective Walker, he asked me if I ever quit," I replied. "But overall, I think okay. They take what I tell them seriously. I hope they followed up with my tip about Nikolaidis wanting to cancel the wedding only days before his death."

Carolyn walked up to a new board with a sheet of paper on which she wrote RICO in large letters.

"Questions," Carolyn said. "Would Rico testify willingly or would we have to subpoena him? How credible would he be as a witness? What do we know about the bracelet?" She asked for my phone again and looked at the photos. Then she set it down. "Can I get a copy of those, please?"

I nodded.

"Why does he have this thing?" she said. "It's kind of fascinating as objet d'art, but it's also pretty ugly. It doesn't match the décor in Nikolaidis's house, at least according to the crime scene photos I've seen."

"Why is the bracelet important?" Tristan asked.

"Because it establishes the link between Nikolaidis and Rico," she said. "If we can firmly establish Nikolaidis gave it to Rico, it helps substantiate his story."

"What about different motives?" I asked.

"What do you mean?"

"We still don't have a clear idea of what Nikolaidis was actually doing at the lab in addition to the work he told AthenaLibre about."

"Can we rule out someone else at AthenaLibre as a suspect?" she said.

"Not yet we can't."

"Then we need to keep up that line of questioning," she said. "If possible, we also want to get some of this on the record and in the papers. In my experience, nothing lights a fire under a reluctant police force like headlines about what other people are finding out."

"Okay, my two highest priority lines of questioning are about AthenaLibre and the bracelet, right?"

"Sounds right to me. Keep pressing on both."

"What should I do?" Tristan asked.

"Keep out of trouble," Carolyn said. "If you want to contribute, you can work for me here in the office. I don't want to give any overeager policeman a reason to charge you with violating your bail conditions."

"Tristan," I said, "you were one of Dr. Nikolaidis's assistants, even if you weren't full-time. Did you think he was doing anything off the books, so to speak?"

"I'm almost sure he was. I wasn't involved very much in a lot of the actual research, but I became the lab's key logistics person. There were two different kinds of supplies. One was chemical compounds and analysis kits I recognized as belonging to Dr. Nikolaidis's pesticide work, but some other deliveries didn't seem to have anything to do with the projects I knew about."

"What would he get?"

"Weird stuff. Every fourteen to twenty days there would come this sixty- or eighty-pound box from Purina."

"Purina? As in dog food?"

"Actually, the company makes all kinds of pet food, but yeah.

And that's not all. He also got organic compounds that act as catalysts and reagents for organic chemical reactions, a box of spray bottles, twelve large beach towels, and lots of distilled water."

"What did you do with all this stuff?"

"That was just it. The biodegradable plastic research items were distributed to various supply cupboards and closets in the labs, but the other order stuff always went to the cabinets in the back of the lab, and he had the only keys."

"If he had the only keys, how did you refill them?"

"I didn't. I just left the unwrapped pallet by the cabinets, and it'd be gone when I came in next."

"I've been puzzling about how the killer got Dr. Nikolaidis to return to the lab late at night," I said, "but maybe they didn't. If he often worked at night, he might have already been there."

"I can't tell you how often he did it," Tristan said. "But I know he did it a lot. Workers in his labs were always getting emails from him time-stamped midnight or one or two in the morning."

"So, did the killer or killers come to the lab because they knew Dr. Nikolaidis was there," I wondered out loud, "or was his presence there a surprise?"

❖

I had one contact in the jewelry business that I genuinely trusted. Helen Trang inherited Coastal Jewels and Watches from her father after growing up helping him in the store. If anyone could identify Rico's bracelet, she could.

I stepped into the cheerfully lit shop on the corner of Monroe Street and Ninth Avenue at about three p.m. A bell jingled, and Trang came out from her back room wearing a bamboo-patterned shawl over a white blouse and plain black slacks. Her face lit up when she saw me.

"Ah, Mr. Porter, so good to see you again. Getting in some shopping for the holidays?"

"Good morning, Ms. Trang. I only wish I was here to shop. I wondered if you could look at some photos of a piece for me?"

She came around the counter and locked the door, putting up the Closed sign. I pulled up the photos of the bracelet on my phone and passed it to her. She pursed her lips as she thumbed through them, increasing the magnification on some and going back to view others two or three times. She handed the phone back to me.

"I like having friends who bring me curious things," she said with a smile. "They keep my day from getting boring. Is this yours?"

"No, I ran across it while reporting a story. What can you tell me about it?"

"What do you want to know?"

"Well, to start with, where did it come from?"

She picked up the phone again and looked at the first picture. "Eastern Europe or Russia."

Could someone have bought this in a jewelry store?"

"Ha!" She let out a sharp laugh. "Maybe. But one hundred twenty or thirty years ago. This piece is old."

"How can you tell?"

"Three ways. First, the style. It has been many, many years since stylish ladies would be seen wearing such large jewelry as this. Second, the value. Tell me, have you held it in your hand?"

"Yes."

"And I bet you were surprised at how heavy it was."

"Yes, I was."

She flew through the phone images until she reached one she had magnified before. She enlarged it again. "The bracelet has two marks," she said, pointing at the screen. "See the little five-eight-five in the box?"

I nodded.

"That tells me it was most likely made in Russia before the revolution, and that it's made from an alloy that is fifty-eight percent gold with some other metal. Something to allow the gold to articulate that way. I imagine it lay flat when it was unclasped?"

"I believe so, yes."

"Then it is very valuable," she said, "and far more expensive than a bracelet an average contemporary woman would have purchased or received."

"And the last sign?"

She looked at me slyly. "The hidden chamber in the head, of course. I don't believe jewelry makers have put secret spaces in anything other than lockets since 1900." She looked at the image containing the marks again. "I don't believe this would have ever been sold new in a jewelry shop," she said. "No, this is what my father called an intentional piece. Wait here."

She got up from her stool and headed into the back of the shop, returning momentarily with a thick, black book.

"This is an index to all the European and Asian jewelry marks up until about 1960," she said, setting it down on the counter with a quiet thud. "My father used to swear by it." She opened the book and began leafing through the pages.

"What are you looking for?"

"If you look at the image again, you will see the second mark is a triangle with two lowercase b's in it. I think that mark might be very important—aha! It is."

"What is it?"

"That is the mark of Burletski Brothers, a jewelry firm in St. Petersburg, active from about 1800 up until 1919."

"What does that tell you?"

"That it's almost certainly made to order. Most jewelry firms, both then and now, make pieces for sale in their own shops or under contract to retailers. But some makers, like Burletski, made items solely to order and not for general sale. That means this design and decoration arose not from a jeweler's whim but from a customer's desires."

"That might explain some of the item's details," I said.

"Quite right. What else struck you about the bracelet?"

"The clasp in the snake's mouth," I replied immediately.

"Yes, that was certainly clever. What else?"

"Its lack of ornamentation."

She looked hard at me. "What do you mean?"

"I mean except for those few small pieces of jade on the head, the bracelet doesn't have any precious stones."

"Look again." She laughed quietly.

I studied the snake's head. "What am I not seeing?"

"You're right that the green stones on the snake's head are jade. Of themselves, not very valuable. But look at the eyes. Can you see they are a little different than the stones on the head?"

"I guess. They're a little darker, a little smoother."

"Those are emeralds. Small and given only the most basic cut, so they don't catch the light, but they're emeralds nonetheless."

"Wow."

"And look more closely at the jade stones on the head. Do you think they were just applied randomly?"

"I suppose they could be in sort of a circle," I said.

She laughed. "If you look more closely, you will see—"

"A spiral."

"That's right. And you probably see the spiral points the way to opening the hidden space in the head."

"Wow."

"Like I said before, you have really brought me something interesting."

"Would you care to share an idea of how much it's worth?"

"Nope. Since a large part of the value will be in the gold, I'd need to weigh it first. Then we'd want to research its history. Some of the St. Peterburg jewelers kept records that survived the revolution or their exile. I seem to recall Burletski popping up in France or Spain at the end of the war. For all we know, this might have been a gift to a mistress or another person involved in an intrigue of some sort."

"Where could a person have picked it up recently? An antique store? A pawn shop?"

"I would guess either one of those," she said, "but not an ordinary one. A specialist antique or pawn shop, I would think. I mean, consider its aesthetics alone. It's actually a little ugly, isn't it? How many sweethearts do you suppose would be thrilled if their man brought them a bracelet in the shape of a snake?"

"That's a good point, but doesn't it guide us back to its origins? If this really was an intentional piece, who was it intended for and why? Was the chamber in the snake's head filled with something lethal? Was it meant as a warning?"

"Or did a wealthy, powerful woman commission it for herself as a warning to others who might try to take advantage of her? Can you text me those images? I have contacts in the higher-end pawn and antique world. I'd like to share them and see if anyone recognizes it. It's so distinctive. If anyone has been shopping it around or sold it, they should remember."

"Good idea," I said, texting her the complete set of photos.

"Are you certain this is not yours?"

"It's not mine. Why?"

"Some objects have a certain power. My father felt it sometimes, and now that I'm older, I can too. Tell your owner she should not keep this bracelet in the house. A safe deposit box would be better. Or maybe even better, sell it or give it to a museum. She should not underestimate it. It contains some deep malevolence."

I decided not to tell her that its current owner was a sixteen-year-old call boy living and working about eight blocks from her shop. But I did resolve to suggest Rico put it in a more secure location. I'd pay for the safe deposit box. I didn't claim to have Helen's powers, but I found the bracelet unnerving too, and I'd feel better about Rico once it was someplace else.

Reluctantly I pulled myself away from Lyle and our warm bed to face a cold and clammy St. Michael's Harbor morning.

"Ugh. You're up early. I was hoping for a morning romp before we have to head out."

"Rain check," I said. "Bernie called and left a message last night, so I want to get in there to see him before he moves on to something else."

Lyle groaned and rolled over. "Leave the heater on the bathroom, please."

Compared to other places I lived, the South Georgia coast

would never qualify as cold. You could count the number of times our thermometer dropped below freezing each decade on the fingers of one hand. But forty-degree air off the ocean combined with a high humidity level and chilly wind out of the north could still make the place damned uncomfortable.

Consequently, I felt particularly grateful, as the jets from the showerheads beat my body with ribbons of warm water, that Lyle had put so much time and attention into planning his home and bathroom. Thus refreshed and armored behind a close shave, clean teeth, and a bespoke shirt and trousers, I stood, Badda-Bean coffees in hand, on the big red X in the hall outside Bernie's door. At exactly eight o'clock, I pushed the button.

"Who calls on the lowest and most pestilent man in the history of the world, formerly known as Bernie Sluice?" he asked from the tinny-sounding speaker attached to the wall above the button.

"Bernie. Good morning. It's me, Manny. You called me last night and said you had something for me."

"Enter if you so desire." The heavy portal swung open with a whoosh of escaping air. As usual, I stood for a moment inside the door to let my eyes adjust to the gloom. As Bernie had promised, a lot of the computer clutter that ordinarily made the place a minefield had been cleared away, leaving a small table and chair with a terminal and Bernie standing beside them, dressed in sandals, a white robe, and a yellow headband.

"What's all this then? I bought you a café au lait from Badda-Bean."

Bernie bowed to the terminal, then spoke to me.

"Last Friday, playing *Shogun's Palace*, the all-powerful and most noble force of Tokyo Firehouse Number 16 completely defeated me, conquering my stronghold and capturing my treasure. This is part of my humiliating punishment for being such a worthless creature who dared to challenge the all-powerful and most noble Tokyo Firehouse Number 16."

He took the coffee I offered him, but instead of drinking it he turned to the terminal again. "This beverage is a gift to this most unworthy creature, who, in awareness of his unworthiness, offers it freely to the all-powerful and most noble victors." A red light beside the machine camera blinked twice.

"Thank God," Bernie muttered to me sotto voce. "Walk past me and meet me at the working terminals."

I walked deeper into the gloomy space until I reached the part of the room Bernie used as an office. He arrived soon after.

"""Isn't this a bit much for just a video game?" I said.

He stood up straighter. "The Japanese leagues are the best in the world. I'm one of just five non-Japanese to have been recognized as a League Competitor there. The stakes are higher."

"How long does your punishment last?"

"Another eight hours. I feel grateful I didn't put down any stakes on this match or I'd be out that as well."

"How much we are talking?"

"About a thousand," he said. "It's all in yen, so it's hard to keep precise track of gains and losses. Last quarter, though, I netted almost twenty thousand dollars."

I whistled. "But on another topic, what do you have for me?"

"Quite a bit," he replied. "Where do you want to start?"

"Let's start at the most recent and work backward."

"Okay. The landline you gave me rings in a largish property with the address of 856 Monroe Street, so in Tinker Creek. No one called Eduardo was listed as the owner. It's owned by a corporation named Copacabana LLC, which is a Colombian corporation with headquarters of record currently on the island of La Palma, which is one of the Canary Islands and, thus, a province of Spain."

"Wow. Terrific. Thank you, Bernie. Anything else about it?"

"Copacabana LLC has a boardinghouse license from the city that allows them to offer six rooms on the property plus one apartment for the landlord/manager. It's renewed the license annually for seven years. The police have never been called there, nor is there any record of neighbor or neighborhood complaints."

"It sounds like they keep a very low profile," I said. "That may have been part of what Nikolaidis liked about it. What else?"

"On to your good doctor's work," he said. "Based on an analysis of the information you provided about the materials the lab was ordering and your source's report about the use of laboratory monkeys, I believe Nikolaidis was trying to develop a new and different kind of opiate."

"Like a new kind of heroin?"

"Heroin is the well-known opiate, but a lot of synthetics are already out there. For example, fentanyl, the drug that killed Prince, is a synthetic opioid, as are the drugs in OxyContin and other opiate pills."

"I hear the names of these drugs all the time, but then I forget they're classified as opiates. But if abundant opiates are available, where's the sense in making another one? Despite his faults, I don't sense Phillip Nikolaidis wanted to become a drug lord."

"I agree with you. But I think he wanted to develop one with very specific properties."

"Such as?"

"I think Nikolaidis was trying to invent a knockout gas."

"What's a knockout gas?"

"Didn't you watch *Batman* in syndication when you were a little kid?" Bernie asked.

I shook my head.

"Well, if you had watched it, you would have seen how the Penguin or the Joker or the villain of that episode would plan to steal all the jewelry and money from guests at a fabulous party by pumping the space full of some sort of gas that puts everyone to sleep. That was a knockout gas. Of course, it never existed in the real world, but that doesn't mean people haven't been trying to create it."

"All right, but aside from criminals, who would want such a thing?"

Bernie looked at me, surprised. "Only every law enforcement organization in the world," he said. "Think of how much better it might be to toss a canister of sleeping gas into a hostage situation instead of tear gas. Plus all the possible military applications. And the thing is," he said, lowering his voice though no one else was there, "there are already one or two prototypes."

"Really?"

"Yep. The Russians have a fentanyl derivative they used when that Chechen gang took over that theater in St. Petersburg or maybe Moscow. Hostage situation. Russian authorities pumped in a bunch of this stuff and then sent in commandos wearing gas masks. It worked well on the terrorists. No shots were fired. But it worked too well on some of the hostages, including children. It killed like fifteen of them."

"My God."

"That's one of the persistent problems—dosage. How do you set a dose when you might have a room full of physically different people? And then how do you make sure they only take that amount? A panicky hostage, for example, might gasp for air and take in way too much."

"And you think Nikolaidis was trying to make this stuff?"

"I'm not sure about a new prototype. He might have been trying to refine one of the existing prototypes, and I think he was testing it on the monkeys to build a dosage system."

"What could he have done if he'd been successful?"

"Patent his discoveries. He never signed an agreement with AthenaLibre about patent rights—at least not that I could find. Or he could just approach one of the current patent owners and sell it to them."

"What could that have brought him?"

"Either path could have brought him tens of millions of dollars," Bernie said. "Patenting it himself would have rewarded him lavishly over time, but it would have taken longer and involved a good deal more work. Selling to an existing patent holder would have given him enough to set up his own research lab in a shorter time and the freedom not to have to seek sponsors."

"That would explain his comment to his fiancée about wealth in the future. How confident are you about all this?"

"About his researching an aerosol opiate, very confident, like ninety-five percent. Whether he was seeking a whole new prototype or just looking to modify an existing one, about seventy-five percent."

"Can you write me a report that says that and explains why

you think so? It doesn't have to be exhaustive, but it would help if a layperson could read and understand it."

"Sure thing. I sort of thought you might want something like that, so I already have a rough draft. I'll polish it up and get it to you today."

"Thanks, Bernie, awesome job as usual." I turned to leave. "Good luck with your remaining punishment today."

"Thanks, but it's really nothing. The last time I won, I made the losing team leader walk around Tokyo all day wearing a sandwich board that declared 'I am a LOSER' on it. It wouldn't have been that big a deal, but his day job was in a Tokyo bank."

❖

As I rode the elevator from Bernie's basement back up to my office, I decided I had enough to seek an interview with the AthenaLibre leadership about Nikolaidis's research focus and how the company decided to view it.

Anna Fin Chow picked up on the first ring. "Mr. Porter, what a pleasant surprise!"

"Thank you, Ms. Fin Chow. I hope you still have that opinion at the end of this call."

"Oh, work, is it?"

"I'm afraid so."

"Before we get started in all of that, how is Tristan doing?"

"About as good as can be expected, given everything that's happened."

"I'm glad to hear it," she said warmly. "You might be surprised to learn Tristan has a lot of supporters at AthenaLibre. In fact, I and a couple of others are circulating a petition asking the company to offer him another internship once he's been acquitted."

"That would be very generous. Do you think the company would do that?"

"As the director of public relations, offering the internship will be my official recommendation. His acquittal will show he had nothing to do with the death, and why should he lose the internship opportunity for something he didn't do?"

"I agree."

"The police have been back as well," she said quietly. "They took Niko's personnel file and some of the lab files too."

"I'm sure they're doing a good job," I said, hoping my words could keep my own spirits high.

"Well, what's the news question?" she asked, putting on her more official voice.

"We know Nikolaidis was working on developing an opiate that could be delivered in an aerosol or mist," I said. "We want to know if AthenaLibre was aware of his research focus or whether he was conducting this inquiry on his own."

There was a silence on the line. "Really?" she said finally. "I have to admit, of all the things you might have said, that was about the last I would have expected. May I ask what led you to this conclusion?"

"Statements from his staff as well as analysis of the materials he ordered for the lab. Some of those compounds are very specific."

"I'll pass it along. I'm not sure what they'll do with this, but thanks for bringing it to us and not just springing it on us."

"Please," I said. "We aren't fly-by-night."

"I know. I know. I just don't know what they're going to say upstairs," she replied. "But I'll let you know."

She called me back in less than an hour.

"Mr. Fuller and Mr. Billings will be able to give you a half hour over video conference from their individual locations," she said brusquely. "Mr. Billings is attending meetings in New York and Mr. Fuller is presenting at a conference on London. We'll begin the call in twenty minutes."

A few minutes later, an email appeared in my box offering me a link to the meeting. At precisely 10:30, I clicked on the link and was admitted to the session. Both executives looked uncomfortable.

"Gentlemen, thank you for agreeing to speak with me on such short notice," I began.

"Not at all," Billings said. "We want to know whatever you use for your reporting. We just received a report about this very topic this morning, so you almost beat us learning about our own company."

"If you only found out this morning, what are you prepared to discuss now?"

"We can confirm your facts," Fuller replied. "During the last two years, Dr. Phillip Nikolaidis was researching the practicality of using an aerosol system to deliver an opiate drug as a fine mist."

"Was this drug an existing opiate compound, or was he working on developing a new one?"

"Honestly, we don't know yet," Fuller said. "Two of his research drives were encrypted with a password he didn't share with the company—against our regulations, by the way. That's one of the questions we hope to answer soon."

"How far did he get with the research?"

"Pretty far. As I understand it, he'd developed an opiate that could exist as a fine mist, but we don't know how far he got in developing a delivery system."

"I understand Dr. Nikolaidis had declined to sign a patent agreement with AthenaLibre, is that so?"

"All of our new researchers have to sign a patent agreement as a condition of employment when they first arrive," Billings said. "But the agreement expires in two years. Dr. Nikolaidis had signed the agreement three times but declined to sign it this year."

"Didn't that send up a red flag with the company about what he might be doing?"

"Not necessarily," Fuller said. "We try to maintain an attitude of openness about scientific inquiry here. We're aware many of our researchers have projects they pursue on their own. But as long as they meet their commitments to the company, we haven't wanted to shut down those other inquiries."

Billings cut in. "The researchers who work here are naturally curious people. The fact that we don't seek to stifle curiosity is, frankly, one of the things that makes our company a highly desired place to do scientific research."

"I can see that, and I agree it would make AthenaLibre almost an idyllic place to be a scientist, but what if a researcher started researching something potentially dangerous—like an aerosol opiate?"

Both of them paused for a moment before Fuller jumped in.

"One of the things we've discussed is the need to tighten up our research guidelines. In general, we've operated on an honor system, assuming our researchers were all honorable men and women who would work for positive research."

"But our counsel has advised us, just yesterday in fact, that a reform of our guidelines might be necessary," Billings said. "We agreed and have started assembling an team to take on the project."

"Circling back to Dr. Nikolaidis's research, if he succeeded in developing an opiate that could be delivered in an aerosol form, I presume that opiate would have a formula. Have you found it yet?"

Another long pause. Billings this time.

"We've identified references in Dr. Nikolaidis's notes to a formula for the opiate, but we have not yet found the formula itself. Like we said before, two of his research drives have yet to be decrypted."

"That means a formula for a new form of aerosol opiate that we know nothing about could be out in the world now."

The men nodded.

"Last question, gentlemen. Have you found anything to suggest the formula for this opiate wasn't removed from Dr. Nikolaidis's lab by the person or persons who killed him?"

"Of course not," Billings said. "But we haven't found any evidence such a formula *was* removed either."

The rest of the interview devolved into a discussion of potential liability, where they went to great lengths to shield the company from any responsibility for anything that might have happened. I cut it short, citing deadline pressure.

As I began to review and organize my notes for the story, my cell phone rang with a call from Helen Trang. "Ms. Trang, always a pleasure," I said.

"Oh, I doubt that," she said with a dry chuckle. "But I think I may have some useful information."

"Please share."

"I thought that unique bracelet would stick in the mind of anyone who saw it, and I found someone who says he did."

"Who?"

"A friend of mine named Gilbert Flacks, who owns the Crabby Pawn, down on lower Breaker Street. He says a man brought in the bracelet a few weeks ago to get it evaluated and maybe sell it."

"Did he make an offer?"

"I don't think so. He didn't say he had."

"Will he speak to a reporter?"

"I don't know. Probably, but I'm not sure he'll want to speak on the record. Those pawn guys usually keep their negotiations private."

"Thanks, Helen, you're the best. I'll try to speak to him today."

"Let me know what he says. You've aroused my curiosity about how this turns out."

"Will do," I replied and rang off.

CHAPTER 8

A Sign for the Stocking?

As I had been told, the Crabby Pawn stood out on the 200 block of Breaker Street like a lighthouse on a foggy coastline.

"Can't miss us," Mr. Flacks had said when I called to request he meet me. "We're the only canary yellow building on Breaker. Hell, probably in the whole city. Parking is free behind us, or you can pay to park right out front."

I looked at the narrow alley leading to the rear parking lot and opted to pay the meter. A recording of an orchestra played holiday tunes at a low volume in the background as I walked through the bright blue door.

"Welcome," chirped a young woman wearing a Santa hat from behind a sophisticated-looking computer at the front door. "Can I help you find something?"

"You know where everything is?"

"What I don't know, Basil does." She ran her finger along the top of the monitor.

"Actually, I'm looking for Mr. Flacks. We have an appointment."

Her eyes widened slightly. "You should have said." She picked up the receiver on her desk's antique phone. "Mr.…." She looked up at me expectantly.

"Porter. Jose Porter."

"Mr. Porter is here to see you. Okay, I'll send him back." She hung up. "Follow the central corridor through the toys, and Mr. Flacks's office will be the first door on the left."

I thanked her and set out. I've always had a weakness for antique and pawn stores, particularly the ones that sell odd and hard-to-define items. Within a few feet, I saw three items I would have loved to stop and study but had to leave them behind to make the appointment with Flacks. I knocked on the door and entered to find a short, bald man who looked like he could have doubled as one of Santa's more senior elves.

"Come in, young man, come in," he said in a gravelly voice as he came out from behind his desk to welcome me. I realized my first impression had been mistaken; he wasn't a little man but merely short, coming up to barely my chest and dressed from the turn of the last century. He wore a white dress shirt and slate gray pants with yellow suspenders and the only sleeve garters I had ever seen outside of old photographs. He sported a pale gray bow tie and two of the shiniest black shoes I'd ever seen.

"Pleased to meet you," he said, his grip a good deal firmer than I expected. "Can I offer you something to drink? I've got a little fridge with soft drinks and bottled water or something more adult in my desk."

"No, thank you."

He motioned me to sit down at a chair across from his desk as he returned to his. "Now, how can I help you?"

"Ms. Trang said you might have had someone who wanted you to look at this," I said, passing him the phone with the bracelet photos pulled up.

He took the device. "Oh yes, a gentleman came by with this looking for an evaluation and possible sale, either on its own or as part of its set."

"It's part of a set?" I tried to keep the surprise out of my voice.

"Oh yes. This was just one piece, although it was the only part of the set he actually had with him. But he had photos of the other pieces—two rings, a pair of earrings, and a locket. All shared that particular serpentine motif."

"Really? It's hard for me to imagine a woman ever wearing snake jewelry."

"I agree. From our perspective, pieces like these can seem incomprehensible. But this wasn't made for our time, was it? We can't evaluate everything in the past by our own standards if we expect to understand it."

"Did the gentleman have a name?"

He paused a moment. "In normal circumstances, I'd decline to identify a client, but as he is now deceased, I don't believe there would be any harm. The gentleman was Dr. Phillip Nikolaidis."

"What did you tell Dr. Nikolaidis about it?"

"I told him about what I expect Ms. Trang told you about it," he said. "Likely Russian origin. Almost certainly a commissioned piece."

"Did he tell you where he had gotten it?"

"He told me that a great-aunt of his had died and passed the set on to him. She got it from her mother, who was a Russian refugee after the revolution in 1917. He had no definitive paperwork to prove this, but he told me he had a receipt showing its owner cleared the set through customs in New York when she arrived. He said the customs officer declared one of the rings as not being part of the set and charged her five dollars' duty on it," he said with a chuckle.

"Did you believe him?"

He shrugged in what I thought was a particularly elfin way.

"I didn't disbelieve him. Working in pawn is like laboring in the dustbins of different cultures after a multitude of tragedies. Nothing comes to us as the result of things going well. I get used to hearing a lot of stories."

"Did he want you to buy the bracelet?"

"I wasn't sure. Initially, he said he didn't want to sell it, but then later he acted as if he did. I was prepared to offer him a low price for it in case it turned out to be stolen, but in the end, he didn't take it."

"What was that price, if I may ask?"

"It was above seven thousand but below twelve," he said, "and that's as narrow as I will go on the price."

"And what did you really think it was worth?"

"Well, that was the problem, wasn't it? Without knowing more about it, it was hard to account for its value. Plus, I have to consider the market for this thing. You said it yourself. Not many men will pick it up as a Christmas gift to the girlfriend, wife, or mistress, now will they? And I told him that too."

"Told him what?"

"That he probably needed to take it to a bigger market if he wanted to find a really interested buyer. Let's face it, I love living here, but this is not New York or even Atlanta. The pool of people here who would appreciate the real quality of this item and have pockets deep enough to buy it for what he would want is exceedingly small. May I ask you a question now?" he said.

"Of course."

"What is your interest in this piece? Do you believe Dr. Nikolaidis was killed by someone stealing it?"

"Not at all. The piece is currently with someone who says Dr. Nikolaidis gave it him. Like you, I have no reason to disbelieve my source. But I remain curious about where the piece might have come from and who else might be interested in it. Why?"

"In some ways, it was a very troubling item," he said. "So many precious things either found or created in Europe during this period have violent and terrible histories. I don't believe these items were created in joy, and I'm not sure they should be in general circulation, but they might belong in a museum."

"I don't really have an opinion about that, other than to say I couldn't see myself ever wanting to buy it," I said. "But you're not the first expert to express some misgivings about the bracelet."

I thanked Mr. Flacks for his time and secured his permission to call him again should I need more information, then headed back out into the shop.

I had some extra time, so decided to take a tour through its two floors of objects, bric-a-brac, and antiques. Most of the items were the sort of things that are usually found in such stores, but a sign on a wall of a section dedicated to local memorabilia grabbed my attention.

"Bonne Chance Motors" appeared in red cursive letters in the corner of a blue rectangular sign above the legend "Make your car a lucky car. Bring it to US for service" in red.

I dragged a sputtering sales assistant wearing a Santa hat to the shingle and demanded to know what he knew about it.

"I don't really know, sir," the clerk said, lifting it off the wall. "But we can find out."

He brought the sign to a large table in front of the cash register and laid it face down. On the back a small label carried a code and a price of fifteen dollars. He typed in the number and read off the screen. "We purchased the sign six years ago at a local estate sale, sir. That's all the information I have about it."

"I'll take it. Do you gift wrap?"

"If you're okay with red paper, we do."

"Then gift wrap, please."

The sign fit neatly into my car's trunk when I left the shop, and I felt happy to have gotten Lyle such a personal gift.

❖

Bernie had called while I was out, so I called him back first thing.

"Happy holidays, Mr. Sluice. You rang?"

"And merry Christmas to you," he replied. "I just wondered what the executives said."

"You were right. They're still trying to get into two of Nikolaidis's encrypted computer drives to get the actual formula, but they admitted he was trying to develop an aerosol opiate."

"Excellent!" Bernie whooped. "We make a good team, you know."

"I agree, but it would be really cool if we could pin down the whole story."

"Like?"

"Like figuring out if Nikolaidis was looking to sell his discovery outright and who his buyers might have been."

"How would we do that?"

"Look at people we know are already researching it," I

suggested. “You mentioned a Russian firm has been trying to come up with an aerosol opiate. Or listen to some traders and see if they know anybody who might be in the market.”

“This is a little delicate,” Bernie said.

“How so?”

“Because Nikolaidis was murdered. How do we know the ones who killed him might not be someone who wanted the formula but didn’t want to pay for it?”

“We don’t.”

“Hence the delicacy.”

“Do you have contacts?”

“A few.”

“Well, start making a few inquiries. Gently. And see if anything comes to the surface.”

“Will do.”

❖

Later, I called Chief Detective Walker and got his voice mail. He phoned back in about an hour.

“This is Walker.”

“If I buy the coffee again, can I come to see you this afternoon?”

“I’m on duty all day, so that won’t work. You want to ride around with me for a while? That’s the best I can do.”

“If it’s the best we can do, it’s good enough. What time?”

“I’ll pick you up outside Badda-Bean at two. You buy the coffee. Try to get one of those holiday ones, but no pumpkin spice.”

“Got it.”

At 2:00 exactly, Walker pulled his white Ford over to the corner, and I hopped inside, placing each of our coffees in the respective cup holders.

“What’d you get?” he asked.

“Hello, Detective. Nice to see you too.”

“Shut it. It’s already been a shitty day.”

“Sorry to hear it. Peppermint latte, whole milk, whipped cream, peppermint candy chips on top.”

"Hmm," he said. "Creek side of MLK park?"

"Sure, but I'm not following you into the bushes to feed the ducks."

"Ha! Like I'm the one who'd be leading that parade." He smirked and deliberately adjusted himself.

"You're so crude."

"And you love it."

I examined the car. Contrary to my expectations, it looked well-kept. No trash on the floors. The seats were in good shape. Nothing hanging from the mirror. No suspicious odors.

"Before you say anything, ordered spaces help maintain an ordered mind. You should remember that."

We pulled through the Washington Street entrance and took a right on the drive that led past Tinker Creek. After a few twists and curves, we turned into the first gravel parking lot and took a spot overlooking the water. He rolled down his window, shut off the car, and picked up his coffee.

"So, what you got?"

"I interviewed the two execs at AthenaLibre this morning," I said. "It's gonna run in a day or two, but I wanted you to know our murder victim was trying to develop an aerosol form of opiate."

"Aww, shit," Walker said, glaring at me. "What for? Aren't we up to our asses in overdose deaths?"

"Money, of course. I can't tell you much more than that because they're still digging details out of two encrypted computer hard drives, but you might put a bug in the ear of your drug detail chief so she knows about it."

"Yeah. Good idea. What else?"

"This expands our universe of potential Nikolaidis murder suspects again."

"How do you figure?"

"It provides another motive for someone to kill him. They wanted the formula for the opiate."

"Nice try. See, for us to consider looking for suspects with an alternate motive, we need to have some evidence such a suspect exists."

"You never told me whether you followed up with Nikolaidis's priest."

"As a matter of fact, I did. Father Ampleforth was quite forthcoming about his former parishioner. He confirmed what you told me."

"Told you!"

"Congratulations, you're one for one in reliability."

"I have another one for you." I reached into my pocket and brought out my phone, showing him a photo of the bracelet. "I believe Nikolaidis gave this to one of my sources," I said.

Walker studied the photo. "Ugly enough, ain't it? Who'd he give it to?"

"That's not as important right now as where he might have gotten it from."

"Why?"

"Look at it," I said. "Was there anything at all about his lab or his house or his car that suggested he would be interested in this sort of object?"

He looked blankly at me.

"I don't think there is," I said. "I think it's much likelier it came as a gift from someone who might have gotten it from an elderly relative and who didn't want it either."

"Like who?"

"Nadia Elena Reznikov."

"The grieving fiancée again? Dude, you've got to let your bad feelings toward this woman go. It's starting to look a little weird."

"Not at all. She's the most obvious source." I started ticking off my reasons. "First, the experts say it's a bespoke Russian piece made for a client, not just purchased in a shop. Second, she comes from a family of Russian émigrés with the wealth and station in life to have the means to pay for such an object. Third, the bracelet only shows up with Nikolaidis after Nadia Reznikov agrees to marry him, and fourth, the bracelet is only one piece in a set of four, which strongly suggests it was once a wedding present."

"But even it does turn out to be hers and she gave it to him, so what? People give each other lots of things when they think they're in love. How does this tie into Nikolaidis's murder?"

"I realize lovers often exchange gifts, but how do you think she or her family would feel if she found out he was evaluating this family heirloom with an eye toward selling it? Or, worse, that he gave it to someone with whom he was already having a relationship?"

"Did he?"

"Yep."

"Man, that's low," Walker said. "And this person is your source?"

"Yep."

"And let me guess—based on Tristan's statement, this person is not a female."

"Right again," I said. "House-only call boy, lives and works down on Monroe Street in Tinker Creek."

He sat quietly for a moment before thumping the steering wheel. "Damn it," he said.

"I thought you'd be happy and maybe a little grateful," I said, feeling disappointed.

"I *am* pleased. Thank you. But don't underestimate how pissed off I am that a civilian has done better detective work than we have—again." He remained silent a bit longer; then, when he spoke again, it was in a more normal tone of voice. "What do you know about Nadia Elena Reznikov?"

"Almost nothing," I said. "I met her, her brother, and a family friend at the interview. The brother gives me the creeps. He's a control freak who came across as being wound way too tight, and the friend came across as a thug. I've done a little bit of digging into the family. They're spread out across six states in the US and four countries abroad. Wealthy but without any obvious connection to wealth-building activity."

"Are you thinking Russian mafia?"

"I don't know what I'm thinking exactly. My social media sources tell me there are no mob rumors at all, but I was hoping that an organization with a few more resources and expertise might investigate."

"I suppose we can do that much for you. You know there's a good chance we might need to talk to that kid?"

"I figured as much. I can contact him, and I was hoping we could arrange something more private than a raid on the house."

He arched his eyebrows. "You don't want much, do you?"

"I do, but it's not so much considering what a knowledgeable source I am."

"I can work on it, but I'm not making any promises."

"That's fine. As usual, I'm not asking for any."

❖

I had just started writing the article about AthenaLibre, Nikolaidis, and the aerosol opiate when Susan Owen asked me to come to her office.

"Happy Hanukkah," I said as I walked into her office.

"You're two days early, but I appreciate the thought," she replied. "And merry Christmas to you. Now for some not-so-merry-news." She held up an official-looking thick off-white envelope.

"Oh, man. What now?"

"First, let me offer my congratulations on the AthenaLibre interview. Your father and I saw a replay of it after the fact and enjoyed seeing them squirm a bit. But I offer those congratulations in advance because of this. It's from Patrick Mahoney, AthenaLibre's in-house counsel, joined by Benjamin Longstaff, a partner at Longstaff, Elgin and Harris, the company's Atlanta-based law firm. Essentially, they're warning us against publishing anything that might 'sensationalize the recent tragic events at the AthenaLibre headquarters or give the public any reason to doubt the sincerity of this corporation's commitment to basic research to benefit society.' In particular, the company 'will object to any suggestion it has been involved in research into opiate compounds and their delivery systems' or that it knew of and approved of 'any such research being conducted by a rogue researcher.'"

"Wow. Isn't that a little hard to demand if the company's two executives just admitted that such research was going on and that Dr. Nikolaidis was involved in it up to his neck?"

She looked at me with a pained expression. "Obviously, but just be careful, please. Triple-check your research and know that the paper will fact-check this one several times over, even if holds up publication. Make sure everything is documented and be ready to answer questions."

"Understood. How long before we have a transcript of the interview?"

"Tomorrow morning. Write from your notes for the first drafts, then check the quotes against the transcript before you file."

"All right. Anything else?"

"Yes. I've been talking to the production people, and we want to run this story as a two-part series. There's a lot of meat in there, and we think it will have a greater impact if we run it on two consecutive weeks. We haven't decided yet whether we like Friday or Sunday for a drop date, but we're confident we want it in two segments."

"Okay. What I file first will be the first story," I said.

"Now a question from me," she said, peering at me over her reading glasses.

"Shoot."

"How are you holding up? We haven't had a chance to connect lately."

"Lyle and I are fine. The garage is hopping with all the charity work they're doing this year, and I'm busy too. The AthenaLibre story just added to it. It's hard to believe Christmas is so close. It doesn't feel much like a holiday."

"You know the young man indicted in that case, don't you?"

"I do. He's a mentee of mine. That's probably our biggest downer this season. It's hard to feel jolly and happy when this is hanging over Tristan's head."

"I can totally see that," she replied softly. "It's hard to think of Hanukkah lights and freedom when so many things in our world seem headed toward darkness and confinement. But as one of the

Talmud scholars wrote thousands of years ago, the oil in the lamps lasted, and so will we. Maybe that will be our miracle."

I headed back to my office to call Pierre Chamel on WhatsApp to make sure he had the digital supply receipts of Dr. Nikolaidis's supply orders and to ask him to print them out.

He picked up on the second ring.

"Maybe we're long-lost twins," Pierre said when he took my call. "I was about to call you myself."

"Hello, Pierre. Maybe we are twins in spirit. Why did you want to talk to me?"

"I wanted you to know you really stirred things up at Athena. None of the material they had in their system before is still there. They copied it off and deleted it."

A cold finger of fear moved down my spine when I heard this. I kept my voice steady and light. "Pierre, please tell me you still have everything you said was there before they deleted it."

"Of course!" He sounded genuinely shocked that I would suppose it might not be. "Not only do I still have it, but I have the receipts in chronological order if you want them that way."

I let out a sigh of relief and a brief prayer of thanksgiving to St. Thomas More, patron saint of journalists. "Pierre, you are worth your weight in fine chocolate."

"Nonsense. Emily and I talked about it and made sure we got it all."

"Can you do me a favor and put them on an encrypted USB drive for me? I can send a messenger for it if you let me know it's ready."

"Sure thing. Does this mean we might see an article soon?"

"With any luck," I said.

He lowered his voice. "I told Emily last night I don't think we can count on having this backdoor access for too much longer. There used to be several ways I could get in under their defenses, but those holes are getting sealed, and I haven't found any new ones. They haven't locked me out…yet, but I wouldn't count on my having access indefinitely."

"Pierre, don't worry about it. You've already helped more than I had any right to request. And don't take any risks. I'd rather you pull out right now, today, than risk getting caught."

We hung up, and I sat back in my chair to think about the people like Emily and Pierre, people who were curious about what went on around them, moral enough to recognize when they saw something questionable, and brave enough to put their skills to good use when they saw something that needed confronting. People like them had helped me break some of my biggest stories, and I wondered if I had ever done enough to really thank them.

Pierre texted me when the USB drive was ready, and I sent a runner from the mail room to get it. I had her take it to Bernie's office first so he could check it and then deliver it back to me.

Aside from the final check of my quotes against the transcript, the first half article was ready to go. I filed the rough draft with Susan so she could get fact-checkers started and told her I had the information to answer questions as they arose. Then I headed out.

❖

I set out across the *South Georgia Record*'s half-empty parking lot toward the Electric Blue Gumdrop, a damp and clammy wind blowing in from the east, putting the lie to the city's slogan that "you never need a hat in our harbor." I could have used a hat and then some as I reached the car and climbed in.

Once inside, I sat for a moment, enjoying the shelter from the wind and letting the car warm up a bit. But the sense of melancholy that had tugged at the edges of my mind since I left Susan's office grew stronger, and none of my usual defenses could vanquish it. Our remaining days to trial were ticking away one by one, and we still had no clear, decisive avenue to clear Tristan of murdering Dr. Nikolaidis.

True, the circumstantial evidence appeared formidably in his favor. But how would a mostly white jury weigh such evidence? The days when all-white juries pardoned whites for lynching Black men and women felt like they had passed many years ago, but I knew some of the oldest, most entrenched attitudes toward Black and mixed-race citizens were among the slowest to pass away.

Tristan's only really secure path to safety lay with our finding out what really happened that night and who was involved since it wasn't him. But those discoveries remained almost as far away now as they had been the morning I spotted the dead scientist's body through the window.

The discovery that Nikolaidis had been researching a very dangerous and addicting chemical worth hundreds of millions of dollars if it made it to the street was tantalizing. But that's all it was. Like mirages in the desert, this information's ability to save Tristan's life kept vanishing as his trial date drew near, and I had no idea how to make it remain substantial.

Likewise, how did the mystery of the scientist's personal life fit into the case? Clearly Nikolaidis had been a closeted bisexual man, if not full-on gay, but was his murder a hate crime? If so, it was among the least obvious hate crimes in history, without any evidence of the contempt and malice that usually accompanied such killings. Something felt both deeply personal and amateurish about the act, like a crime of passion that had been unconvincingly dressed up to look like something else.

The lateness of the hour convinced me to put the car into gear and head home to Lyle and Bonne Chance. But the prospect didn't fill me with any of its usual comforts, and I hoped I could chase the blues away before I got home.

Traffic was heavy with commuters and holiday shoppers, so I left the freeway early instead of taking the usual Tinker Creek exit. This meant I'd have to cut through some neighborhoods I didn't visit often, but even with stoplights, I'd probably make better time than sitting in bumper-to-bumper traffic.

The streets were mostly clear, fronting modest bungalows set close together with small backyards. While remaining humble in size, almost all of them sported some little piece of holiday cheer, whether a wreath on the door, a string of lights around the porch rail, or holiday candles in the windows. Several offered a lot more, including one that demanded cooperation from the residents of four houses. Santa's sleigh, complete with reindeer and overflowing with packages, all done in lights, appeared to land on the roof of the far right house, then it ran along the roofs of the middle two buildings until it took off again from the house on the far left.

The better mood the decorations brought me faded a bit when I arrived at Washington Boulevard to find traffic every bit as backed up as it had been on the freeway. I endured the stop-and-go for about a block before I saw the Church of St. Benedict the Moor on the left side of the street. Unlike most nights, light poured from almost all the church's windows, and a steady stream of people appeared to be coming and going. Intrigued, I parked and got out to see what was going on.

After I stepped inside the door to the long sanctuary, a young woman in a blue skirt, black low-rise shoes, and a white blouse approached me.

"May I help you?" she said. "You look a little lost."

I silently cursed the rising blush I felt creeping up the back of my neck. "Ah. Well. I don't know. I was just driving by, and the church is usually dark when I pass it. But tonight all the lights are lit, so I stopped by to see what's going on," I said, trying not to sound as flustered as I felt.

"Well, we're coming up on Christmas, so that's always a busy time for us. And we're transitioning from a children's Mass to the choir's dress rehearsal for its part in the midnight Mass later this week, so that's why there are so many people here."

Just then the organ at the front of the sanctuary let loose with the first notes of "Joy to the World," temporarily deafening us.

"Wow, I hope they adjust that before the next Mass."

She giggled. "The organ is over one a hundred years old, and I think our organist is too. He always starts rehearsals like that. Says the organ needs to clear her pipes."

The numbers of people coming and going had slowed to a trickle, mostly a few hurrying in and then up to the front. Choir members, almost certainly.

"Would anyone care if I stayed to listen to a bit?"

"Mr. Matteaus, the choir master, won't like it, but if you stay out of the first few pews, he won't notice you. And the church is open, so please, be our guest."

"Thank you, I will."

I walked about a third of the way to the altar and sat down in one of the pews. I wasn't the only person sitting in on the rehearsal. Three rows ahead of me sat another younger man, well-dressed and waiting expectantly. Two rows ahead of him were two high school girls along with an older woman across the aisle.

For the first few minutes, all we heard from the front was the bustle of conversation, greetings, and organization. But after a short time, a tall, thin bearded man with glasses stepped out in the front and clapped his hands until the hubbub quieted. Then he stepped onto a short stand that made him appear even taller, and the choir launched into one of my favorites, "O Holy Night."

O holy night,
the stars are brightly shining...

The choir carried me back to the church in Little Havana, when my mother and her friends bundled me into too many clothes for the warm Florida night and brought me with them to their long and passionate Christmas Eve Mass.

Long lay the world,
in sin and error pining,
till He appeared and the soul felt its worth.

With each line, I remembered something else: the short, slow drive through crowded nighttime streets, the hundreds of relatives and friends who would not be satisfied until they hugged and kissed me even when I didn't want them to, and the mixed odors of incense, wax, and spices inside the sanctuary.

I wondered what happened. How did I let all that beauty slip away from my life? I never had a screaming match with the Church. No dramatic showdown when I stomped out over this or that. I attended Mass regularly until I left high school and, for a fleeting amount of time, fancied I might have been called to the priesthood. But then, in college, the Church and going to Mass felt less and less relevant. The Church's ongoing hostility to any positive expression of gay sexuality played a part, of course, along with her inability to police her own leadership. But in the end, we merely drifted apart.

As the musicians segued into an instrumental version of "Silent Night," I thought about Tristan and how he had so bravely put everything on the line rather than participate in a lie. I thought about the residents from Romero House that we fed, and Ms. Dass and her wards at Baldwin House, and how many prayers we all needed just to keep going.

"Lord, I don't even know anymore if you exist," I prayed quietly as the music drew to a close, "but if you do, there are sure some folks down here who could use a bit of your help."

CHAPTER 9

The Snake Exits

"I was about to come out to look for you," Lyle called out from the kitchen when the elevator clattered to a halt at the apartment.

"I'm sorry I'm late. I stopped on the way home and let myself get distracted." I hung up my coat and entered the warmer space. It smelled wonderful.

"Distracted enough you weren't answering my calls or texts? Where were you?"

"I stopped in at St. Benedict the Moor on the way home. Their choir was practicing for the Christmas Mass in a couple of days, so I sat and listened."

"Really?" Lyle said, his unspoken *why* lingering in the air.

"Because it's Christmas but doesn't feel like Christmas," I said. "Tristan is still in awful trouble, nothing feels like it's getting much better, and I don't feel like I'm contributing much at all."

"That's nonsense," Lyle said with a snort. "Most of what we have to defend Tristan so far is because you dug it out."

"Yes, but it doesn't feel like enough. I need a hug," I said, gasping with pleasure as I felt his strong, familiar arms pull me in close.

"Feelings aren't facts," he whispered to me as he rubbed my back, then cupped my ass. "You might have already launched events that will provide us with a whole mess of facts that get Tristan's charges dropped. We just don't know, and that has to be okay for right now."

"Ugh," I said, but he was correct.

He released me and dipped a wooden spoon into a pot for me to taste. "Meanwhile, I've made your favorite beef stew."

"The one with Guinness?"

"Absolutely."

It tasted so good, I felt myself moan with pleasure, and I realized how hungry I had become. "Whatever happened to the man I met who couldn't really cook," I asked, chuckling.

"He met someone who showed him how and made him want to," Lyle replied with a kiss and another hug. "After dinner, I thought we might stay in and have a little alone time. Tristan called to say he's eating at Baldwin House tonight, so I thought we might—"

"Sounds like a plan. I've missed you lately. It'll be nice to stop thinking about criminals and clues for a bit." I disappeared into our bedroom to change clothes. I had replaced my work shirt with a polo when my phone rang. The number was local. I picked it up half expecting a robocall or scam. Instead, I got Rico.

"Mr. Porter, can I come visit you and hang out for a while, please?" he said, sounding both depressed and frightened.

"I guess so, Rico. What's up?"

"Nothing, really. I want to talk to you more about Niko, and I just want to get out of here for a while."

"What's going on? Is Eduardo not treating you right?"

"Eduardo always treats us right," he said in an annoyed voice.

"Is he standing right there?"

"No. He's always cool with us. For real."

"So, what's going on?"

"Things have just gotten really slow for me. Eduardo's only letting my regulars see me, and I don't have a lot of those. I used to count on two or three new clients a month to help me make rent, but I haven't seen any new faces since Thanksgiving really."

"How come?"

Rico explained that Eduardo's rules included that no client could book time with any of the residents without attending one of his socials, and that outcalls were strictly forbidden. At first Rico thought this solely protected the house's share of a boy's earnings, but lately he had come to appreciate the policy's role in keeping him safe.

"Yesterday, Eduardo came to my room and told me he had gotten several calls from wannabe clients looking for me who didn't like either the socials or the no outcall rule," Rico said. "Normally, clients either hang up or make a reservation for one of the socials. But these guys got very aggressive and demanded to be able to see me. Of course, he refused and is double-checking clients at the socials, but that just slows up business for me. Plus, now I can't even leave the house without his pre-approving where I'm going."

"But don't you think that's a good idea, considering the safety question?"

"Yes and no. He's a good guy, and I appreciate he wants to look out for me. But it's not like I started in life this year. I took care of myself before I came here, and I can look after myself now."

"You're probably not going to like that I agree with Eduardo on this."

"I already figured, but that's because you don't really know the life like I do."

I wanted to ask what he meant but decided to let that comment slide for now. "By the way, how can you be sure that Eduardo's going to be cool with your coming over here?"

"He's already approved it. I already told him all about you, and he likes you."

"You did? He does?"

"Of course. Your name is in the *Record* all the time, remember? He reads what you write, so he already knows you're not a cop or a wacko."

I decided to consider later how I felt about having gained the approval of a keeper at a teenage brothel. "You'll need the address."

"No, I won't. You live over that big car repair place on Jackson. I know where it is already."

"How did you—"

"I saw you a few weeks ago at the community center and followed you home."

"Okay. Be careful. Don't make me wish I'd come to pick you up."

"God, I'm not six years old. Be there in ten."

I sighed, pulled on a pair of jeans, and went to tell Lyle.

In the light of everything that happened later, I think both Lyle and I agreed that the evening we hosted Rico carried a special place in our memories. It wasn't that Rico charmed us—though he did—it was how he helped us to see each other in a different light.

At first Lyle felt put out to have an unexpected guest for dinner, but Rico made a good impression in his black sneakers, jeans, white button-down shirt, and narrow black tie. Lyle also guffawed when Rico said to me, "Wow. You got yourself a hunk."

"I like to think Manny and I both got ourselves hunks," Lyle said with a smile.

"Oh yeah, of course," Rico said, blushing. "I didn't mean to suggest Manny wasn't handsome too. I just didn't expect you to be so big."

To be fair, Lyle's size might have impressed Rico because Rico had relatively small stature. If he stretched up to his full height, the top of his head cleared Lyle's chest, a difference I caught in a photo of the two of them later that evening.

We shared our dinner, amazed such a small person could eat as much.

"I guess you don't eat well," I said.

"Not anything as good as this," he said, looking into his empty stew bowl. "Eduardo makes a house dinner on Mondays, Wednesdays, and Fridays, but he's not that great a cook, so I grab fast food sometimes."

Later, while Lyle tidied the kitchen, Rico told me he was considering leaving the life but didn't know how to do it. "I have almost ten thousand dollars in savings, but that's not really enough yet," he said.

"I don't mean to ask too personal a question, but where are your parents?"

"Franklin Episcopal Church," he said. "Buried in the graveyard.

A drunk driver on a rainy night killed both my parents when I was ten. I lived with my granny for a little while, then she had a stroke. They sent me to foster care for a few months, but that was hell. They didn't really want me, just the money having me brought in, so I ran away when I was eleven and never looked back. I've been in the life for almost four years now."

"Why are you thinking of leaving?"

"I'm getting older. That's one reason I ain't drawing as many clients as before. I'm losing that look, you know? Plus, I'm not stupid. I know it's got no real future in it. It's time to do something else."

"Like what?"

"I don't know. Get a GED. Maybe go to community college. I have some art skills. I wouldn't mind being a graphic designer or an illustrator."

Lyle came back in with a plate of the holiday cookies he bought at a bake sale that morning and three mugs of hot chocolate.

Rico almost squealed. "Oh, yum. I haven't had these in ages."

Lyle cleared his throat. "I've already seen the photos Manny has on his phone, but do you think I could maybe get a close look at the bracelet?"

"Sure," Rico said, getting up to get it from his jacket pocket. He brought it back to the table and handed it to Lyle.

"You're right, Manny, it is really heavy," Lyle said. "And the level of detail is amazing. If you touch one of the snake's fangs, it's sharp."

"You were just speaking about resources and future plans, Rico," I said. "That bracelet would be worth quite a lot of money to the right buyer. Have you thought about selling?"

"No," Rico said immediately, then paused. "At least, not for a while. Maybe in the future, if I meet a man and settle down, I could see selling it. But not while it's all I have to remember Niko."

I escorted him down the elevator a short while later. He showed off his skater skills by staying on his board as the old lift clattered and lurched down the shaft. At the street level, I accepted his shy hug. I didn't tell him I'd started to consider how Ms. Dass might feel about having him as a resident of Baldwin House, at least until he finished his schooling.

"I'm out," he said over his shoulder as he rode the skateboard out of the elevator. "Catch ya later." And he was gone.

"You know, I think I got a glimpse of why Ms. Dass works so hard to make Baldwin House a success," I said to Lyle, whose reassuring bulk spooned up against me in a loving hug later in bed.

"I think I know what you mean," Lyle said. "I had a couple of weird moments over dinner when I felt almost parental."

"I know, exactly. That mix of admiration and concern, fear and responsibility…and love. Even though he's not even our son."

"One thing for sure," Lyle said. "If he was our son, there's no way he would have to make a living in a brothel."

"Amen," I murmured, slipping into sleep.

Later, sometime between two thirty and three, I awoke to my phone's persistent buzz. A feeling of dread settled into my stomach as I put the phone to my ear.

"Manny Porter," I whispered.

"Chief Detective Walker here."

"Chief, it's two thirty in the morning. Don't you ever sleep?"

"I'm on Adams Avenue between Thirteenth and Fourteenth," he said. "There's been a…severe mugging I thought I should tell you about."

"We have a crime reporter. His name's Abner Smalls, remember? Call him." Behind me, Lyle grunted in his sleep before settling into me again.

"Already come and gone," Walker said, lowering his voice. "Manny, the victim had your name and number in his phone."

"What?" In a moment I was wide awake, and my sense of dread moved from my stomach to my chest.

"What is it?" Lyle mumbled. "What's going on?"

"I wouldn't call you if it wasn't serious, but I think you should come down here."

"On my way," I replied, sliding out from under the warm covers as carefully as I could, but Lyle jerked awake.

"What are you doing?"

"Walker called. Someone who has my name and number in his phone was attacked. It sounds pretty bad."

"Did he say who?"

"No, so it sounds like the victim might be unconscious. I might be able to give them an ID."

"God, it's always something," Lyle groaned.

"I know." I pulled a sweater on over my T-shirt. "Promise me you'll go back to sleep."

"I'll try. Where did it happen?"

"Adams between Thirteenth and Fourteenth. What's down there?"

"Not a lot. The towing impound lot, for one. Also the municipal bus yard."

I grabbed my keys and wallet, kissed Lyle's cheek, and headed out. The dread I felt on the phone call continued to grow the more I contemplated who the victim could have been.

"Please, no," I prayed with greater intensity as every minute passed. "Please don't let it be."

I saw the accident scene in the distance before I arrived. A dozen police cars clustered in the middle of the block, their red, white, and blue lights casting the scene in a sort of macabre patriotism. A patrolman behind a barricade at Twelfth Street waved me down but allowed me to enter after I gave my name and showed my license. He directed me to park behind a line of unmarked police cars.

I found Detective Walker beside his car talking on the phone, and when I cast my eyes into the car's back seat, my spirit plummeted. There, badly scraped and with one wheel broken off, was Rico's beloved skateboard.

"Thanks for coming," Walker said. "The whole department is out on this one. It's a kid, about fourteen or fifteen."

"His name's Rico," I said. "Jaime Rico Pelado. He's a source of mine, and a key witness in the Nikolaidis story."

Walker spoke into the phone. "I'll call you back." Then he looked at me hard. "Maybe we should find a place to talk," he said finally. "Get in."

❖

"Can we please head to the emergency room? I need to find out how he is."

"We can talk on the way."

"What happened?"

"One of the residents on the street, a Mrs. Darkoy, said her dog kept pestering her, so she let it out in the backyard. The dog ran straight to a back gate and kept barking there. When she went to get it to come back in, she found the boy."

"How hurt was he?"

"He wasn't dead, which is the good news, I guess. But he wasn't conscious, and the EMTs had to stabilize him, so it didn't sound great."

I leaned back in the seat and absorbed this news, silently willing the old car to greater speed. I was going to bring him up to date when he stopped me.

"Wait," he said, "let me fill in some gaps."

"Okay."

"This Rico kid was Nikolaidis's male love interest? The one he gifted with the ugly bracelet?"

"Correct. Did you find the bracelet?"

"Nope. It wasn't on him, but we won't be able to really search the alley until after sunrise."

"I don't expect you'll find it, damn it!"

"I wish you had gone ahead and given him to me when we spoke earlier," he muttered. "Now a potential witness might die, and an important piece of evidence has gone missing."

I held my tongue. He was right. My interest in keeping Rico as a source for my story might have cost him his life. Guilt washed over me in a torrent.

"Give me the address now," he said.

"What for?"

"So I can do my job as I should have done before and send some of my guys around to search his room in the house and take a statement from the pimp landlord," Walker said. "The bracelet might be there right now, and the landlord is a witness who might be able to verify at least some of Rico's statement."

I gave him the address and listened in as he made the assignment.

"The landlord's name is Eduardo," I said. "Tell your guys Rico said he never treated him badly."

"Why should that matter?"

I felt my face color a bit. "Because sometimes your guys have been known to be a little overzealous when making arrests."

Walker dismissed my comment. "Nah. Municipal possibly, but not my guys. Besides, who said anything about making arrests?"

"Really?"

He shot me a frustrated look. "We're not vice. We're not bringing anyone in on a morals charge. Unless this dude up and confesses to killing Nikolaidis, we aren't interested in him as a suspect. All we want is honest answers to our questions."

We pulled into the hospital parking lot.

"You might be interested to learn I followed up on your tip," he said out of the blue. "I asked a buddy of mine on the state organized crime team to look into Nadia Elena and the Reznikovs."

"And?"

"And nothing yet. He hasn't gotten back to me. But that's a good sign."

"Why?"

"Because the other times when I've asked him and he's found nothing, he's gotten back to me right away."

At the hospital, we learned little more than we knew before. Doctors had Rico in surgery, repairing something damaged in his chest, and no one was available to give us a prognosis.

As a familiar face due to my previous time in the hospital, I was able to get myself listed as an interested party on Rico's file, to be contacted whenever his condition changed, but that was all I could get done.

Walker drove back to the attack scene to supervise the search of the alley, and after a few hours with no updates on Rico's status, I took a rideshare to collect my car. Before I set out, I texted Lyle, outlining what had happened and letting him know I was safe. I was just pulling up to the *Record* offices when an incoming text buzzed my phone. It was from Susan.

Meeting in Mr. Porter's office as soon as you arrive. Urgent.

When I arrived at my father's office, I stopped at Rosa's desk to drop my bag and hang my coat. "What's up?" I asked in a low voice.

"I don't know," she replied. "Susan arrived about an hour ago looking upset and asked to see him. She hasn't come out since, and he's had me reschedule his two morning conference calls."

"Thanks, Rosa," I said. Then, squaring my shoulders, I went in.

My father sat behind his desk, but he had removed his jacket and rolled up his sleeves, something he did when he was upset. Susan stood up, and I thought she appeared pale. My father waved me into the other seat opposite his desk and Susan sat down again. He nodded to her.

"Manny, this arrived addressed to me in this morning's mail," she said, passing me an envelope.

I examined the plain white envelope, the kind available in many drugstores in boxes of ten or twenty. As she noted, it had been addressed to her, care of the *Record*, on a typewriter. A first class stamp had been haphazardly applied to the upper right corner, but there was no return address. The envelope had been slit open.

I pulled out its contents, one sheet of plain white paper with a single, undated, message, typed.

To whom it may concern:

You should know that your reporter, Immanuel Porter, is involved in an inappropriately intimate and ongoing relationship with the young man (or should I say, thug) who awaits trial for the murder of dear Dr. Phillip Nikolaidis. As this relationship has been neither disclosed nor explained, an attentive and careful reader might wonder how much Mr. Porter can be trusted to faithfully report news about the Nikolaidis case or AthenaLibre, as he appears to have firm convictions about each. For example, Mr. Porter paid the bail bondsman's significant fee so this thug could walk our streets until trial. I am a longtime and usually very happy subscriber to the Record *and would hate to see our proud newspaper compromise its ethics in the search for lurid material.*

It was signed, *a faithful reader.*

I flipped it over and examined the back. Nothing.

"Well?" my father said.

"An obviously venomous and ghastly poison pen note," I said. "Thoroughly horrible, but not surprising and, I would have thought, not that unusual."

"Not the letter itself. What it says. Is it true?"

"Is *what* true?" I asked, aghast. "Of course it's not true. Tristan is a mentee of mine, nothing more. I'm shocked you would even suppose otherwise for a moment."

"Not that, Manny," Susan said. "I think we all know about and approve of your mentoring Tristan. What Mr. Porter and I are asking about is the last bit. Did you pay the fee for Tristan's bail from the bonding agent?"

I looked up at them, suddenly feeling like a twelve-year-old boy who'd been caught pinching beers out of the party cooler. "Technically—"

"*No!*" my father said flatly. "This is not the time to go all Jesuit on us. Did you pay the fee for Tristan's bail?"

"Yes," I said quietly. "I put up some of the money myself, but Lyle and Bonne Chance Motors put up the bulk of it."

My father looked at me hard, then dropped his gaze. "My God, what were you thinking?"

"That Tristan is not a thug and might not last three days in an adult jail or prison. That I was partly responsible for getting him into this mess by pushing for him to take the AthenaLibre internship, and that I was brought up not to turn my back on the weak if I can help it."

"Yes, damn it," my father roared, standing up. "All well and good, and I agree, but why didn't you come to us first?" He paced to the far wall and started back.

"Why?" I asked, bewildered. "What's the big deal if I helped Tristan or not?"

"Because AthenaLibre was stung by your story," Susan said. "Their law firm has sent a letter demanding a retraction and filed the preliminary notice of a complaint in court."

"So what? Why should that matter? I sent over the data when I filed the story. Your fact-checkers went through it. Everything I reported is true."

"They won't contest the facts, they'll contest the interpretation and nuance of the facts," my father said in a tired voice as he came to his desk. "And when they find out you helped Nikolaidis's alleged murderer make bail, they'll have something they can call a motive."

"But—"

"Not another word! It's time to let the adults do what needs to be done. Susan, get with the lawyers and go over that retraction demand with a fine-tooth comb. Work with them to see if you can find some compromise language we can tolerate that we can use in a statement."

"Yes, sir."

"And you—you're off any future reporting on AthenaLibre. None. I don't want to hear that you have been anywhere near the company or that murder case. Is that clear?"

"With all due respect, sir, that's not fair. I reported nothing in that story that was not true. I believe we're in a strong position."

"Yes, we are," Susan said, "when it comes to the facts, but your father is trying to say facts don't mean the same things as before. Perception matters a lot more now. And your actions may have given this paper's enemies an important assist."

"But—"

"Enough!" my father said. "We've already spent too much time discussing this. As of January first, I'm suspending you from this newspaper for a week without pay. Some time away will help you consider the dilemma you have presented us. You will finish your stories that do not relate to AthenaLibre before that time and then you will go."

"But—"

"Before you say another word, you should know I can make it a month suspension."

I shut my mouth, then opened it again. "Yes, sir."

"Dismissed, both of you. Susan, I want an analysis and report from your conversation with the lawyers on my desk as soon as possible."

"Yes, sir."

We both left the room.

❖

I stopped at Rosa's desk to pick up my bag and coat. Susan kept going, and I didn't stop her. I wasn't sure if either one of us felt like sharing an elevator with the other.

"Manuclito, what's wrong?" Rosa asked, using a term for me she hadn't used since I was a little kid.

"I've made a serious mistake," I said, looking at her sadly. "I'm suspended from the paper for a week without pay as of January first."

She didn't speak, but her face registered her shock. "But he can't—"

"He can and he should, if he feels as the publisher it's what the paper needs. He cannot be my father in this situation. He has to be my boss."

I sighed and left her office. I contemplated what to do next. I had a couple of stories not related to AthenaLibre in the hopper, but they weren't ready to write yet. I thought about calling my data team to let them know they'd have to work with another writer on part two of the story but realized Susan would want to do that herself.

I decided to swing by Tommy's office and tell him before I left. He deserved to hear it from me, not through the grapevine. But his space was empty, despite his lights and computer being on. I considered leaving a note, but then decided against it and headed home.

At Bonne Chance I ran across Felipe in the delivery lot, buffing out a wax job. "Hey there, Mr. Porter, come and look at this beauty."

I didn't want to but walked over. He was right, it was a beauty, a baby blue Cadillac from the early 1960s.

"What was she in for?" I couldn't tell from looking at the nearly perfect automobile.

"Right front fender. Some bastard hit her while she was parked outside a party and put a right deep dent in. So we made her right again."

"Looks great, Felipe. Great work."

"What's up with you, then?" he asked. "You look like your dog died, you've been fired, and then dumped all at once."

"Just a hard day. I'll get over it."

"Hope so," he said. "Christmas Eve tomorrow!"

I nodded and headed for the elevator, approaching it from the outside to avoid anybody else. Upstairs, the apartment's silence disturbed me until I realized I wasn't here often during the day. How would I know what it usually sounded like? I poured myself a glass of the good burgundy from an open bottle and sat in one of the comfortable living room chairs to consider my options. Then I promptly fell asleep.

I woke up later to a gentle kiss from Lyle and his worried face hovering over mine. "Hey," he said. "Welcome back."

"God, what time is it?" The light in the room was different but I couldn't tell the hour.

"About two," he said with a smile. "Parker told me you were home, so I came up at ten thirty to say hello, and you were already asleep. I didn't want to wake you, and you've been out for hours."

I groaned and stretched. The living room chairs provided comfortable seating but were not much good for sleeping.

"You feel okay? What's going on?"

I stood up facing him.

"First, may I have a hug?"

"Of course." And I sighed as he wrapped his familiar strength around me.

"So, what's going on?"

"I fucked up, Lyle." I pulled myself away and started walking back to the bedroom to change clothes.

"How so?" he asked again, familiar with my occasional bouts of pessimism.

"Remember when we paid the fee so Tristan could post bail?"

"Only every time I get a statement from the emergency fund," he joked as he followed me, "which does not mean I wouldn't do it again in a heartbeat."

"And that is a major part of where we—I—fucked up. Instead of rushing so quickly in where angels fear to tread, I should have spent more time considering why angels might fear to tread there."

"Will you please start making sense? Start at the beginning."

"AthenaLibre is making noises about suing the *Record* over my coverage of the company."

"All right. Sucky move on their part, but I'm sure the paper has faced lawsuit threats before."

"And the publisher, my father, believes the fact that we paid the fee for Tristan's bail will help them build a case that I was too involved in the story to be evenhanded and that I bear a grudge against the firm."

"But that's dumb. It's not like you came on the beat and started gunning for AthenaLibre. This story pretty much fell in your lap, almost literally. Plus, even if that were true, everything you have reported about the company has been factual, so motivation isn't really a question."

"But facts and good reporting don't carry the same weight as they used to," I said. "People can turn on their computers and find alternative theories to explain all sorts of facts, and even find their own sets of alternative facts. And he thinks people will use our support of Tristan to help them do just that—even people who may be placed on a jury."

"Wow. What does that mean?"

"Susan is meeting with the paper's lawyers this morning to draw up a conciliatory statement that might allow the paper to back away from the story as published so far without issuing a retraction. And I've been taken completely off any story involving AthenaLibre and suspended for a week without pay starting January first."

"What? But who's going to write the story's second half?"

"I don't know," I said, feeling suddenly tired despite my napping. "All I know is that it's not going to be me." I turned away from him quickly, dangerously close to tearing up. I felt him approach from behind me and put his strong hands on my shoulders.

"Damn, Lyle, this is the worst day of my career so far. And I brought it all on myself. I can't even stamp my feet and blame Dad for being unjust, because he's right. By helping Tristan, I may have dropped the paper in the shit. I would have suspended me too."

He rubbed my shoulders. "Now, I might push back a little on this Hate Manny-fest," he said. "First, you and I both believed Tristan is innocent. Do you still believe that?"

I nodded.

"Good, so do I. And neither one of us thought Tristan deserved to spend weeks, if not months, in an adult jail, right?"

"Right."

"In light of that, what did we do? We did a good thing without necessarily thinking it out fully first. That was a mistake. I'll even give you that it was a serious mistake. But it wasn't something we did out of malice, nor do I imagine you will ever do it again."

"Are you going back to work?"

"Honey, it's December twenty-third. Bonne Chance shut at noon today. We won't reopen until December twenty-seventh."

We decided not to tell Tristan about my suspension from the paper so he didn't feel any more guilty than he already did, but it didn't matter. The Tinker Creek grapevine had already spread the news.

He came off the elevator like a shot at five thirty, fresh from helping Ms. Dass finish last-minute shopping for Baldwin House. Lyle was marinating steaks for dinner and I was surrounded by bowls as I made my mom's recipe for homemade eggnog when Tristan appeared in the kitchen.

"Is it true?" he said, dropping two shopping bags on the floor.

"Is what true?"

"Is it true that the paper fired you?"

In his corner of the kitchen, I heard Lyle chuckle.

"No. I've been suspended for a week, but not fired. Where did you hear that?"

"Miss Dass got a text. I told her it couldn't be true, but I came home to check." He got his phone out and wrote a brief message. "Now she knows I was right." He picked up his bags and took them to his room but reappeared soon.

"Eggnog," I told him.

"Is it polluted or clean?"

"It's Christmas, so you can have either."

"What's it poisoned with?"

"Bourbon."

"No thanks," he said with a smile. "I think I'm still too young to like those grown-up drinks."

"Suit yourself," I said, pouring him a glass of the virgin mix. "Now why don't you pull up some nice music for us on that smartphone?"

"Deal," he said, disappearing back into living space. Soon, Bing Crosby's "White Christmas" came wafting into the kitchen.

"Huh, that's surprising," Lyle said. "A little old-fashioned."

"I don't know. There's nothing that says young people can't be sentimental."

"I guess."

We finished in the kitchen and had settled in to enjoy the music and the tree when the doorbell rang. The outside camera revealed a middle-aged man of medium height wearing a brown suit with white shirt and no tie. Beside him stood a young policeman.

"Detective Norton and Officer Tangiers," the man said, holding a shield up to the camera. "May we come in?"

I scrutinized the pair. I vaguely remember seeing Detective Norton down at the station, but I didn't recognize Officer Tangiers.

"Of course," I said, sending down the elevator.

"Who is it?" Lyle called out.

"Cops," I said. He came out of the living room as the lift door slid open and the two officers stepped out.

"Jason," Lyle exclaimed. "Merry Christmas. This is a surprise."

"Oh, hey, Lyle. Merry Christmas to you too." Norton looked embarrassed.

"Do you want to come through and sit down?"

"No, thank you. We're here to see Mr. DeJesus. Is he around?"

"Yes," I said, starting to turn around to go get him.

"Did I hear my name?" Tristan said as he approached.

"Are you Tristan DeJesus?"

"Yes."

"I'm Detective Norton and this is Officer Tangiers."

"Yes. How can I help you?"

Norton turned to Tangiers, who handed him a clear evidence bag he gave to Tristan.

"Mr. DeJesus, do you recognize the object in this bag?"

Tristan held up the bag and then smiled widely.

"Of course I do. That's the pendant Manny gave me that got stolen. Look, Manny, it's my pendant. Thanks, guys. I didn't think I would ever see it again. Where did you find it?"

"A forensic team found it at the site of a robbery assault," Norton said.

"Where was that?" I asked.

"I'm sorry, it's an ongoing investigation. I can't share that. Mr. DeJesus, where were you last night between eleven and one this morning?"

"Here," Tristan said. "I spent most of the evening at Baldwin House and got back here about eleven. I went straight to bed until I woke up this morning."

"Can anyone verify that?"

"No. I knew I was coming in late, so I deliberately kept from waking anyone. What's all this about?"

Still looking embarrassed and directly at Lyle, Norton announced, "Tristan DeJesus, I have a warrant for your arrest for violating the terms of your conditional release. Officer Tangiers."

"What the fuck?" Tristan shouted as the policeman got behind him.

"Hands behind your back, sir."

"Jason, what's this all about?"

"I'm sorry, Lyle, Mr. Porter. All I know is that this comes from the prosecutor's office after that necklace thing was found at the scene of the attack on that boy. It has Mr. DeJesus's fingerprints on it."

"Of course it does. It's mine," Tristan said, still in a loud voice but not shouting. "But I haven't seen it in almost a week, since it was stolen out of my locker at the community center. Manny, you were there. You saw the broken locker."

"It's true, Detective. I was there, and I can attest that someone burgled Tristan's locker while he and I were shooting hoops on the court. I'm confident the rec center manager will say the same thing."

"I'm sorry. If I was doing this based on my own investigation, I could hold off until I gathered more information, but like I said, this comes from the prosecutor's office."

I sighed, and Tristan put his hands behind his back to accept the handcuffs. "I'll follow in my car," I said. "Lyle, please call Carolyn and ask her to meet me at the station."

Guiding Tristan between them, Norton and Tangiers stepped onto the lift along with me, and we headed down to the cars. The last thing I saw before the elevator doors closed was Lyle speaking into his phone.

Following Detective Nolan's shabby Ford Focus through dead quiet St. Michael's Harbor streets ranks among the more surreal experiences of my life.

I don't know what I expected. It was almost Christmas Eve! Yet in other places, folks were moving about, holiday haters coming back from bars, gifting procrastinators speeding to find that one last thing, guests arriving late.

But these streets remained quiet and still except for our two-car parade, which dutifully made a full stop at every traffic light and stop sign, though the nearest cars on any of these streets moved slowly blocks away.

In front I saw Tristan glance from the back seat out the window.

I knew he recognized my car, and I hoped he could see it despite my headlights and at least know I had kept my word, and he was not abandoned.

I pondered what had happened as I drove. Nolan had said the arrest order came from the prosecutor's office, not from his higher-ups. Did Detective Walker know about it? I sensed protocol would have demanded he be kept in the loop on anything as big as an arrest. But this wasn't an apprehension, more of a return to custody.

And how the hell had Tristan's pendant gotten to the site of Rico's attack? I generally don't believe in conspiracies. Most fall apart well before their conspirators commit any crimes, and it becomes exponentially more difficult to hide a cabal with each new person you add to it.

But what had happened with Tristan was enough to make me revise my thinking. Clearly someone had either planned to make him the lead suspect or sought to make sure he remained in that role. But who?

We reached the corner of Washington and Branch. Nolan turned right to take Tristan down to the intake office. I didn't follow. Experience had taught me that unless I was family or legal counsel, I wasn't getting through that door. I parked in the visitors' lot, then took the stairs two at a time.

At the front desk, a young policewoman named Officer Wright looked at me quizzically.

"My name's Immanuel Porter. My friend Tristan DeJesus was taken into custody this evening."

She typed quickly on her keyboard. "He's being processed now. That's all the information I have. You can take a seat in the waiting room if you want."

"Thank you."

I found a seat on one of the overstuffed but battered chairs. These looked like they could have graced an elegant hotel lobby or gentlemen's club once upon a time, but now they were faded and patched. A large television on the far wall played an old movie, and a bank of vending machines occupied the inner wall.

I sat on the edge of the chair and tried to call Lyle, but couldn't find a signal. After about an hour, Carolyn arrived.

"Thank God you're here," I said.

"I'm sorry. I came as fast as I could, but I'm babysitting my niece while my sister and her husband are at a party. I got one of my neighbors to watch her until they can make it back. What can you tell me?"

"He was taken into custody at Bonne Chance. It was a two-man team, Detective Nolan and an officer. They said it was on a prosecutor's order, not a police order, and they said forensics found Tristan's pendant at the site of an attack."

"What pendant?"

"A gay pride pendant I gave him," I said. "But what's so weird is that pendant was stolen out of a community center locker while he and I were on a basketball court. I was there when he found his locker broken open and the pendant gone."

"We'll deal with that later. Now, let me talk to the duty officer and see what's going on. The important thing is to keep Tristan from being placed in with the adult jail population."

"Is that possible?" I felt my voice shake.

"I'm afraid so, yes," she said. "The juvenile wing might already be closed for the holiday. But hope for the best."

I nodded as she walked to the front desk and was admitted to the back. I settled in my chair to watch the old movie, a Christmas tale starring Barbara Stanwyck and a cute male lead, and hoped for the best until Carolyn returned about an hour later.

"You're back!"

"I've got good news and bad news," she said. "The good news is that while the juvenile facility wasn't accepting any new detainees, neither was the adult because of overcrowding. That left the drunk tank, so that's where he is."

"That's better how?"

"More monitoring. Plus, he might be released if more detainees come to the drunk tank."

"How likely is that?"

Carolyn looked at the wall clock that read half past ten. "Unlikely, but not impossible," she said.

I settled back in the chair. "I know you can't stay, so I will," I said. "That way if he gets released, I can make sure he gets back to BCM. Do me a favor, please? Call Lyle and let him know? My cell phone doesn't work here."

"Will do. Nobody's cell phone works here. They jam the signals as a security measure." She hugged me awkwardly. "I'm so sorry this happened," she said. "Please try not to worry. I'm sure we'll get to the bottom of it."

Then she was gone.

I got up and perused the wall of vending machines. I opted for a large mocha coffee drink and a small box of ginger cookies and returned to my chair to wait.

The next thing I knew, I felt a gentle tapping on my shoulder, and I looked up to find Lyle's face gazing down into mine.

"Oh, hey," I said.

"Hey yourself," he replied.

I sat up and looked around for the clock. "What are you doing here? What time is it?"

"It's about seven on Christmas Eve morning," he said, standing up to let me stretch. "As for what I'm doing here, I just got tired of waiting for my boyfriend to come back from the police station and decided to come find out what he's been doing all night."

"Didn't Carolyn call you?"

"Nope."

"Oh God, I'm sorry." I groaned. "She was supposed to let you know I stayed here to give Tristan a ride home if they sprang him from the drunk tank last night."

"The drunk tank?"

"It's a long story, I'll tell you on the way home."

We paused at the front desk on the way out. Officer Wright had gone, replaced by a policewoman named Alice Bowers.

"I see you found him," she said, smiling at Lyle.

"Of course. I knew he could only be in the waiting room. It was so nice to see you again."

“Oh, I know,” she said. “For me too. And I’ll bring that damned minivan by after the holidays.”

“Do that. I’m confident we can make it run a whole lot better.”

“Sorry to interrupt this reunion,” I broke in. “But can we be sure no one else is coming into the drunk tank today?”

“Oh, honey, it’s Christmas Eve morning. The last bars closed four hours ago, and they won’t open again until the day after Christmas. No guarantees, of course, but if the D and D facility fills up and we have to release Mr. DeJesus, he will be able to call you.”

We left and headed to my car, the only civilian car in the parking lot.

“Is there anyone in this town that you don’t know?” I said.

“Of course,” he said as I opened the door. “We used to take care of her grandfather’s cars, and she used to come with him. After he died, we didn’t see her anymore, but she remembered me and lit up when I came in.”

“Not a surprise,” I said. “What’s the D and D facility?”

“The Drunk and Disorderly facility is the formal name for the drunk tank.”

Chapter 10

Knows When You've Been Bad or Good

I hit the shower to try to wash off the previous night so I could get right back to work on getting Tristan out. But the reality of the time in the waiting room hit me with the warm water, and I couldn't keep my eyes open after I dried off, falling asleep on our bed soon after I got out.

I woke up to Lyle's gentle kisses up my chest and onto my throat.

"Mmm," I growled.

"Shh." I felt him suppress a chuckle. "As sexy as you look wrapped in only a towel, I thought you probably wanted some lunch."

My nose picked up the delicious smell of onions sautéing. "What time is it?"

"After noon on Christmas Eve. I thought I'd better wake you up or you won't sleep at all tonight."

I stretched and looked up at him. "Or you could stay in here, and we could have afternoon delight for lunch," I suggested with a leer.

"Or you could join me in the kitchen so we can eat and then come back in here. Especially since I've already started cooking."

Conceding his point, I got up, pulled on a pair of shorts and a T-shirt, and padded after him to the kitchen redolent with the smells of cooking onions, bacon, and freshly baked bread. My stomach growled with an audible sound. Lyle jumped slightly.

"Wow. Someone's hungry. I guess you didn't hit the vending machines, huh?"

"What's on the menu?"

"Mushroom and onion omelet, applewood-smoked bacon, fresh toasted brioche, and apple crumble with café au lait."

"Sounds lovely. I haven't seen this side of Lyle before."

"I know. He doesn't get out very much," he said with a chuckle. "But Christmas just seemed like the right time." He poured some of the beaten eggs into the pan. "This one is yours. You'll find warm toast and bacon in the oven. Make yourself a plate and pass it over."

I went to the oven and collected two golden brown slices of toasted brioche and three large pieces of bacon. Then I passed Lyle the plate, and he slid the fat, yellow omelet, oozing onions and mushrooms, beside them.

"Café au lait is already mixed in the thermos on the table," Lyle said. "Go ahead and pour yourself a mug."

The food was delicious, both quieting my growling insides and spurring new guilt over Tristan. "Lyle, this is great, but I feel like crap for eating it. God knows what Tristan got for lunch."

"Chicken soup, saltines, and a piece of fruit, usually an apple at this time of year," Lyle said.

"What?"

"Chicken soup, saltines, and an apple. I guarantee that's what Tristan got for lunch. And if he was smart, he ate it and asked for seconds if they had more available."

"How do you know?"

"What? Did you think I never saw the inside of the D and D facility?" Lyle said with a smile.

"When?"

"Oh, a long while ago when I was young and stupid and thought I could handle what my old man couldn't."

"Yeah, but that was years ago. Don't you think they've stopped serving chicken soup for lunch?"

"Nope."

"Why not?"

"Because experience has shown that chicken soup, saltines,

and a piece of fruit are about perfect for a hangover. The broth is warm and homey while still gentle enough for tender stomachs, the crackers provide needed sodium, and the apple gives some roughage and sweetness."

I admitted to myself that sounded better than I expected, but I still felt bad for Tristan. "Lyle, what are we going to do?"

"As soon as we can, we'll get with Carolyn and help her gather what she needs for Tristan's defense—and yes, that might include finding out who killed Nikolaidis, but we can't count on that."

"I know." I looked down at my empty plate, poured another mug of café au lait, then jumped when the doorbell sounded.

"Who the heck is this on Christmas Eve?" I grumbled. I wasn't in the mood for visitors today and wanted to stay in, away from the world.

"I'll get it," Lyle said. I heard a brief conversation with a muffled voice, then Lyle's cheerful "C'mon up."

"Aw, man." I shot Lyle a look as he entered the kitchen.

"I think you'll want to talk to this visitor," he said. "Or at least listen because he definitely wants to talk to you."

I heard the elevator door open and then a heavy tread on the floor. I tried to recall where I had heard it before. As I put sound and person together, Detective Walker's bulk filled the entrance.

"You've got some nerve showing up here on Christmas Eve," I said. "What's the matter? Run out of people to lock up before the holiday?"

Walker's face flushed, but he didn't answer my challenge, nodding first to Lyle and then to me.

"Morning, Lyle, Manny," he said in a soft voice. "Thanks for letting me up."

"You're welcome," Lyle said. "The hardworking men and women of law enforcement are always greeted at our table. Coffee? We have café au lait in the thermal pitcher, or I could brew you up fresh and black if you want."

"No thank you, Lyle. If I could have a little glass of that good Irish stuff you had a few months ago instead, I'd sure appreciate it."

"Of course. I'll fetch the bottle."

Lyle walked out to his office and left us in the kitchen. Not only did Walker look embarrassed, but he was more rumpled than usual and needed a shave. I motioned to the chair next to mine. "You're here now," I said. "You might as well sit down."

He sat. "Smells good in here," he said. "You must have gotten up early to start cooking."

"Nope, this was all Mr. James. I was way too tired from spending the night in the police station waiting room to fix any of this."

He winced as Lyle came back carrying the bottle and three shot glasses. "A toast," Lyle said, putting a tumbler in front of each of us and pouring a generous serving.

"I don't know…"

He ignored me. "A toast to returning friends and those who can help them come back."

"Hear, hear," Walker said.

And we drank, the amber liquid burning down my throat and sending its warm glow into my toes. "Wow," I said.

Walker stood up suddenly. "When I heard about what happened last night and after I read the reports, I knew I had to come by here to apologize—particularly to you, Manny. Just to be clear, I could not have prevented Tristan from being returned to jail, as that order came from the prosecutor's office. But I could have made it happen in a different way."

"Why didn't you?" I said.

"I didn't know," he said. "The city attorney's office deliberately left me out of the loop because they knew I didn't agree with their using a relatively powerless young man for political grandstanding. Norris is detailed specifically to that office, so they didn't have to go to the trouble of getting me to sign off on it."

"This sounds like you don't believe the pendant is the sort of evidence they say it is," Lyle asked.

"Please!" Walker said with a snort. "I never pretended to be Sherlock Holmes, but I'm not stupid either. What is the one thing this case has consistently lacked since the very morning after the murder?"

Looking into our blank faces, he continued. "Direct evidence! Solid, uncircumstantial proof linking our prime suspect to the crime. We have Tristan's fingerprints on the spool of wire, but not on the actual wire around the victim's throat. We have evidence that Tristan had after-hours access to the AthenaLibre building without alerting the security system, but we have no proof he used it. Finally, we have a sworn statement from Tristan alleging romantic advances from the victim, but we can't even verify that these took place, much less that it was reciprocal. Now, all of a sudden, out of the blue, we find a personal item from Tristan with his fingerprints on it, at the scene of a savage attack on a potential witness in this case? Just like that? That doesn't pass my smell test."

"So, just for the record, if you had been in the loop would you still have put Tristan back in jail?"

"Manny, I'm sorry, but yes," he said. "I couldn't have refused the order. But I would have done it differently. The next business day after Christmas, Tristan could have turned himself in at the station. I would have made sure he went into the juvenile division."

"Thank you, I appreciate your telling me this. I was hating thinking I had lost my status as an informed source." I smiled at him.

"That reminds me, the organized crime team finally got back to me about the Reznikovs."

"Oh?" I tried to keep the excitement out of my voice. "What did they say?"

"The bad news is that the Reznikovs are *not* a Russian mob family. But the better news is that they *are* a leading Belarusian crime family. One of the guys called them kissing cousins to a couple of the biggest crime syndicates in St. Petersburg."

Lyle and I looked at one another, stunned at the news.

"Which brings me to the grieving fiancée," he said, reaching into his back pocket and pulling out a notebook. "According to a specialist at Interpol, Ms. Reznikov has no formal police record but has been a person of interest in over twenty-six criminal investigations covering everything from drug smuggling to art theft, antiquities looting, human trafficking, and confidence schemes.

Essentially, whenever someone in the family needs a front for something underhanded, she's been available to help."

"It looks like we might finally have another candidate for prime suspect," I said.

"But how do we keep the investigation going?" asked Lyle.

"I have an idea," I said.

❖

Christmas Day passed quietly and poorly for me and Lyle. My looming ban from the *Record* put a damper on any holiday festivities with coworkers, and Lyle sent his regrets to the usual round of party invitations that he received as one of St. Michael's Harbor's most successful businessmen.

"It's not like I'm missing much," he said. "I usually just go pro forma anyway. Some people urge me to attend for the networking opportunities, but that feels even worse, in my opinion, taking yet another aspect of the holiday and subordinating it to making money. Yuck."

But Tristan's absence from home and presence in jail was what made it a day for staying in and enjoying each other's company.

Our pace picked up the day after, when a couple of well-placed calls from Lyle won us two seats at the St. George Hotel's ninetieth annual Boxing Day brunch. The event began in the 1930s to recognize, thank, and provide holiday cheer to the working men and women of St. Michael's Harbor, particularly those in the hospitality industry.

Held the day after Christmas in the St. George Hotel's exclusive cocktail lounge, the Dragon Bar, the occasion had gradually begun welcoming people from across the city, not just servers, maids, and cooks.

Lyle and I wrangled our way in because I believed there would be few other places downtown to get a bite to eat the morning after Christmas, so we had a high chance of running into Ms. Reznikov and her small entourage.

I arrived at nine under the pretext of preparing a piece on the event, given its nine-decade history. Lyle would enter at ten as the guest of one of his business clients. As much as I disliked the idea of needing his assistance, my brief encounters with Nadia's brother and "family friend" left me open to having some trained outside muscle on my side.

The Dragon Bar at the St. George Hotel is one of the city's more divisive venues. Fans find it elegant, Old Worldly, and high class, with its long bar that runs the length of the east side of the room and the many old-fashioned mirrors that decorate the opposite wall. Detractors find it heavy, imperial, and stodgy. They often point out the bar's long history of being primarily open to rich, white patrons for the other 364 days of year, a policy the hotel abandoned only under pressure in 1968.

I tend to fall somewhere between the two camps, but usually wind up seduced, like Nadia Reznikov, into approving of the establishment by its superbly trained and creative bartenders.

I had finished interviewing the current manager and was considering pausing for a drink when I heard Ms. Reznikov's unmistakable voice in one of the room's corners where she, her brother, and a man I took to be the family friend were being seated at one of the more remote booths.

"Yes, darling, this will do nicely," she said to a young maître d', then she fixed her gaze on the second companion.

"Drinks," she announced to the family friend. "Gregor?"

"Mimosa."

"And get yourself something."

The family friend stood and strode to the bar. I took up a position at one of the two-seater rounds diagonally behind them. From this vantage point, I could watch them without being easily seen. A few moments later, he returned with a tray holding one of the bar's trademark golden chalices that they used to serve the Dragon's Blood, along with a champagne flute containing the mimosa and a cup of coffee with a creamer.

For a while we all watched the flow of people enter the bar and find their tables as the smells of breakfast gradually began to swirl around the room.

"Merry Christmas!" A perky voice burst from behind my right ear, making me jump. It belonged to a cute, elf-costumed brunette girl who didn't look old enough to work in a bar. "Welcome to the Boxing Day breakfast here at the St. George. I'm Holly, and I'll be helping you this morning. What can I bring you to drink?" She paused to catch her breath.

"Since the Dragon's Blood seems to be the thing here, I'll have one of those."

"They *are* popular. While we're at it, do you know which one of our five breakfasts I can bring you this morning?"

"Which one is the smallest?"

"That would be our Elf's Feast, sir. Cinnamon oatmeal with dried fruit and nuts, two slices of toast with butter, and a small fruit salad."

"I'll take one of those."

"Very good."

After a few minutes, another server brought me a golden chalice, and I got to taste what the excitement was about. At first the flavor was overly sweet and fruity, as though someone had infused the essence of fruitcake into a drink. But then the sugar faded, leaving a rich and nourishing savory flavor that felt like it ran clear through to my toes and almost wrapped me in a shawl of warmth. Wow, I thought as I realized I had consumed half the chalice. I could see how this could be addicting.

"Of course, I could only advise you on mechanics and reliability, not aesthetics." Lyle's voice came at me from somewhere on my left, letting me know he and his party were seated nearby.

My trio of oatmeal, toast, and fruit arrived, and I tucked in while the cereal was hot. As I ate, I watched a team of servers deliver the Reznikovs' much larger meal, observing how hungry they all seemed, and that Nadia had ordered herself a second chalice.

If possible, I wanted to get her away from her companions long enough to have an uninterrupted conversation, but I wasn't sure how to do that. Their table had an empty seat, as did mine, but I didn't expect her two chaperones to leave any time soon, nor did I see how to get her to visit my table.

In the end, Mother Nature intervened on my behalf. I had chosen a table on one of the direct paths to the women's bathroom. Sure enough, a little more than an hour after they had been seated, she asked a server a question and then unsteadily got to her feet.

As she started toward me, I took care to both edge my chair apparently carelessly into the gap between tables and to bury my head in a copy of the latest *Record* I had brought with me. I had to wait a moment or two.

"Merry Christmas, Mr. Porter. Such a surprise to find you here."

"Why, Ms. Reznikov, the pleasure is mine. I thought you had already left our little seaside town."

"Ugh, I wish." She twisted her bottom lip into a parody of a baby's pout. "Your police chief and prosecutor are the most pig-headed of men."

"Why, what's happened?"

"They've told us we cannot go home until the prosecutor has decided whether he will call us as witnesses or not. And they still don't know when they will release dear Niko's body so we can give him a decent burial."

I made a show of pulling my notebook out of my pocket. "Why don't you sit down and tell me about it? I might be able to help if I call around asking some questions." I got up and pulled out the spare chair, which she sank into heavily.

"It all started when that rude chief of detectives came to our suite here at the hotel and began asking a lot of very personal and impertinent questions."

I let her go on for a few moments, dutifully writing down her comments until I managed to get in a remark of my own. "I see," I said. "Well, that might explain a couple of things."

"What things?"

"One reason they might not have sent you home is because this case has had some funny twists and turns to it, that's all. Having you around will probably help them sort it all out."

She peered at me closely. "What twist?"

"Oh, for example, all that uncertainty from some of Niko's friends about whether he genuinely wanted to get married."

"What friends? What foolishness is this?"

"Ms. Reznikov, I didn't mean to upset you, but I thought you knew. A few of Niko's friends have told police he'd been expressing doubts about the marriage. He even canceled his bachelor party."

"What nonsense!" Her face quickly assumed a tomato-like hue. "Of course he was a little nervous, afraid even. Show me a single man who is not afraid of the altar a least a little. I don't believe these so-called friends knew my Niko very well at all."

"But, Ms. Reznikov, they maintain the source of Niko's reluctance to marry was his prior relationship with this person." I laid a recent picture of Rico on the table.

"Relationship? That's only a boy. What, was Niko supposedly wanting to adopt him and feared what I would say? This is absurd."

I took a deep breath. "Ms. Reznikov, like I said, I'm not looking to upset you, but I'm afraid the police believe the nature of the relationship to have been a bit more intimate than usual between a parent and child." I watched as the full meaning of what I was saying took root in her mind, and her face transformed into a mask of repugnance.

"This is monstrous!" she almost shouted. "They are saying that I almost married a prancing, boy-diddling faggot? Liars! It's untrue! Mr. Porter, you must understand, we have a tiny number of those filthy perverts in my country. It is almost impossible my Niko could have been one."

I had one more card left to play.

"Ms. Reznikov, have you ever seen this before?" I placed a photo of the bracelet on the table between us. The color drained from her face.

"Where did you get that photo?"

"From the police," I lied. "They believe Niko gave it to the boy, whose name is Rico, by the way, as a token of his affection."

"Liars!" She stood up and grabbed the edge of the table, flipping it up and back onto me before she went rigid and fell to the floor, where her body twitched in spasms.

"Get a doctor," I shouted, pushing the small table off me and reaching for my notebook. "She's having a seizure!"

I had barely regained my feet when a powerful force jerked me around, and I found myself face-to-face with an enraged Gregor.

"You bastard, what have you done!" He pulled back to hit me when a familiar muscular forearm reached around and put him in a choke hold.

"Run," Lyle said. "I'll see you at home."

Seeing a hole in the crowd, that's exactly what I did.

❖

All the way home I replayed the conversation with Nadia Reznikov. Could she not have known about the relationship between Niko and the boy and been genuinely shocked? Or had she simply been appalled that I brought it up in public? One thing was for sure. She recognized the bracelet, and she did not appear to have known the police knew about it.

That snake bracelet is key, I thought. It had to be how she found out about Nikolaidis's other life.

On a hunch I tracked down Gilbert Flacks's card from the Crabby Pawn. Fortunately, he had written his personal number on the back. He picked up on the third ring. After I introduced myself again and apologized abundantly for disturbing him at home, I asked his permission to ask two more questions about the snake bracelet.

"You don't need to apologize," he reassured me. "Today's a day for eggnog, mulled wine, and phone calls. I'm pleased to talk to you."

"Do you remember that snake bracelet we discussed a few days ago?"

"Of course. Ugly thing. Do we have to discuss it again?"

"Not in detail," I said. "I just need to ask you a couple more questions about the timing of your evaluation of it. Is that all right?"

"Ask away."

"Do you remember what day the gentleman first brought in the bracelet for you to look at? I don't have to know the exact day, but you might recall a general date or one that could have been nearby."

"It was the Saturday after Thanksgiving."

"How are you so certain?"

"Because that was our highest sales day in months," he said. "There was so much sales traffic, I debated having him come back on a quieter day but decided to deal with him after I saw the item."

"Thank you, sir. Only two more questions. You told me earlier that you had taken photos of the bracelet and sent it around to major pawn shops and galleries in other cities, right?"

"That's right."

"Were any of those in New York?"

"Of course."

I tried to keep the excitement out of my voice. "Of those, do you remember any expressing particular interest in the piece? Was there a firm that sought a follow-up with the owner, for example?"

"Only one," Flacks replied. "The Berodin Gallery expressed a strong interest in the piece and urged me to direct the owner to them if we couldn't reach an agreed price on our own. But of course, they would."

"Why?"

"Because the Berodin Gallery specializes in items from Eastern Europe and western Russia, particularly those dating from before the Russian Revolution."

"Could you spell their name sir?"

"B-E-R-O-D-I-N Gallery. Google them. They have a website."

"Thank you, sir. You can go back to the eggnog now. Merry Christmas!"

"Merry Christmas to you too."

❖

As I hung up with Flacks, the elevator came clanking to a stop and Lyle got off. His clothing was more rumpled than usual, but otherwise, he looked fine.

"Hey," he said, a moment before I kissed him.

"My hero," I replied.

His face darkened. "Your irritated coach," he said. "What happened to everything I taught you? That lug yanked you around because you were in the wrong place with the incorrect stance. What if I hadn't been there?"

I looked at him. He was right, of course. I had been caught up in the situation and hadn't considered my defensive stance.

"You can't let your mind go like that," he said. "Always be thinking, *Who's around me? What's my best way out?*"

"I know." I felt let down. "Thanks for helping me out."

He smiled and gave me a hug. "Don't let it get to you. I didn't mean to rain on your parade. You were excited before I came in. What have you found out?"

"Gilbert Flacks, the pawnbroker Nikolaidis approached to evaluate the bracelet, did that evaluation two days after Thanksgiving. He sent photos of it to large pawn shops and galleries in other cities, including New York."

"So?"

"I believe Nadia Reznikov's family gave that bracelet and other jewelry pieces to Nikolaidis as part of the betrothal and marriage ritual, and they found out he was trying to sell their gift."

"And that was enough to get him killed?"

"Maybe. Or it might have just been enough to get him followed, but once they found out he'd given the bracelet to Rico, or even that Rico existed, his fate was sealed."

He considered a moment. "Talked to Walker yet?"

"That was my next call."

"Good luck."

Detective Walker picked up on the second ring. "You are a menace."

"Merry Christmas to you too," I replied.

"You know, half an hour ago I had a long phone call from Dominic Berkshire. Do you know who he is?"

"Not a clue."

"He's the general manager of the St. George Hotel. He called to ask me to investigate how a record had been broken today."

"What record?"

"I'm explaining that. Did you know that this year is the ninetieth anniversary of the Boxing Day breakfast at the St, George Hotel's Dragon Bar?"

"I think I read that on a poster."

"Well, it is. That means that the hotel went through the Great Depression, World War Two, the Red Scare, the civil rights movement, the sixties and seventies, up into today, and in all that time, not until this year has the St. George Hotel's Boxing Day breakfast been disrupted by a riot. Would you know anything about that?"

"No. At least not directly."

"So, you didn't goad a woman at the event into becoming so angry she slipped into an epileptic fit, the very first in more than a decade?"

"I didn't goad anyone into anything," I said. "Nadia Reznikov sat down at my table and expressed confusion about why she hasn't been given permission yet to return home. I suggested that it might be because some loose ends in the Nikolaidis case needed to be resolved. When she asked what those were, I told her."

"Oh my God."

"I didn't know she would have that reaction," I said. "I really didn't. But I called because I'm more certain than ever she recognized Rico's bracelet, knew who Rico was, and knew Nikolaidis was involved with him."

"How?"

I told him about my conversation with Gilbert Flacks. "I think the Reznikovs gave Nikolaidis the jewelry set, including the bracelet, as part of a dowry. I believe he hated it because nothing about his house or workspace suggested he'd like it. So he took the bracelet to the Crabby Pawn to see what he could get for it, and when it wasn't as much as he hoped, he gave it to Rico. We know from Rico that Nikolaidis was in a crazy sentimental mood about him in the weeks before he was killed. When the Reznikovs found out he not only tried to sell their gift but gave it to his male lover, they hit the ceiling and sealed his fate."

"But how did the Reznikovs find out?"

"Because Gilbert Flacks circulated the photo around to other pawn shops and galleries, including some in New York. In fact, I believe if you look into the one who expressed a real interest in the bracelet—the Berodin Gallery—you'll find it has ties to the Reznikovs, who we know have been involved in the looting of antiquities. I think Flacks inadvertently tipped them off to the attempted sale and then they found out Rico had it. The first time I met Rico, I noticed he was very free and open about exhibiting the bracelet, so it wouldn't have been hard."

"Some parts are a stretch, but it's not impossible," he said. "Where do you think the bracelet is now?"

"The Reznikovs have it," I said. "It wasn't in the alley, and Rico didn't have it. The Reznikovs wouldn't have thrown it away after all the trouble they've gone to to get it back."

"Okay, Judge Mittsy owes me a favor. I'll get a warrant. You and Lyle meet me at the St. George."

CHAPTER 11

Cutting to the Chase

The lobby of the St. George bustled like an anthill on a summer day as Christmas visitors checked out and the New Year's guests arrived. Lyle and I paused at the entrance, taking it all in. The front desk looked swamped under two queues of departing clients wanting to settle bills and one line of arriving guests seeking to check their bags until they could be assigned rooms later.

Lyle sauntered over to a bellboy waiting for a client to pay their bill. "Hey, Billy, how's it going?"

"Hey, Mr. James! What are you doing here?"

"Oh, just meeting some friends for a drink. Or at least I hope so. Have they cleaned up the bar yet from this morning?"

"OMG, wasn't that wild? The biggest thing to happen in this joint in ages, and I wasn't here," he said in a disappointed voice.

"Was there much damage?"

"Nah, the bar'll open in like half an hour. If you just want a drink, you should be fine. I don't know how many tables will be available."

"Anyone hurt?"

"I don't think so. One lady had, like, a seizure or something and an ambulance came, but she wouldn't let them take her to the hospital. I think she's back in her room already."

"Well, thanks, Billy. How's that old Mustang running?"

"Still running good," he said, reaching behind Lyle to rap his knuckles on a wooden table. "I'm saving up for some modifications that I might come see you about next year if that's okay."

"I'll be happy to see you," Lyle said as he walked away and returned to me. "My pal Billy over there told me an ambulance came for Ms. Reznikov, but she declined to be taken to the hospital," he said in a low voice. "Supposedly, she's resting in her rooms. Which ones are they again?"

"The Peacock Suite. Ninth floor, I think. We should wait here for Walker and brief him when he arrives."

"Good idea."

As we stepped back outside to wait on the stoop, a dark gray sedan pulled up in front of the hotel. Detective Walker got out and walked up the stairs to us. Two other figures remained in the car.

"Gentlemen," he said gravely.

"Detective," I said. "We've established she's still on the property, likely in her suite. The hotel staff is overwhelmed right now, but I expect the manager will verify they're in the Peacock Suite."

"Great. We're short-staffed because of the holiday today, so I've got a new officer named Wilson, fresh from the academy, and Sergeant Sands, who usually oversees the evidence locker for us."

"Are you sure that'll be enough? I don't think she'll be physically dangerous, but she's with two men who appear fit and trained."

"You execute warrants with the people you have," Walker said. "We'll make sure we have a hotel employee with us in case we need a passkey."

"I'd be glad to go up with you if you needed an extra body," I said.

"Not a chance. You're a civilian, and our mutual friend Smalls just informed me you've been pulled off anything to do with this story. Funny how that little detail slipped your mind when you called me to get me down here."

"It wasn't relevant since the facts were the facts. Anyway, you're here now. What's the plan?"

"You and Captain America here keep watch on the lobby, and we'll head up," he said. He waved to the car and then went inside.

Officer Wilson and Sergeant Sands locked the car, then headed up to us. Wilson was an extremely tall man with a face like twelve-year-old boy's, and Sands could have been his grandfather.

"Where's Detective Walker?" Wilson asked.

"In the hotel, getting the manager," I said. "He'll let us know when to send you in."

"My first actual search warrant," Wilson said.

"Yeah, and I was supposed to stop doing them years ago," Sands complained.

My phone rang. It was Walker. "Tell Wilson and Sands to meet me at the main elevators. I'll have Miss Tang with me from the hotel. Then you and Lyle take up positions where you can see the front and side entrances. I don't want to risk losing them."

"Will do," I replied and rang off. I relayed his instructions to Wilson and Sands before turning to Lyle. "He wants us to keep an eye on the front and side doors in case they try to get away."

We all went back inside, and I watched Sands and Wilson meet up with Walker and a young Asian woman. I stayed at the front door and sent Lyle across the lobby where he could see me as well as have a clear view of the side entrance. The elevator came, and Walker's team boarded it. We waited.

After about five minutes, three members of a cleaning crew got off an adjoining elevator. They wore light blue coveralls and darker caps with the word "Sanitall" lettered in red. I looked at them closely but decided they were not the Reznikovs, in part because they all sported off-season tans. The Reznikovs had been bone china white.

A hotel maid came up to them and engaged the shortest of the three in an active conversation that ended when he shrugged and pointed to the elevator. She looked frustrated but summoned a lift and boarded it as soon as it arrived. The three headed across the lobby to the side entrance.

Walker called again. "We had to use a passkey because they aren't here," Walker said. "But bags packed and ready to go. Has anybody passed by you guys?"

I looked across the lobby, but it was empty. "I'm afraid so, Detective, but they were made up and disguised!" I hung up. "Lyle, get the car, meet me at the side door," I shouted, heading across the lobby. I burst through the doors and looked up and down the street. At the far end of the block, I caught sight of three figures in blue getting into a black Prius.

"You there, stop!" I ran down the sidewalk, but the car pulled away from the corner and zoomed down Clement Street. I stared after it helplessly until Lyle pulled up in one of the garage's souped-up beaters. I jumped in, and we were off in pursuit.

The streets were mostly empty the day after Christmas, so we could easily keep the Prius in view until they scooted through a light at Washington Boulevard that we missed.

"Damn it, where are they?" I said as we kept moving down Clement.

Walker rang. "Where are you?"

"On Clement, just crossed Washington, but we lost them. Where are you?"

"On the way to the car with Wilson. I left Sands to keep searching the room. No bracelet yet, but Sands found a half-empty box of ammunition, so be careful."

"Will do." I rang off as we stopped at the light at Clement and Oak.

"So if I was running, what down here would help me run?" Lyle asked. "The airport is the other direction, as is the interstate."

"Amtrak!" I said. "In fact, I think a northbound Southern Crescent comes through around now. I thought we might take it back the next time we went to New Orleans."

We pulled into the station lot to find it overflowing. I texted Walker.

Amtrak!

"There's the car," I said, spying the black Prius parked illegally in front of a fire plug. Lyle pulled into an open spot. "Wow, so many people."

"Look, two trains," Lyle said. "That's why."

Sure enough, there were trains on both the north and southbound tracks. No wonder so many people were on hand.

"But which one will they take?" he said.

I thought about for a moment. "The northbound. The Southern Crescent ends in New York, and that's home for them. The southbound is the Disney Express, and that only ends in Orlando."

We got out of the car and ran into the station, looking for the light blue of a coverall or a darker colored cap. The announcer's voice hummed overhead: "Amtrak 137, the Disney Express for Jacksonville, Palatka, DeLand, Winter Park, and Orlando, will depart in five minutes. Allll aboard Amtrak 137."

"Quick, find the stationmaster and get them to stop the Crescent from leaving until Walker gets here," I said to Lyle. "I'll keep looking for them."

Lyle dashed toward the offices while I headed to the northbound platform. Most of the crowd had gone by this point. An older couple moved slowly down the floor toward the station and two porters looked at me curiously.

"All passengers on the Southern Crescent with stops in Charleston, Greenville, Charlotte, Richmond, Washington, Baltimore, Philadelphia, and New York should be aboard now. The Southern Crescent is leaving momentarily. Allll aboard."

I kept running toward the end of the train until, almost imperceptibly at first, I saw the cars give a slight jerk. Then another. Right at the point the rattler began to pick up speed, the last door came into view. I grabbed the bar, hit the button, and with a whoosh stepped into the shaking, clattering space between the two cars. The carriage portal shut behind me. What had I done?

❖

I felt the shaking beneath me increase as the train picked up speed, and I pondered what to do. I needed to contact a conductor. I hit the entrance bar to the door on my left that read "Amtrak Personnel Only." Nothing. I hit the open bar to the portal on my right and it opened up into one of the standard cars.

I started to move up the center aisle. There weren't many

passengers in this one, and most were reading, listening to headphones, or sleeping. I continued through to the end, navigated a space between the cars again, and proceeded into the second. Still no conductor. I reached the far end of the second when I finally found a tall, hefty Black man wearing a blue Amtrak uniform and cap. He stood in a small alcove at the end of the car, writing earnestly on a paper attached to a clipboard. I waited for him to finish.

"Yes, sir, how may I help you?" he said finally, after signing his name at the bottom of the page.

"Are you the conductor on this train?"

"I am a conductor," he said. "Augustus Quimby at your service." He touched the edge of his cap.

"Mr. Quimby, my name is Jose Porter, and you have to stop this train!"

"Whoa now," Quimby said, looking shocked. "That's a big request. Why would I want to do that?"

"Because I believe three fugitives from law enforcement boarded in St. Michael's Harbor. All three are dangerous and one is likely armed, that's why."

"Shh, young man," Quimby said. "Keep your voice down. Passengers are always listening, and we don't want to start a panic. Now, let's take three deep breaths."

I looked at him, incredulous, as he gazed expectantly at me. "Oh, all right," I said, joining him in taking three deep, slow breaths and feeling, I admitted to myself, much better at the end of the last one.

"Now, you said you believe these people are on my train. Why is that? Did you see them board?"

"No, sir, I didn't actually see them, but I'm almost positive they got on this one rather than the Disney Express."

"But how do you know they got on a train at all? They might just have hidden in the bathrooms until the train left with you on it. I can't stop the train based on just your suspicions of what might have happened."

"Sir, I can't go into all the reasons, but I'm a reporter and I've been reporting on these people for a while, and I'm almost positive they got on this train and are trying to get away. Will you help me or not?"

"Now, you didn't ask me that before. You asked me to stop the train, which I can't do, but I didn't say I wouldn't help."

"What can we do?"

"I'm not sure we are going to do anything," he said. "But we do have an armed US Marshal among the passengers."

"Really? Who is it?"

"We never know which passenger it is, but they started putting an armed marshal on major passenger routes after the September 11 attacks, just like they do on planes," Quimby said.

"But if we don't know who it is, how do we let the marshal know?"

"I'm not sure yet, but it's better to have one on the train than not, right?"

"Right."

"And tell me, do these folks know what you look like?"

I responded that, sadly, they did.

"Okay, let's do this. I've got to finish taking tickets anyway. You can stay here out of sight until I get back. Tell me what they look like."

I did my best to describe Nadia, Gregor, and the family friend as the conductor listened attentively. "Are you sure they wore blue coveralls?" he said.

"Those were the last clothes I saw them in, and they didn't have time to change."

"The reason I ask is because those are going to make them stand out clearly," he said. "What should I do if I come across them?"

"Nothing," I said. "They're probably going to want to pay for their passage on-site, so you can take their fare and give them tickets. Don't let on you recognize them, and please don't forget at least one of them might have a gun."

"Trust me, sir, I am not about to forget that," he replied with a shudder.

I retreated into the alcove shadows and watched him move up the aisle, taking tickets and answering questions until he was out of sight. About forty minutes passed before he returned.

"Anything?" I asked anxiously.

"Nope. Not unless you count a negative response as an answer. I've been up this train until the dining car, but I didn't see anyone who matched your description or was wearing blue coveralls. Not a one."

"And what cars are past the dining car?"

"Freight and luggage next, and then locked and sealed mail, and finally the locomotive, but that's about it."

"Any sign of the marshal?"

"Nothing definite. I saw one or two that I thought might be, but that's not something you can just walk up and ask about."

My face must have registered my disappointment.

"Now, my section didn't include the two sleeper cars," he said. "My friend Henry is the conductor there, and he told me he had a female volunteer in Sleeping Compartment 3 who hadn't shown a ticket yet."

"What's a volunteer?"

"That's someone who gets on and takes an open sleeper without a reservation, then pays the difference between their seat fare and the sleeper fare," he said. "It doesn't happen a lot, but some folks on these long routes like it."

I felt a thrill of excitement. "Gus, please go up and ask Henry to position himself outside that compartment. Don't let that woman go unless she pays the fare," I said.

"What are you going to do?"

"I'm going to check the baggage and freight car," I said.

"I can't give you permission for that."

"That's why I didn't ask you for any. What can you tell me about it?"

"It's divided into four sections for luggage and freight, but the handlers often ignore those. Be careful because it's easy to trip, and the lights don't always come on."

I passed through the late lunch diners quickly and soon stood in the shaking, rattling passage between the dining car and the baggage car.

I took a moment to quiet my mind, remembering as much as I could of what Lyle had tried to teach me. Then I calmly reached out and gave the button a push. The door slid open, and I stared into the darkened car.

I entered, felt the door whoosh shut behind me, and stood for a moment, letting my eyes adjust to the gloom. I reached into my pocket for my phone to give me some light, but then reconsidered making myself a target. I focused instead on bringing my breathing under control.

Finally, I took a few steps into the compartment. If I was correct, I was about midway past the first of the four baggage areas when I felt, rather than saw, the attack come from behind my left shoulder. As Lyle had taught me, I dropped slightly to give myself a lower center of gravity and turned to drive my right elbow into where I guessed my assailant's face or throat might be. I felt and heard a soft crunch, followed by a gurgling sound, as his body fell against me, and I realized he was trying to pull me to the floor. I reached for the first thing I could find in the shadows and brought the heavy suitcase down on his head. I felt his grip relax as he slumped away from me.

I was trying to push him farther away when a shot rang out, and I dropped to the floor of my own accord. At least we know where the gun is, I thought.

❖

Lyle stood frustrated on the platform looking after the northbound Crescent when Walker and Wilson ran up.

"Train left two minutes ago," Lyle said. "I couldn't convince the pigheaded station agent to delay its departure for as little as five extra minutes."

"God damn it," Walker said. "Where's Manny?"

"With no evidence to the contrary, I believe he's on that train."

"Come back to the stationmaster with me," Walker ordered,

and they returned down the long platform to the offices. The stationmaster, Fredrick Harrison, a short, wiry, balding man dressed in a shabby Amtrak uniform, was no happier to see Lyle the second time around.

"You again!" he said. "I already told you I lacked the authority to hold up that train. Now, unless you have some other business with this station, I suggest you leave this office before I call the police."

"I saved you that step," Lyle said. "I brought the police with me."

Walker flashed his badge. "Chief Detective Walker with the St. Michael's Harbor Police Department. I thought stationmasters had the authority to call angels out of heaven if they needed them to protect health and safety."

Harrison groaned and pointed to the small sign on his desk that read Stationmaster. "I guess literacy is not a requirement for chief detectives or grease monkeys," he sneered. Attached to the front of the sign was a yellow sticky note with the word "Acting" written on it.

"Yes, gentlemen, I have been the acting stationmaster of St. Michael's Harbor station for five months and four days. I have license to keep this place running on all its established routines, but that's it. I lack the authority to purchase a new coffeemaker without prior approval, much less order a train delay."

"Then what's the earliest station where we could get a stop?"

"Charleston."

"What's the procedure for doing that?"

"There isn't one!" Harrison said. "Trains might halt for weather, for damaged tracks, for poles down and even, heaven forbid, for an accident, but they don't stop to fulfill requests—even from law enforcement."

"Then we'll go up the chain of command," Walker told him. "Who's your boss? May I have his number, please?"

"Gladly." Harrison began flipping through a large Rolodex on his desk when the phone rang. A young woman at another writing table picked it up but hit a button and called out.

"It's for you, Mr. Harrison, Central Schedule says it's urgent."

"Gentlemen, please excuse me a moment. I have to take this." He punched a button at the base of his phone. "Harrison…What?" His face paled, and he dropped into the wooden chair behind him. "Yes, of course. I'll post the notice right away. Thank you for calling."

He looked up into their inquisitive faces. "You won't have to talk to my boss after all," he said. "Central Schedule has ordered a full traffic stop at Charleston."

A sense of foreboding filled Lyle's chest. "Did they say why?"

Harrison nodded. "There's been a report of gunshots on the Southern Crescent."

❖

In her seat about a quarter of the way back in the third passenger car, Special Duty US Marshal Judy Davenport jerked out of a daydream. Was that a shot? She straightened up in her seat and tried to attune her hearing to the usual train sounds, the clacking of tracks, bursts of conversation, the occasional whoosh of a door opening. But those noises were disrupted. People sitting nearby looked about them uneasily.

I wasn't alone in hearing it, she realized. Time to take a tour of the train.

❖

While lying belly down on the dusty baggage car floor, I considered what to do. Somewhere ahead of me in the dark was the thug with a gun. The other thug was either unconscious or worse, someplace on the dark deck behind me. As much as I wanted to crawl back over him and out of the car, I realized I couldn't leave an armed criminal on a train full of unarmed people.

I took stock of my supplies. One phone, not much help in this situation; one pocketknife, ditto; some loose change from yesterday…Now, *that* might help. As quietly as possible, I fished a few of the coins from my pocket and clenched them in my sweaty hand. Rolling onto my side, I quietly tossed the coins as far as I could to the front left of my position. They landed clinking on the floor, and two more shots rang out like thunder in the enclosed space.

"That's three," I thought, taking advantage of the echo to crawl forward another couple of feet to where a large trunk provided a good deal of shelter. I carefully moved from my belly to my knees.

The shots had given me a good idea of my opponent's location, and I peered cautiously over the trunk to try to see him. I spotted his head in a corner of the boxcar, walls protecting him on two sides and a small mountain of luggage defending his third. Unfortunately, this gave him an almost perfect defensive location. From there he could see and fire into the whole boxcar while only facing attack from one direction. What to do?

A clanking sound came from the near wall of the car, from behind the sealed door to the mail car and locomotive. I watched him brace himself against a shelf of suitcases and take a shooting stance aimed in that direction. If anyone came through the door, they would be right in his line of fire. Please don't let anyone come in, I silently prayed as I dropped to my belly again and crawled to the suitcases that made up his third wall of protection.

He was close enough now that I could hear him muttering to himself as I peeked around the pile and saw him. It was Gregor. He had moved up slightly, and I was positioned diagonally behind his left ear.

Another series of clanks came from beyond the wall, along with muffled curses. Someone was trying to come into the car. I saw Gregor grip the gun more tightly and readied myself. I launched my body with as loud a scream as I could at his midriff, aiming for his gun hand. As I charged, he partially turned and tried to stiff-arm me with his left, but that was his weaker side, and he failed to stop me. His gun went off with another thunderous explosion as he dropped it, and we fell heavily together into the shelves of suitcases. He was fast. Before I could move, he was up on his feet, about to stomp on my crotch until I swung my right leg hard into the back of his knee. He howled and dropped to his knees again while swinging at my head as I concentrated on moving inside and landing thumping shots to his chest and ear. I thought I had him until he swung around with some kind of package and used it to clock me hard on the side of the head.

I saw stars while he got back on his feet to look for the gun. I tried to make my body move to stop him before he found it, but at the point I thought I failed, I heard a woman call out "Freeze!" And when he turned to face her, her gunshot shook the car as he dropped to the floor clutching his leg. The marshal had arrived.

❖

I looked to the far end of the car and saw Gregor's shooter was a petite African American woman in low-rise heels, a smart gray pantsuit, and a white blouse. She held a Glock in one hand and an identification shield in the other.

Behind her came Gus Quimby and about six burly men in the Amtrak blue uniform. She paused to kneel beside the first thug who'd attacked me but came to her feet almost immediately.

"This man is dead," she said, addressing Gus. "Please seal the car and limit access. The only people I want in this car going forward are law enforcement and authorized medical personnel and evidence technicians."

"Yes, ma'am," Gus said.

She came through the car to Gregor, whimpering on the floor. "You. What's your name?"

Gregor merely stared at her, his eyes flashing hatred and pain in equal measure.

"His name's Gregor Reznikov," I said from my seat, slumped against the suitcases. "Originally from Belarus but most recently from New York City. I think you'll find his sister Nadia is in Sleeping Compartment 3. They're both wanted for questioning in the murder of a research scientist in St. Michael's Harbor earlier this month."

"You filthy bastard," Gregor croaked from the floor. "I told Nadia we should have dealt with you after the funeral, but she was soft. She never could recognize the nancy boys." He tried to spit on me.

"Enough of that," Marshal Davenport said. "Mr. Quimby."

"Yes, ma'am?"

"I'm taking over the dining car as a command center until Charleston. Please clear all the passengers out and move Mr. Rez... Rez..."

"Reznikov," I said.

"Move Mr. Reznikov into one of the booths and see if you can find someone with medical training to take a look at his leg."

"Yes, ma'am."

Gus motioned two of the conductors, who came forward with an emergency stretcher and removed Reznikov on it.

"And who are you?" she said, looking down at me with a hawkish expression. "Can you stand or are you injured too?"

"No, I can stand," I replied, "but Gregor there caught me with one of those packages, and it seemed like sitting was better."

"Well, please stand when I am addressing you."

Gradually, using the shelves for support, I brought myself up.

"Now, who are you?"

"My name is Jose Porter," I said. "I'm a reporter for the *South Georgia Record*. I followed Mr. Reznikov and his sister Nadia and that dead fellow onto this train to prevent them from escaping a murder charge."

"So, you don't know the identity of the dead guy?"

"Not definitively, but I think his first name is Pyotr."

"How did he come to be dead?"

"I believe I killed him."

"What? Let's start at the beginning. When did you follow these three onto the train?"

"When the train was in the St. Michael's Harbor station. If you don't believe me, Mr. Quimby can verify my story, as can the chief of detectives for St. Michael's Harbor, a man named Walker."

Gus stepped forward. "What he's saying is the truth, ma'am, at least as far as that's what he told me when he came on board."

"So you followed them on the train and decided to enter the baggage car. Why?"

"Because Mr. Quimby told me conductors had taken tickets from everyone on the train and not found them. The baggage car was the one part of the train where they could reasonably have hidden."

"So, when do you think you killed this Pyotr?"

"Shortly after I stepped into the baggage car, I was attacked from the rear. I deployed a defensive strategy, and I believe one of my blows landed in an especially sensitive spot and killed him."

She tapped her foot. "All right, seeing that Mr. Quimby vouches for you, I'm not going to arrest you for now. But don't leave the train without my permission, understood?"

"Understood. One more thing, ma'am."

"What?"

"Have you interviewed the woman in Sleeping Compartment 3 yet?"

"No, she was farther down on the list. Why?"

"Because I believe she has items in her possession that would be valuable evidence in the murder case. It would be a shame if those items were to go missing."

"Quimby!"

"Yes, ma'am?"

"Find another strong conductor, and the two of you come with me to the sleeping car. Our work is not over yet."

After Marshal Davenport and her deputies had cleared out, I slowly went through the dining car and into the nearest passenger space. On my way I passed Gregor, sleeping peacefully, attended by a young woman wearing civilian clothes but with an EMT cap.

In the passenger space, I found the nearest empty row of seats and slumped across them. Outside, the day had yielded to evening, and the increase in house lights and traffic suggested we might arrive in Charleston soon. It felt like I closed my eyes a mere moment when someone shook me awake, and I looked up at Marshal Davenport again.

"We're coming into Charleston soon, so I needed to wake you," she said by way of apology. "I need you to identify this object."

She held up a clear evidence bag with the serpentine bracelet.

"That," I said, "is a key piece of evidence in a murder investigation. One man was killed because of it, and a boy was almost killed."

"This?" She looked at it again and sniffed. "I wouldn't have it."

"Where did you find it?"

"The lady in Sleeping Compartment 3 was trying to open her window to throw it out when we entered," she said. "She has refused to cooperate so far, and we don't know who she is or why she had it."

"Detective Walker can fill you in," I said wearily.

"I expect so. We did reach out to him, and though he couldn't spend much time on the phone, he did confirm the outlines of what you told us. He's on his way here now to see about the situation."

"What's going to happen to Nadia and Gregor?"

"Truthfully, I don't know. That's a little above my pay grade. Now they're in federal custody. Gregor will likely go to the University Health Center to get his leg looked after, then he'll join Nadia at the Charleston city jail."

"Where will they be tried?"

"That's up to the US attorney and the local prosecutor," she said. "Definitely not me."

She took her leave at that point. I was surprised to find myself alone with Nadia one more time when Quimby parked her in the row of seats opposite mine as we waited for the train to enter Charleston station.

After Nadia sat down, she gazed at me with a baleful expression. "I expect to get off, you know," she said. "Daddy has an army of lawyers, and I'm sure he will begin calling them as soon as he learns we have been arrested."

"He might. Though it may take him some time to find federal lawyers."

"Yes, well, I didn't kill him or order him killed, but I am not surprised or sorry he's dead."

"Isn't that a little harsh? After all, you were going to marry Nikolaidis, and you told me you loved him."

"Not at all," she said. "I did love him—when he was not

deserving of my affection and knew he was not entitled to it. A man with so few scruples deserves everything that happens to him."

I had nothing to say to that. We rode through several starts and stops in silence until she suddenly spoke again. "They told me Pyotr is dead. Is that true?"

"If you mean the man in your entourage other than Gregor, yes."

"Now I am shocked," she said. "You know, he held several medals for his special forces service to the Russian Federation against terrorists. How did he die?"

"He attacked me from behind in the dark, and I defended myself."

"You?"

"If it makes you feel any better," I replied, "I think luck plays into any kind of conflict. Maybe today was my lucky day and his unlucky one."

She remained silent after that until we entered Charleston station, where one of the conductors took her off the train and turned her over to the US marshals waiting there.

I stayed on board a couple of more hours, telling my story to different law enforcement officers and at least two FBI agents until, finally, when the last one gave me back my phone and told me I could leave, I realized I had nowhere to go. The officer recommended the Charleston Court hotel around the corner, and so I checked in there and fell into bed fully clothed in a dead sleep.

After what seemed like a few moments, I awoke to someone pounding on the door. "Wha…what," I said. "Hold your horses. God."

"Not God, but maybe a close second," Lyle said.

"Lyle!" I flung the door open, and there he stood in loafers, jeans, and a T-shirt. I stumbled into his arms.

"There, there," he said, "I'm glad to see you too."

"I was shot at. A bunch of times. And a Russian special forces soldier tried to kill me, but I killed him and we caught all three of them and Nadia had the bracelet and she said she didn't care Nikolaidis was dead because he broke her heart because he was gay—"

"Hey there, slow down." He pulled me away from him so he could look into my face. "Thank God you're okay," he said, pulling me close again. And for a time, we simply stood there, hugging and kissing in the open door, in front of God and everybody, giving thanks for each other.

When we finally moved into the room, I started to tell him everything, but he insisted on getting me clean first. Thus, I recounted meeting Quimby on the train while we showered together and finished describing Ms. Davenport's great shooting as we lay entwined on the bed.

"So, you're telling me all the Krav Maga mat time was worth it," he said with a smile.

"Oh my God, Lyle, totally!" I said, tearing up a little. "I don't even remember deciding to do anything. I sensed the attack, and my body went on automatic. I didn't mean to kill him."

He stopped me there. "Manny, look at me. Look at me. You did nothing wrong. That man would have killed you and others if he could. You didn't mean to kill him, but the fact that you did while defending yourself is his fault, not yours. Understand?"

I nodded.

"Now, let's get some sleep. We'll drive home tomorrow."

As I drifted off to sleep, I suddenly remembered. "Tristan! Lyle, what happened to Tristan?"

He hugged me closer. "Calm down. By now he's been out of the drunk tank and in the juvenile facility for like four hours."

"Oh. Okay, thanks."

Tommy's car was in the Bonne Chance Motor drive when we pulled in late Monday morning, and we found him sprawled out in the back seat. I shook his shoulder.

"Dude, did you sleep here?"

"Not much. It took you long enough to get back. I've been waiting for ages."

"Waiting for what?"

"For you to get back and help me," he wailed. "I can't just do the second part of this story on my own, I need your input. Please!"

I shook my head. "Sorry, dude. I'm off the story. Dad made that very clear. I've already fucked things up a lot. I don't want to make it worse."

"Hold on," he said. "I thought you'd say that." He brought out his phone, hit a button, and put it on speaker. I heard a ring, then Rosa's voice.

"Hold, Mr. Kingsolver. He's expecting your call."

After a few moments my father's voice came on the line. "Well, young Kingsolver. I take your call to mean it's as you said it would be?"

"Yes, sir. He's here now and refuses to help me because you told him he can't."

"Manny, speak up and let me hear your voice."

"Yes, sir, I'm here," I said, stunned.

"Son, young Kingsolver called me so I could tell you myself I want you to help him complete the AthenaLibre story. The news from Charleston hit here yesterday and reversed the legal outlook. We're no longer under the threat of lawsuit, and frankly, Kingsolver could use some help matching your style in part two. What do you say?"

"Tommy is my best friend. If it's okay with the paper, of course I'll help."

"It's fine with the paper," he said. "In fact, I want to rescind the—"

"Don't!" I said. "You were entirely right to ban me. I was wrong. If I had to do it all over again, I'd still want to help Tristan make bail, but I'd approach my editors to talk about it before I took any action. Besides, I think I need a week away."

"If that's the way you feel, okay. Your mother asks that you please come to dinner soon so she can give you all the hugs she thinks you deserve. And she says be sure to bring your boyfriend too."

"Tell her thank you and we will," I said, then I hung up before I started to cry.

After the call, Tommy went into Lyle's office to get ready to work on the story, while Lyle turned on all the lights. Our tree looked particularly glorious with all the packages arranged underneath its boughs. We'd decided we wouldn't open gifts or take any decorations down until Tristan was out of jail, but there was one package I wanted Lyle to unwrap today. I carefully slid the long, flat parcel wrapped in red paper out from the others and brought it to him.

"Go ahead and open this one," I said. "I hope it brings back only good memories."

Lyle unwrapped the sign with a puzzled look on his face, then turned it over to the front. "I'll be damned. I love it. But where on earth did you find it?"

"At the Crabby Pawn. They brought a while back at an estate sale."

"This is so wild. It even predates my coming on board here," he said with a chuckle. "I think my dad bartered his mechanic services to get this sign done since he had so little capital."

I joined Tommy in Lyle's office and started reworking the second part of the AthenaLibre story when Lyle came in to announce we had a visitor coming.

"Arundhati Dass just called," Lyle stuck his head around the partition to tell us. "You're not to leave the house for half an hour. She's bringing you a surprise."

"I bet it's one of her Mumbai wonder cakes," Tommy said. "She gave us one last year, and it took like a month to eat it all."

"Why, isn't it good?"

"It's delicious, but it's huge and so rich you only a eat a little piece at a time."

"I'm sure the Bonne Chance staff can deal with one," Lyle said confidently.

But when the elevator door clanked open to reveal Ms. Dass,

she held not a cake but the hand of one Jaime Rico Pelado, standing at her side looking paler and skinnier, if that was possible, with his other arm in a sling.

"Rico!"

He looked at everyone in the room and then stepped in with Ms. Dass. "Mr. Porter, Mr. James. Merry Christmas," he said in a quiet voice.

And that was all we needed to rush them both with hugs.

"Oh my God, dude, when did they release you?"

"Today," Ms. Dass said. "This morning. I picked him up from the hospital because there was no one else to do it and because he's the newest resident of Baldwin House."

"Woohoo!" I yelled. "Fantastic, Rico! Congratulations!"

"Of course, we still have some details to work out," Ms. Dass said, and I caught a glance between Rico and his new landlady. "But the fundamental decisions have been made, and I feel comfortable having him move in this coming week."

"I want to thank everybody," Rico said. "For real, this was something I wished I could make happen, but I had no way of seeing it through. The love and caring you all have shown me is what made it possible."

"Rico, welcome to the family, to *my* family," Ms. Dass said. "Years ago, when I came to Baldwin House, it was to help young people like you. I am honored and excited you've chosen to live with us, and I look forward to helping you take your next steps."

"I think this calls for a drink," Lyle said. "How many eggnogs do we have?"

It turned out all the adults wanted the punch, even Tommy, who didn't usually touch the stuff. We were engaged in quiet conversation when the doorbell rang again.

"Good Lord, it's like an open house," Lyle said, walking to the lift. "Who's there?"

"Merry Christmas," Carolyn almost sang on the intercom. "I come bringing gifts—may I come up?"

"Why not? Everyone else has," Lyle said with a chuckle.

But when the elevator arrived, it brought the best present of all. Standing next to Carolyn Mondial, wearing the same clothes he wore almost a week ago, was Tristan DeJesus.

Lyle let out a whoop, and the apartment exploded in cheers and applause as Tristan stepped forward with a smile a mile wide.

"Merry Christmas, everyone!" he shouted before he turned to start tearfully hugging as many people as he could.

Carolyn Mondial grabbed a decorative bell from a side table and rang it to bring order to the din. "And a special merry Christmas to Judge Matthews," she said, "who wrote this morning that he could see no reason why one Tristan DeJesus should spend another hour in jail for a crime he clearly did not commit. Then he dismissed all the charges."

Thus began one of the greatest Yuletide parties Lyle and I have ever thrown and ended my most challenging season yet as a reporter and as an adult. While I might have gone to Thanksgiving as a young man uncertain of himself and of his calling, I came away from Christmas feeling sure-footed about both.

About the Author

An avid reader, traveler, cook, and occasional public speaker, D.C. Robeline didn't try writing a novel until challenged to do so.

Now he writes suspenseful stories featuring strong LGBTQ characters fighting for justice that reflect many of his readers' life stories and inspire others.

Manny Porter and The Yuletide Murder is his second novel. He plans one hundred more.

Books Available From Bold Strokes Books

Felix Navidad by Nathan Burgoine. After the wedding of a good friend, instead of Felix's Hawaii Christmas treat to himself, ice rain strands him in Ontario with fellow wedding guest—and handsome ex of said friend—Kevin in a small cabin for the holiday Felix definitely didn't plan on. (978-1-63679-411-2)

Manny Porter and The Yuletide Murder by D.C. Robeline. Manny only has the holiday season to discover who killed prominent research scientist Phillip Nikolaidis before the judicial system condemns an innocent man to lethal injection. (978-1-63679-313-9)

Corpus Calvin by David Swatling. Cloverkist Inn may be haunted, but a ghost materializes from Jason Dekker's past and Calvin's canine instinct kicks in to protect a young boy from mortal danger. (978-1-62639-428-5)

Calvin's Head by David Swatling. Jason Dekker and his dog, Calvin, are homeless in Amsterdam when they stumble on the victim of a grisly murder—and become targets for the calculating killer, Gadget. (978-1-62639-193-2)

Murder at Union Station by David S. Pederson. Private Detective Mason Adler struggles to determine who killed a woman found in a trunk without getting himself killed in the process. (978-1-63679-269-9)

A Champion for Tinker Creek by D.C. Robeline. Lyle James has rescued his dad's auto repair business, but when city hall condemns his neighborhood, Lyle learns only trusting will save his life and help him find love. (978-1-63679-213-2)

Heckin' Lewd: Trans and Nonbinary Erotica, edited by Mx. Nillin Lore. If you want smutty, fearless, gender diverse erotica written by affirming own-voices folks who get it, then this is the book you've been looking for! (978-1-63679-240-8)

Inherit the Lightning by Bud Gundy. Darcy O'Brien and his sisters learn they are about to inherit an immense fortune, but a family mystery about to unravel after seventy years threatens to destroy everything. (978-1-63679-199-9)

Pursued: Lillian's Story by Felice Picano. Fleeing a disastrous marriage to the Lord Exchequer of England, Lillian of Ravenglass reveals an incident-filled, often bizarre, tale of great wealth and power, perfidy, and betrayal. (978-1-63679-197-5)

Murder on Monte Vista by David S. Pederson. Private Detective Mason Adler's angst at turning fifty is forgotten when his "birthday present," the handsome, young Henry Bowtrickle, turns up dead, and it's up to Mason to figure out who did it, and why. (978-1-63679-124-1)

Three Left Turns to Nowhere by Jeffrey Ricker, J. Marshall Freeman & 'Nathan Burgoine. Three strangers heading to a convention in Toronto are stranded in rural Ontario, where a small town with a subtle kind of magic leads each to discover what he's been searching for. (978-1-63679-050-3)

One Verse Multi by Sander Santiago. Life was good: promotion, friends, falling in love, discovering that the multi-verse is on a fast track to collision—wait, what? Good thing Martin King works for a company that can fix the problem, right…um…right? (978-1-63679-069-3)

Fresh Grave in Grand Canyon by Lee Patton. The age-old Grand Canyon becomes more and more ominous as a group of volunteers fight to survive alone in nature and uncover a murderer among them. (978-1-63679-047-3)

Loyalty, Love & Vermouth by Eric Peterson. A comic valentine to a gay man's family of choice, including the ones with cold noses and four paws. (978-1-63555-997-2)

Bury Me in Shadows by Greg Herren. College student Jake Chapman is forced to spend the summer at his dying grandmother's home and soon finds danger from long-buried family secrets. (978-1-63555-993-4)

A Different Man by Andrew L. Huerta. This diverse collection of stories chronicling the challenges of gay life at various ages shines a light on the progress made and the progress still to come. (978-1-63555-977-4)